Christmas at Embthwaite Farm

Christmas at Embthwaite Farm

A Mowbray Sisters Romance

Kate Hewitt

TULE
PUBLISHING

Christmas at Embthwaite Farm

Tule Publishing First Printing, November 2023

The Tule Publishing, Inc.

First Publication by Tule Publishing 2023

Cover design by Rhian

ISBN: 978-1-961544-80-2

Chapter One

SHE FELT LIKE Little Red Riding Hood. She had the cape—well, technically, a red coat, but still—and the basket, made of wicker with a gingham cloth covering the top, looped over one arm. She was making her way through the woods, or at least a part of the North Yorkshire countryside that looked woodsy—a sweeping drive that snaked past fir and yew trees as well as some towering rhododendrons, up to the Mathering Manor House Hotel, where the Big Bad Wolf awaited her.

Well, Harriet Mowbray told herself, she didn't *know* that the owner of the hotel was Big Bad Wolf-esque, but it felt as if he held her fate in his hands, and that was plenty scary enough.

She didn't normally do stuff like this. She didn't go out and solicit strange men—with *cookies,* nothing else, mind—and she didn't make bold approaches to anyone, anywhere, ever. She didn't 'grab life with both hands' or 'seize the opportunity' or 'suck the marrow out of life', or whatever else you wanted to put in a meme or on a mug. Harriet knew she had lived her life safely. Smally, if that was even a word. She'd done it first out of fear and then later as a choice. Why risk and get hurt? Try and fail? Oh yes, she knew those quotes, too. *Failure is success in progress*, said Albert Einstein. Or Walt Disney: *Everyone falls down. Getting up is how you learn to walk.*

Easy to put on a bumper sticker but less so to live out day by day. And Harriet had chosen not to—yet here she was, standing at the bottom of the sweeping drive up to Mathering Manor House Hotel, about to try, at least in this.

What on earth had she been thinking?

Her sister, Rachel, had been the one to chivvy her along, telling her she should expand her fledgling, barely there bakery business, solicit new customers, find new avenues of revenue, speaking like the investment manager she was, when the truth was, Harriet didn't even *have* a bakery business. Not really.

"I've done some cookies and scones for a couple of functions," she'd told Rachel flatly, as they'd stood on opposite sides of the kitchen table, facing each other off like opponents in a boxing ring. For a long time, that was exactly how her relationship with her sister had felt—a low-level, and sometimes not so low, thrum of antagonism between them, a hum of resentment in the air, whenever they saw each other, which had been rarely.

Harriet knew she was to blame for it, at least in part. Maybe even a large part. Since Rachel had come back from her high-flying life in London to Embthwaite Farm, tucked in the rolling moors of North Yorkshire, they'd managed to find something of an equilibrium, but it had taken a while. Rachel had returned home to help care for their ailing father, and Harriet had felt she'd swanned in at the start, believing she knew best, and that Harriet had just been sitting on her hands and being useless. As usual.

Those first few weeks had been fairly fraught, and a couple of painfully honest conversations—the kind Harriet *really* didn't like—had helped to expose old wounds, and then hopefully begun to heal them. Two months on from her sister's arrival, the healing was still in process, but at least it was happening. Harriet knew she and her sister would always be very different people; Rachel was a go-getter, utterly focused on career and ambition, at least until recently. Since coming back home, she'd fallen in love with an old flame—their neighbour Ben Mackey—and he certainly had helped to soften a few of her edges.

But her sister still sometimes became impatient with Harriet's endless doubts and dithering.

"What do you have to lose?" she'd demanded in exasperation, as they'd stood there in the kitchen. "Just *ask*. If they don't want your baked goods, they'll say so. End of."

And that will crush me, Harriet had thought but not said. She knew Rachel wouldn't understand. She didn't know what it was like to feel utterly rejected, even if she thought she did, because back in year seven, Ben Mackey hadn't sat with her on the school bus. Harriet had heard the whole story and she'd sympathised, she *had*, even as part of her had thought, *Really?* That's *what held you back all this time?*

Because meanwhile she'd had a mother who had abandoned her—and yes, she'd abandoned Rachel, too, *obviously*, but she'd at least waited until Rachel had gone to university—and a father who more or less couldn't stand her—and he *loved* Rachel, as much as he loved anyone, that was—to contend with. *Sorry, Rach, but I think I win the rejection stakes.*

Not that it was a competition anyone, Harriet included, wanted to win, but it explained why she wasn't eager to be rejected by anyone, over anything, ever again. Even over a simple matter of cookies.

Harriet hitched the basket a little further up on her arm as she eyed the steep, sweeping drive. If she went back home now, Rachel would know she'd chickened out. It annoyed her that she still cared that much about what her sister thought, and part of her wanted to stalk back home defiantly and say: *So what? I didn't go. I didn't want to go.*

Except she actually did want to.

She really wanted her bakery business—such as it was—to succeed. She'd been trying to get it going for several months, but every time she felt as if she managed to get a bit of momentum, something set her back. An order was cancelled. A bakery she'd approached to supply with fresh bread had backed off, claiming her kitchen wasn't up to the necessary hygiene standards (it was now, and they still weren't interested). Each time she worked up the courage to ask someone if they would like to collaborate with Embthwaite Treats, a little part of her died when they said sorry, no, and sometimes not even sorry. *No good, love. We've got a contract with another supplier.* Or: *I'm afraid we decided to go with someone else.* Or simply: *Nope, not interested.* All those rejections hurt. A lot. And it had taken a lot to make herself get back up again, steel herself to try again. She'd started to wonder if she should even bother. She hadn't in the past, so why now?

The truth was, she'd had more than a sneaking suspicion that the gigs she had got—a couple of parties and supplying a nearby tea shop—were out of pity. It felt like everyone in Mathering, population four thousand, knew about Harriet Mowbray, the sister who hadn't left to make something of herself. Who hadn't even managed to get her A levels. Who had been living at home, picking up occasional work when she could, and going absolutely nowhere.

Besides all that, now that Rachel was home, watching her on the sidelines, telling her to try harder, her failure wouldn't be the quiet slinking away that it usually was. It would be even more shaming. Rachel would tsk and shake her head and say: *Harriet, you are your own worst enemy.*

As if she didn't know that already.

Harriet took a deep breath as she transferred the heavy basket to the other arm. She'd made five separate batches of Christmas cookies as samples for the manor house hotel, hoping they might want her to be a regular supplier after their grand opening the week before Christmas.

Rumour was the hotel had been bought by a mysterious millionaire, someone from far away, London maybe, or even abroad, who had been seen out and about on rare occasions although no one seemed to be able to say much about him. The whole town had been abuzz with the news, although Harriet couldn't be sure how much was true and how much was the usual village gossip. What was true, was the manor house *was* being renovated, *was* opening before Christmas, and *maybe* needed cookies.

She was doing this.

Taking another deep breath, Harriet started up the lane. It was steep and curving, and her calves had begun to ache along with her arm by the time she made it to the grand entrance of the hotel, a rambling edifice of weathered golden stone, first built in the 1500s and then added onto over various centuries and decades, so the result was a house that looked like a history lesson, complete with squat Georgian squareness, Gothic towers, and a modern monstrosity of a wing out back. Harriet had always been intrigued by the place, which had been owned by local aristocracy until their line had died out over a hundred years ago. Before the First World War, it had been a school, and then a nursing home, and then nothing. It had been empty for thirty years, with the requisite rumours of being haunted or cursed, before Mr Mystery Millionaire had bought it.

It was certainly looking busy and occupied now, at any rate, with construction workers coming and going from various entrances. There were several trucks parked out front—one that was for flooring, according to the logo on its side, and another offered to fix any and all of your plumbing problems. Considering the inn was meant to open in just over a month, Harriet hoped it lived up to its advertising.

She squared her shoulders and, gripping her basket of cookies tightly, headed to the front door.

QUINN TAYLOR WAS having a bad day. He'd had a lot of bad days lately, because renovating a derelict manor house on something of a shoestring budget—although it certainly hadn't seemed shoestring at the start—he was discovering, did not lend itself to good days. Today's problem was the plumbing. Mathering Manor's ancient, creaking system had more than a few leaks—something he should have dealt with before laying carpets in several bedrooms, which were now soaked and probably unsalvageable. A waste he could most definitely not afford, and one that annoyed him because it could have been so easily avoidable, if he'd just *thought*.

He could almost hear his father's voice, see the slow, familiar, and despairing shake of his head.

Where's your common sense?

Not readily available when it came to carpets, it seemed. Or anything else, really. Time and time again he'd shown just how *un*-sensible he could be. Quinn sighed and raked his hands through his dark hair, left a little too long, before letting it flop back on his forehead. He glanced down at the various bills and invoices on his desk, as well as his latest bank statement, which had two fewer zeroes than he'd been hoping. Amazing how quickly you could burn through a massive pay-out when you had a will to. He would have thought blowing through that much money would have taken some effort, but it turned out to be surprisingly easy. Mathering Manor was the definition of a money pit.

A yelp from outside had him turning to the window of the room he'd chosen to be his office, tucked in a front corner of the higgledy-piggledy house, with its many corridors and alcoves, nooks, and crannies. A woman who had been walking towards the front door had let out the sound as she'd been forced to dodge out of the way of a man with a stepladder on his shoulder who hadn't seen her; if she hadn't moved, she might have been decapitated.

Quinn stood up, his grey eyes narrowing as he took in the sight of the woman in her red wool coat, a basket over her arm like Little Red Riding Hood, dark curls erupting from underneath a blue bobble hat. She looked familiar, and he couldn't think why. He hadn't met many residents of Mathering yet, doing his best to keep a low profile, although he had gone to the pub a few times for a pint, and that ceilidh, as well, about a month ago, when he'd heard the sound of the pipes and fiddle and had felt a longing to lose himself, just for a little while, to let loose, to forget everything he'd left behind, including his own ignominy.

Had he met this woman there? Danced with her, even? In the darkened blur of the village hall, he couldn't remember many faces, but her springy curls that surrounded her face like a dark, out-of-control halo made a memory spark. He recalled her laugh, something bubbling up and generous, her head thrown back, curls cascading down her back. Yes, he *had* danced with her, he was sure of it. But what on earth was she doing here at the hotel?

Having recovered from the near-miss with the ladder, she was now starting towards the front door, looking doggedly determined but also a little bit as if she was approaching the gallows. Quinn was intrigued. There was something about her—that determination as well as the obvious fear or at least nervousness—that sparked something else in him.

Sympathy. It was how he'd felt for most of his life, not that he'd ever admitted it to anyone, or would. He had his own way of dealing with his deficiencies. But that look on her face was enough to have him rising from his desk to go to greet her, only to be stopped by the insistent buzz of his mobile. The number flashing on the screen made him pause. It belonged to Amy Robbins, a reporter at a national newspaper who had responded to an initial inquiry about publicity for the hotel. He knew he couldn't afford not to take the call.

"Hello?"

"Is this the Mathering Manor House Hotel?"

"In process, but yes." He kept his tone light, jovial. "Ms Robbins? I'm so glad you called."

"You have an interesting proposal, Mr…?" Her voice held the lilt of a question.

"I believe you've communicated with my assistant previously," Quinn replied smoothly. "But the hotel is being run by Real Incorporated."

"Real Incorporated?" She sounded dubious; he'd come up with the name himself, filed it as a limited company two months ago.

"Yes." He didn't want to give her any more information than that. He had no intention of telling her his name if he didn't have to. "You were interested in the specifics?"

"Yes, especially regarding the technology—"

"Indeed, indeed—"

"A bold move, Mr—?"

"A wise one, I hope. Ms Robbins." He cut her off with a jocular laugh worthy of his father at his smug best. "At least, I hope you'll think so, when you come and visit." He glanced out the window; the woman had gone. She must have come into the house, met his assistant—Perry. But what did she want? Quinn refocused on the call. "We're holding an opening party on the seventeenth of December. You're invited, with a complimentary night at the hotel, breakfast and dinner included."

"That's very generous."

"My pleasure." He needed to get some publicity for this place if it was ever going to get off the ground. "Can we expect you, then?"

"I'll check my schedule and ring you back."

"Wonderful." He ended the call, releasing a pent-up breath, glad he'd navigated a potentially tricky situation. It was surprisingly hard to start your own business without giving your name away. Not, of course, that he was famous enough to elicit a response, or even so much as a raised eyebrow. But all it would take was one internet search for Quinn Taylor to give results he wasn't particularly keen for anyone to see. This was meant to be a new start, a blank page. He didn't need his past, with all its mistakes, catching up with him.

In any case, the people who did know who he was—like his own family—thought he was crazy enough for buying this place. It was certainly a bit different from what he'd been doing before. In fact, *completely* different… *Was* he crazy, buying this place and trying to turn it into a hotel? He'd been a game designer, for heaven's sake. He knew nothing about hotels, or hospitality, never mind this forgotten corner of North Yorkshire he'd stumbled upon. He wasn't even very good with people; computer code had always been more his style, a kind of refuge. He had the unfortunate tendency to say the first thing that came into his head or get absorbed in something else, so it seemed like he was being rude. He suspected it was more self-protection than anything else, but he wasn't all aware it was happening. So why had he gone into a customer-based industry?

His father certainly thought he was crazy, Quinn knew, but then his father had never been very impressed at how much money Quinn had made from selling Q Games, or really, anything he'd ever done at all. His father was old-school, a finance manager who had never got on board with what he called the dot.com craze, not realising how that phrase had already become dated. He'd bought a mobile phone, very reluctantly, only last year. But when Quinn had told him he was buying a crumbling manor and turning it into a manor house hotel, his father had looked at him in disbelief before shaking his head slowly, the way he always did with Quinn, in something close to despair.

"What on earth would possess you to do such a thing?" he'd asked in the kind of tone that would normally be reserved for setting fire to your hair or throwing your wallet into the ocean. Metaphorically, Quinn supposed, he'd done both.

"I just want to," he'd told his father, which had led to yet more head shaking. Quinn was used to it; he'd been disappointing his father for twenty-seven years, since he'd first started school. He should put that on a T-shirt, he thought with a hint of dark amusement. *Quinn Taylor. Disappointing His Father Since 1997.*

He glanced back outside, and saw that the woman in the red coat, minus the basket, was striding back down the drive, her dark, curly hair flying out behind her. There was something almost angry about her stride, until she suddenly stopped at the first curve in the road, her shoulders slumping, her head bowed. Was she *crying*? His heart twisted with sympathy.

Quinn tossed his phone on his desk as he hurried out of his office, determined to discover just what Little Red Riding Hood had wanted with his hotel…and what had got her in such a state.

Chapter Two

HARRIET HURRIED DOWN the drive of the Mathering Manor House Hotel as if she were being chased. It felt better to be angry rather than hurt, and the truth was she was far too close to bursting into tears. Over *cookies.*

How ridiculous, except it didn't feel ridiculous at all, because of course it wasn't just about cookies. It was about her bakery business, her hope and her future, *herself.* And yes, cookies.

Breathe, Harriet, she told herself crossly. *Breathe and don't fall to pieces, just because something didn't go the way you wanted it to. Just because* you *didn't go the way you wanted to.* She'd been too discomfited by the American woman she'd encountered, a woman with a nose piercing and a short shock of bright pink hair, who was younger than Harriet and seemed absurdly cool for poky, dull Mathering. Harriet had been undone simply by the sight of her, conscious of how frumpy and uncertain she felt…she *was.* And the cool woman seemed to think it, as well, by the way her narrowed gaze had flicked Harriet up and down in seeming dismissal.

She had ventured into the foyer of the hotel, her boots thudding on the ancient, well-worn slate, a large, antique gilt-framed mirror reflecting her pale, scared face back at her.

Bushy dark hair. Brown eyes that looked too large for her face. A strained expression that she feared made her look like a scared rabbit, and older than her thirty-one years, to boot.

As Harriet had glanced around the empty space, she'd realised the hotel's hall had clearly already been refurbished, its walls painted a cool, expensive-looking dove grey, a console table of a deep, burnished cherrywood sporting a few glossy brochures. Meanwhile the rooms going off it in various directions were still covered in drop cloths, with stepladders and buckets of paint lying about.

"Hello…?" she'd called out, feeling a bit like Goldilocks venturing into the bears' house, if she was going to switch fairy tales.

"May I help you?" The woman's voice was sharp but not necessarily unfriendly, more just briskly pointed, but when Harriet saw the shock of pink hair and the piercing, as well as the black Doc Marten boots and the ripped jeans and graphic T-shirt the woman was wearing, she immediately felt taken aback and intimidated, as well as a bit stupid for carrying cookies. In a basket.

"H-h…hi," she'd stammered, blushing before she'd even begun. "I was hoping to speak to the, um, owner of the hotel?" Her voice wavered and then rose to a squeak and Harriet cursed herself for being such a complete ninny.

The woman's eyes had narrowed in instant assessment, and Harriet had felt herself visibly shrink. What on earth was she doing here? The gingham-covered wicker basket that she'd thought looked so cute now only seemed twee and, well, pathetic. She felt like an overgrown child.

"The owner of the hotel," the woman had repeated, and

it had taken Harriet a second to realise she was waiting for a name. A name she hadn't known, and that this woman was clearly not willing to give.

"I'm afraid I don't know his name," she'd confessed, an apology. No one in Mathering seemed to know it. "But I know he's planning to open for Christmas, and I thought he might be interested in my…um, cookies." Now she'd just sounded—and felt—wretched.

The woman's eyebrows had risen. "Your *cookies*?"

She'd made Harriet feel as if she were about six, setting up a lemonade stand. "I've left a few samples…" She'd offered the basket, another apology. "If he's interested. My business card is there on top. I supply a few local bakeries and tea rooms." Well, one, but still. She couldn't just say *one*.

"Oh…kay," the woman had said, sounding so dubious that Harriet had literally squirmed.

"Thanks," she'd muttered, and then she'd thrust the basket towards the woman, who had taken it with obvious, confused bemusement before Harriet had scuttled away, back outside.

As she'd hurried down the drive, her sense of pathetic absurdity had morphed into a self-righteous fury. Couldn't the woman have been a *bit* more friendly? A bit more interested? Asked some questions, at least pretended to be engaged? Rumour was the hotel was trying to get the locals onside and involved, source their meat and veg from local farmers, their furniture and fittings from Yorkshire suppliers, all that sort of thing, but this certainly did not seem the way to go about involving local businesses. Not that she really thought of her little baking endeavour as a local business.

As soon as that blaze of fury rose in her, though, it vanished, like a streak of lightning and nothing more, gone in a flash. The woman wasn't the problem, Harriet knew. *She* was. She should have been confident, assured, smoothly explaining why she was there and what she had envisioned. She could have even asked the woman to try one of the cookies—iced gingerbread, almond shortbread, Linzer stars, lemon slices, or matcha snowballs, and waited, with an expectant, self-satisfied smile already on her lips, as the woman's eyes had widened and she'd exclaimed how delicious they were; they'd have three dozen every two days, thanks very much.

Well, perhaps it wouldn't have happened *quite* like that, but that's what her sister, Rachel, would have done, with the breezy confidence that seemed to come so easily to her. Why, Harriet wondered, far from the first time, did she always have to act like she had to apologise for her existence? She felt as if she had 'failure' indelibly tattooed on her forehead, or maybe seeping out of her like some invisible noxious gas. It poisoned everything.

All right, maybe she was being a bit melodramatic. She was just so *frustrated* with herself. She kept trying—sort of—and failing, all because she didn't have the confidence she knew she needed. When would she get it? It wasn't something that could be magically bestowed on her by a fairy godmother with a sprinkle of sparkly fairy dust, more was the pity. She had to find it in herself, and yes, she'd read those memes and mottoes too. *Believe you can and you're halfway there. Self-confidence is contagious. You sometimes lose by taking risks, but you always lose by holding back.* And on and on, usually accompanied by a picture of a sunset or a wide-eyed kitten trying to climb out of a wine glass.

She could tell herself those and more all she liked, and it still didn't seem to make a difference. She only wished it did.

Harriet let out her breath in a long sigh, the anger replaced by weariness as she walked down the rest of the drive more slowly, the cold air nipping at her cheeks, the sky the colour of slate and matching her mood. She climbed in her car that she'd parked on the street by the manor's gate, and sat there for a few seconds, her hands resting on the steering wheel as she breathed in and out, trying to give herself a pep talk before she had to face Rachel. The trouble was her mind felt dispiritingly empty. She started the car.

By the time she'd driven the three miles back to Embthwaite Farm, Harriet was feeling…not better, no, but a little more in control of herself, at least. She'd left the basket at the hotel, she reminded herself. If someone there tried one of her cookies, maybe they'd be so impressed by its deliciousness that they'd follow up. She could say that to Rachel, anyway, who might be, if not impressed, then at least appeased.

Why, after years of virtual estrangement and only a recent reunion, Harriet still felt the need to impress her sister, she didn't know. It had always been that way between them, ever since they were children, when Rachel had stormed ahead in life, uncaring what anybody else had thought, and Harriet had hung back, trying desperately to make everyone, including her sister, like her.

Older by just fifteen months, Rachel had always been the

leader, the caretaker, the boss; Harriet the follower, the cared for, the baby. She hadn't really minded any of those roles until Rachel had decided to walk away from hers, without apology, without even a backward glance. That was how it had felt, at least, but Rachel—Harriet knew—had seen it differently. It was only in the last few months that they'd shared their very different perspectives on their childhoods and Harriet still struggled to reconcile Rachel's version with her own.

She knew she'd been hostile after Rachel had left Mathering for the big, wide world, and she'd stayed…and stayed, and stayed. Just like today, hostility had felt easier to feel than hurt, the stronger choice. Years had gone by between Rachel's visits and that hostility had bedded down in her psyche, formed a calloused crust over her soul. She'd reverted to it simply as a matter of habit, without making a conscious decision, and she was only now learning to admit just how much she'd been hurt when Rachel had left, when she'd stayed away even after Harriet had begged her to come home, after their mum had walked out on her and her dad.

Harriet had been just seventeen, struggling desperately; Rachel had told her to hold on and wait for university. *You'll be free soon, Hats, like me, in just a couple of months.* She made it sound so simple, merely a matter of time, when Harriet had felt like those months presented an abyss impossible to navigate. Her beloved mother had walked out on her without a word, her father barely wanted to speak to her, and her A levels were looming, seeming like insurmountable obstacles to the future Rachel had so blithely promised.

That had been a quick lesson in seeming, if not always

being, self-sufficient. She'd decided right then she wouldn't need her big sister for anything. She certainly wouldn't ask her for anything. And, in any case, Rachel certainly didn't seem to need her.

She was glad they'd reconciled since Rachel had returned home and they were now in the process of rebuilding their relationship, but that didn't mean she was looking forward to telling Rachel how she'd failed, even at something as small as this.

As Harriet turned up the drive, the farmhouse looked as it ever did—squat and square, made of bleak grey stone, nestled against the hillside rising steeply behind it, along with a long, low stone barn out back that housed their dwindling dairy herd. It was home, and it filled her with equal parts longing and dread. She loved this place right down to its foundations, even as part of her was forever longing to escape it...the way Rachel had.

"Well?" Rachel poked her head out of the dining room door as soon as Harriet came inside the house. She'd taken the rather gloomy room over as her study, first working for an investment company in London and now trying to set up a freelancing business by herself. "How did it go?"

"I left the basket," Harriet replied, trying—and, she feared, failing—to inject a note of enthusiasm into her voice. "So, we'll see." She walked past Rachel, now standing in the dining room doorway, to the kitchen, where she reached for the kettle and began to fill it on the sink as their ancient springer spaniel Fred lumbered from in front of the Rayburn to sniff about her boots. Smiling, Harriet bent down to give his shaggy head a pat before she returned to the kettle.

"Cup of tea?" she called over her shoulder. "Do you think Dad wants one?"

"He's sleeping, but I'll have one," Rachel replied as she came into the kitchen. A few weeks ago, their father had been diagnosed with a terminal brain tumour and given just three to six months to live. He'd taken it in his usual stoic, silent way, but Harriet found the news still had the power to shock her. She'd be standing at the stove, or mixing a batch of bread dough, and suddenly she'd remember and feel winded. Underneath the sense of surprise was some other dark, pulsing emotion, but she wasn't sure what it was, and she didn't think she wanted to name it just yet. Her relationship with her dad was complicated, to say the least.

"You left the basket," Rachel stated, clearly not going to let the matter go. "Didn't you talk to anyone?"

"Yes, a woman," Harriet replied with what was meant to be a breezy shrug but came across more like a twitch of her shoulders. "I'm not sure who she was, but she has my business card, so…"

"Okay." Rachel sounded hesitant, and Harriet knew why. She wasn't fooling her. And, sure enough, a second later, Rachel asked, "What really happened, Hats?"

A sigh escaped her, low and weary. "I chickened out a bit," she admitted, and thankfully it didn't feel as bad confessing it as it had actually felt doing it, just twenty minutes ago.

"So, you didn't give them the basket?" Now Rachel sounded confused.

"No, I did, but I just… Oh, I don't know." Harriet let out another sigh, this one expansive, coming from the depths of her being. "I acted like a—like a ninny. She seemed so...surprised to see me there, and basically unimpressed, you know? And so, I burbled and muttered and then scurried away. Not my finest moment, but you know. Whatever."

"I'm sure it wasn't that bad," Rachel replied, not sounding entirely convinced, and Harriet turned to give her a level look. Her sister smiled and shrugged. "Okay, well, maybe it was."

"Thanks," Harriet said without rancour. It still surprised her, this new way of getting along with her sister. She kept bracing herself for a cutting or at least dismissive remark, ready to return with the resentment and hostility, and somehow neither quite happened. It was a relief as well as a shock; it made her feel off balance, and yet weirdly righted, as well.

"Sorry," Rachel offered with a smile. "Tell me about it."

The kettle began to whistle, and Harriet reached for it gratefully. She was desperate for the comfort of a cup of tea. "There's not much to say," she told Rachel. "I went into the manor, looked around, and this woman came out and asked me what I wanted. She wasn't what I'd have expected from a place like that," she added, remembering the woman's pink hair and nose piercing, the sense of assertive assurance that she wore so easily, like a second skin. If Harriet had tried to act that way, it would have been like a little girl playing dress-up with her mother's lipstick and high heels. She'd have looked—and felt—ridiculous. "Not your usual manor house type at all, actually."

"Ooh, interesting," Rachel replied. "Tell me more."

"There isn't much to tell," Harriet reiterated wearily. She

wanted to move on from that moment as best she could, because it just reminded her of her deficiencies. "She seemed quite sceptical. I panicked, mumbled something about supplying bakeries and pushed the basket at her before practically running away." She was, she realised, making it sound a bit worse than it actually had been. She hadn't *run*. Scuttled, maybe, at least a little, but all in all she hadn't been quite as much of a complete goose as she was making herself out to her sister. That, she supposed, was its own sort of self-protection; if she said it first, no one else could.

"Well, at least you left the basket," Rachel replied with a bracing smile. "Really, Hats, it could have been worse, and who knows? Maybe you'll get some interest, especially if you follow up—drop by to follow up, maybe? Show you're keen?"

Harriet had to suppress a shudder at the thought. She did *not* want to go back to Mathering Manor House Hotel anytime soon. And while she knew her sister was trying to be encouraging, and she appreciated the attempt, doubtful as it had sounded, she also knew she didn't feel it inside. There was no way on God's green earth that Mr Mystery Millionaire was going to sample her cookies and then make the effort of seeking her out. No. Way.

"PERRY?"

Quinn came into the foyer, his heart lifting expectantly although he wasn't sure why. The woman had already gone, and he didn't even know her, but he knew he wanted to know more about her. "Why was that woman here?" he asked his assistant. "And why did she leave so quickly?"

Perry, looking more than a little bemused, rolled her eyes, spreading her hands in ignorance. "She was bringing…cookies? I think?"

"Cookies?"

"I don't know, she runs a bakery or something? I couldn't actually figure it out." Perry grimaced. "This accent is giving me grief, let me tell you. I can only make out about every third word, if that, and she was kind of mumbling, which made it worse."

He smiled at that; they'd both found the Yorkshire accent fairly impenetrable since they'd arrived in Mathering just over two months ago. Quinn, having been born in London, felt he should be able to understand it instinctively, but the truth was he found it almost incomprehensibly charming. "I think she wanted to supply us with cookies," Perry finished. "For the Christmas party?" She shook her head, her expression long-suffering.

Quinn knew Perry had not wanted to accompany him to North Yorkshire on his latest venture but had done so out of a sense of loyalty that was most likely misguided—and because he'd offered her a whacking big salary. They'd met in their first year at Stanford, two geeky computer science majors, and they'd stuck together ever since, starting Q Games together—Quinn as designer, Perry as his executive assistant of everything. She'd handled marketing, publicity, admin, and whatever else came up that Quinn forgot to deal with. Sometimes Perry felt like the only person who had believed in him, especially at the start, but Quinn suspected she was starting to have her doubts now. He'd certainly done enough to test the limits of her patience, as well as her friendship.

"Cookies, though," he mused. "So even with the Yorkshire accent, she didn't say the British biscuits?"

"She definitely said cookies." Perry paused. "I think."

"So where did she go?" Quinn asked.

"She ran out of here like I was chasing her or something," Perry replied. "I wasn't, by the way. I don't know why she acted so spooked."

"You can be kind of intimidating, you know, when you try."

Perry cracked a smile. "I wasn't even trying." She reached down to heft a wicker basket. "But she left the cookies, at least."

"Might as well try one, then," Quinn replied easily, and Perry shrugged and lifted the gingham cloth from the top of the basket, looking somewhat dubious. Quinn knew his second-in-command was not loving the Yorkshire countryside. Perry had grown up in LA, spent her working life in San Francisco, and was not a huge *aficionado* of anything rural. Frankly, Quinn had been surprised when she'd agreed to accompany him on this next adventure; he'd thought she'd stay in the world of gaming and apps, not make the weird lateral jump to the hospitality industry with him, way out in rural England, but she had. Maybe out of concern, or even pity, because Quinn knew he hadn't been at his best after he'd sold Q Games. Gone down in a flaming ball of humiliating disaster was more accurate, but Perry had stood by him.

Maybe she was starting to regret it.

"These actually look pretty good," his assistant remarked as they both inspected the basket of cookies. There were several different kinds—miniature balls, tinted a delicate, pale green and covered in Christmassy sprinkles; what looked like gingerbread heaped with thick white icing; shortbread dusted with glittering crystalline bits of sugar; star-shaped cookies with a deep, ruby-coloured jam in the centre; and then some kind of cake bar that looked as if it were oozing lemony goodness. Quinn lifted a card that had been nestled among all the baked delicacies. The different kinds of cookie were written in gorgeous calligraphy, each letter formed with elegant lines and beautiful flourishes. He showed it to Perry, who read aloud, "Iced gingerbread, Scottish shortbread, Linzer stars, lemon slices, and matcha snowballs."

"Wow. That's some variety," Quinn remarked. "I'm impressed."

"Yes," Perry replied, still seeming dubious, "but how do they taste?"

"Only one way to find out." He bit into a lemon slice, and its tart sweetness burst with flavour on his tongue. It was delicious—soft and rich, melting in his mouth. "Wow," he mumbled through a mouthful of lemon before trying a matcha snowball, which was crisp on the outside, pillowy inside, and delicate in its tea flavour. "These really are amazing."

Perry reached into the basket for another card nestled there, among the folds of tissue paper. "Harriet Mowbray of Embthwaite Treats," she read aloud. "Embthwaite Farm, Mathering. There's a cell number, too, so you know how to contact her. What are you thinking?" She raised her eyebrows. "You want her to supply the kitchen? Because you've already hired a pastry chef, remember."

"I have?" Sometimes Quinn forgot all the people he'd hired, in a burst of goodwill and optimism, back when the money had felt as if it were flowing freely. Housekeeping staff, waiters, bellhops, gardeners, and a chef and sous chef. And, it appeared, a pastry chef. All they needed was an operational hotel, but that was in process. Hopefully. They were meant to open in a month, but it felt like it would take a miracle to get there, especially after the latest plumbing disaster.

At times like this, Quinn seriously started to wonder if he had, in the spirit of blithe optimism—or maybe desperation—bitten off more than he could chew, simply because he'd wanted to do—to be—something different. Wanted to try to create something new and good and unique, away from the world he'd known, that he'd turned his back on because he couldn't stand it anymore. Because turning his back on stuff was, unfortunately, something of a talent of his.

Not this time. This time he was *not* going to sabotage his success. He was going to stick at it, and make it work…for once.

In any case, maybe Quinn *had* bitten off more than he could chew when it came to the Mathering Manor House Hotel, but the point now was he'd bitten into a delicious cookie, and, more importantly, he knew how to find its baker.

Chapter Three

OUTSIDE, THE TUFTY grass of the meadow leading up to the steep hill behind the farmhouse was tipped with frost, every blade glittering under the bright morning sunlight, the sky a pale, fragile blue, already starting to deepen to pure azure. It was a gorgeous day, seesawing between autumn and winter, and Harriet was doing her best to let the weather buoy her flagging mood. She was mixing up a massive batch of scone dough for the tea shop in Pickering; she'd been supplying them on a weekly basis since the middle of October, her one actual, ongoing gig.

She was trying not to think about yesterday's cookie debacle, the humiliation of it. Maybe, like Rachel had said, it hadn't actually been as bad as she feared. And even if it had been, Harriet told herself, trying for some robust pragmatism, who cared? She'd never see Ms Pink Hair again, in all likelihood, and she didn't need to darken the door of the Mathering Manor House Hotel, ever.

Maybe, she reflected, she'd try to sell her cookies at the Christmas markets in York or Scarborough, instead. She'd looked at the application online a few days ago, and while the many sections requiring her to detail how her business was sustainable as well as supportive of the local community were a little daunting, she still thought she might be able to do it. It required her to set up a stall and take a photo of it, and since she'd never even had a stall, that seemed *slightly* disingenuous, but you had to start somewhere, didn't you? *Every moment is a fresh beginning. The beginning is always today. Each new day is a blank page in the diary of your life.* More mottoes to live by…or not.

A knock at the front door had her stilling, wrist-deep in dough. It was barely eight o'clock in the morning, Rachel had gone out for a run, and her dad was still asleep. Who on earth would be knocking on their front door right now?

Another knock, this one a little more forceful, a *rat-a-tat-tat* with intent. Harriet wiped her floury hands on a tea towel before hurrying, somewhat apprehensively, to the front door. Through its frosted glass pane, she saw a figure looming—tall, rangy, male. *What on earth?* Or really, *who* on earth?

Feeling a wave of apprehension as well as a flicker of curiosity, she opened the door, and then gaped soundlessly for several seconds. It was the man from the ceilidh. She recognised him immediately, because he was so different from anyone else she'd ever met in Mathering, not that she'd actually met this man. They hadn't even spoken, just danced a reel together, whirling and spinning in a chaotic blur, before he'd disappeared back into the crowded village hall, and she'd never seen him again…until now.

Still, Harriet knew he couldn't possibly be from around here, with his tall, commanding figure, his slightly long, wavy dark hair, reminding her of a grown-up version of a teen pop idol, or maybe a goth-like movie star. Grey eyes, long lashes, chiselled jaw, broad shoulders. A restless loose-limbed sort of energy about him; she felt as if he were giving off sparks. He was wearing a long, dark overcoat over a white button-down shirt that looked wrinkled and expensive, and a pair of dark blue jeans that were clearly well-lived in, and battered Doc Martens. It *was* the man—she was sure of it.

The ceilidh had been over a month ago, but Harriet still remembered it…*him.* He'd swept in and out again in such dramatic fashion, taking part in the reel with seeming enthusiasm, smiling and laughing and whirling about, but before the music had ended and she'd been able to untie her tongue and introduce herself, he'd slipped out again. Rachel had teased her about the mystery man, and Harriet had pooh-poohed the whole notion, but the truth was he'd bowled her over, dazzled her with his dark, brooding charm…and she'd never expected to see him again. And now he was right here at her front door. How? Why?

These kinds of things just didn't happen to her. Ever.

"May I help you?" she asked when her brain had finally kicked into gear, and then she wished she'd said something else. Something friendlier, because she'd sounded both frosty and frumpy, which was quite a feat in only four words, but somehow she'd managed it.

"Yes, you certainly can," the man replied. He had an indecipherable accent, a cross between British and American, which jolted her a little, because she was so used to the Yorkshire burr. "Are you Harriet Mowbray of Embthwaite Treats?"

What? "Um, yes?" *Do not sound gormless*, she instructed herself, fearing it was already too late.

"I'm the proprietor of the Mathering Manor House Hotel, as it will be, hopefully, that is," he replied with a wry, crooked smile that made him seem a little more approachable, and doubly handsome. "I wanted to talk to you about your delicious cookies."

"*Oh...*" Now she was even more flummoxed. He wasn't here because of the ceilidh. Of course he wasn't! He was here because of her *cookies*. This, she realised with another jolt, was the mysterious millionaire who had bought the manor house, or at least his representative. He didn't *look* much like a millionaire, or what she thought a millionaire might look like, but what did she know? But he wasn't here because of their dance at the ceilidh.

For a second, her emotions seesawed between deep disappointment and wild elation. He clearly didn't remember dancing with her, which admittedly stung a little, but he must have tried her cookies and liked them. A lot, even, to come track her down, which was very good news indeed.

"Come in, come in," Harriet said, a beat too late, and stepping aside, and the man came into the hallway, looking around with an alert, obvious kind of interest that made her cringe a little, because the house was not exactly in manor house hotel territory—far from it.

"Sorry, we're redecorating in here," she explained as he took in the sight of the walls, stripped down to bare plaster, with bits of old, yellowing glue stuck in various places and devoid of the wallpaper she and Rachel, in a frenzy of energised dislike, had taken off a few weeks ago. They hadn't gone around to repapering yet.

"So am I," he replied with an easy smile, and a laugh escaped Harriet that unfortunately sounded almost like a burp.

She resisted the urge to clap her hand over her mouth and turned towards the kitchen, mostly to hide her embarrassed flush. “So, you tried the cookies?” she asked as she walked into the kitchen, the man following with an easy, loping gait.

“I ate the whole basket,” he admitted, unabashed. “They were amazing. I don’t think I can pick a favourite, actually.” He spoke as if he’d spent a significant amount of time considering the matter. “If I had to, I think I’d say the iced gingerbread, but really, they were all fantastic. The lemon was…well, lemony, for lack of a better word. And the shortbread was satisfyingly crisp but also buttery. Perfect. And those little stars—”

“Linzer cookies—” she interjected with a smile, enjoying his enthusiasm. It was a balm for her battered soul.

“*Yes.*” He beamed at her. “Was the jam homemade?”

Harriet could feel herself begin to blush with pleasure. “Yes. Raspberry with a hint of gin.”

“Gin, yes, that was it. Fantastic.” He shook his head as if marvelling. “Truly.”

“Wow.” Harriet turned around to face him, hiding her still-floury hands in her apron. She hardly knew what to do with such fulsome praise; she so rarely received it, but it certainly was nice to hear. “That’s…that’s great. Thank you.”

He cocked his head, his grey gaze sweeping over her like a searchlight. “I danced with you at the ceilidh, didn’t I? About a month ago?”

So, he did remember. She was blushing again, fierily this time, and with pleasure. “Um, maybe, yes? I think so?” As if she didn't know it absolutely. She didn't think she'd fooled him with her pretend hesitation.

He nodded slowly. "I remember that you have a wonderful laugh."

"Oh. Er…" She had no idea what to say to that. After three glasses of rosé, she'd probably laughed quite loudly at the ceilidh, mostly out of nervousness. It was more of a bray than a musical trill, though, and no one else had ever called it wonderful. "Cup of tea?" she blurted when she couldn't think of anything else to say.

"That would be amazing, thank you." He pulled out a chair at the table and sat down, clearly making himself at home. There was a restless energy about him, an enthusiasm and alertness that Harriet found equal parts attractive and unnerving. It was so different from the usual Yorkshire restrained taciturnity. As she washed her hands and then went to fill the kettle, she saw him looking around the room, his eyes narrowing slightly as he seemed to assess every single detail. "I like that picture," he remarked after a moment, pointing to a watercolour of the River Derwent that she'd picked up at a little art gallery in Driffield. She'd loved its cheerfulness, the way the water seemed to sing a song, the bright flowers dotting the banks. It was one of the only things in the room that she'd chosen, that felt as if it was truly hers. And he'd noticed it?

"Thank you," she said after a moment, trying not to show how discomfited she was by his presence, his energy. His *appeal.*

He turned back to face her, those silvery-grey eyes focused on her like a laser, with such unabashed intent. There was no hiding his interest, his scrutiny, no polite glancing away from her own uncertain gaze. She wondered how old he was—mid-thirties? There were faint lines fanning out from his eyes, and a few silvery strands in his dark mane of hair, but his energy made him seem younger. "Are you from here?" he asked, and she almost laughed at the question.

Can't you tell? Surely the accent, if nothing else, gave it away. She'd never been able to lose that Yorkshire burr. "Born and bred," she replied as she put the kettle on top of the Rayburn. "And never left," she added, and then wondered why she'd had to say that. Some part of her seemed to be stuck in self-destruct mode, or at least self-deprecating. One tipped into the other all too easily, she'd found. "You're not from here," she added, attempting to keep up her end of this conversation. "Your accent has me confused, though. Are you American?"

"I'm everything and nothing," he replied with a laugh. "I've spent the last ten years in the States, but I grew up in England and Europe, a stint in Dubai, another in Cyprus…" He shrugged, smiling. "Typical corporate ex-pat kid. My father travelled for work."

He'd certainly been to far more places than she had. "I don't even know your name," she realised aloud. She glanced at him, and saw he looked a little cagey. "You really are the proprietor of the hotel, aren't you?" she asked, her tone caught between accusation and alarm. She wasn't sure how this could be a scam, but something about his manner suddenly seemed suspicious.

"Yes, I absolutely am." He paused and then said, as if offering a concession, "My name's Taylor. Quinn Taylor."

"Okay." Had that really been so hard? She glanced at him uncertainly, and he let out a little laugh.

"Sorry, old habits die hard. I'm trying to keep a low profile here."

"That must be why no one knows who you are," she replied. "Everyone's just been called you Mr Mystery Millionaire." She blushed and ducked her head, afraid she sounded ridiculous.

"Catchy. I like it," he said with a grin, and she looked up with a relieved smile. There was something infectious about his easy attitude, his enthusiasm. It gave her enough courage to ask, only very *slightly* flirtatiously, "So, Quinn Taylor, where have you been living in America?" And again he paused. The man clearly didn't like giving out personal details. Maybe rich people were just like that.

"San Francisco, most recently," he said at last. "But I was travelling through Europe when I heard about the manor house."

"Wow." He really had seen so much more of the world than she had. She'd never even left England, and she could count the times she'd left Yorkshire on one hand, without even using her thumb. Meanwhile he'd just been jaunting through all of Europe, had lived all over the world… "So, do you have hotels in other places?" she asked. She pictured him as some tycoon, swilling champagne as he moved from penthouse suite to penthouse suite.

"Nope, this is my first. In fact, I was in a completely different field before I bought this place, on something of a whim." He spread his hands in a gesture of wry self-deprecation. "Probably crazy of me, since I know literally nothing about running a hotel, but you only live once, right?"

"Right." *That* was not a motto she'd ever put much stock in, but she did her best to smile. He seemed the sort of man who could lend his hand to just about anything and make it work. He was brimming with confidence, with energy, in a way she never had been. She felt both envious and admiring, as well as a bit intimidated. Quinn Taylor was utterly unlike her.

The kettle started to sing, and Harriet whisked it off the Rayburn and set about making the tea. "Mathering must be very different from what you're used to," she remarked as she counted out spoonfuls of loose tea into the big brown pot. "San Francisco…that's a big city, especially compared to this little market town."

"Exactly," Quinn agreed, and she wasn't entirely sure what he meant. She poured the water into the teapot, and then brought it to the table to steep.

"So, the cookies?" she asked, deciding to bring it back to the reason he was here. There was something about Quinn Taylor that unnerved her just a little too much, even as her heart skipped a beat and her blood felt as if it were fizzing when he looked at her. There was only so much of that kind of reaction a girl could feel without worrying about embarrassing herself. Best to keep their conversation to business…whatever that turned out to be.

A DELICATE, ROSY flush had risen to Harriet's cheeks as a

dark curl of hair fell over her forehead when she bent to pour the tea. She was a beautiful woman, in a warm, generous sort of way, although already Quinn could tell that she didn't think she was. She seemed nervous, discomfited, and unsure, although maybe that was just because he'd waltzed right into her house. He'd never really got the whole concept of social niceties, had always preferred simply to cut to the chase.

Who had the time, patience, or inclination for the complicated dance of etiquette, of not saying what you meant because it might come across as too blunt, too eager, too abrasive, too much? He followed ideas like loose threads, wherever they led, barely aware of the loops and twists, or the feet he stepped on, the noses he so often tweaked out of joint, or the bemused looks he received when he seemed too effusive, because if you liked something, why not say so? What could possibly be the harm?

But he didn't particularly want to bemuse Harriet Mowbray. How he wanted her to feel was, at this point in time, somewhat elusive, but he was fascinated by her. And she was undoubtedly curious about him, based on the way she was asking questions—and he was trying not to answer them directly. At some point, he knew, he'd have to give up the pretence. Even this tiny town in the North Yorkshire moors would figure out he was Quinn Taylor, gaming wunderkind who'd flamed out in spectacular style, or really, lack thereof. Still, he wanted to try to delay the release of that insalubrious information for a while, at least until the hotel had opened, and proved to be a success. *If* that even happened.

"The cookies," he agreed, smiling. "Why did you bring them?"

"Why?" She looked startled, and he realised he might have sounded a bit censorious when he was just *interested.* Interested in who she was, what made her tick, what she thought, and yes, the cookies she'd baked.

"I only meant," he rephrased, "what were you envisioning, in terms of the hotel? Proposing, that is? To supply the hotel's kitchen, I hope?" He smiled and was gratified by her shy smile in return, like the unfurling of a flower.

"Well, yes." Cautiously she lowered herself into the chair opposite his, tucking that stray curl behind her ear. "I mean, if that was what you wanted. I supply a few bakeries and tea shops—well, that's not true." She gave a good-natured grimace. "One tea shop, as a matter of fact." She nodded towards the big mixing bowl of dough on the table. "With scones. And I've done cookies and cakes for a few parties and things. But I'm really just starting out with all this. I mean, *really* just starting out. Barely beginning." She finished this list of caveats with a slight wince, like an apology, and as if she was waiting for him to say, *Well, in that case, never mind...*

But of course, he was never going to say that. Quinn loved an underdog. He was one himself—the ultimate academic no-hoper who had managed to make good, if not in his father's eyes, then at least in his own. Of course, that hadn't gone quite the way he'd hoped it to, but he still managed a multimillion-dollar pay-out and here he was again, trying hard.

Already he sensed in Harriet something of what he felt in himself—the burning desire to prove yourself, the decimating fear that you wouldn't. She just didn't hide it nearly as well as he'd learned to. Well, he admired her transparency.

"Great," he replied easily, "then you should have time for a big order from the hotel." He watched as her eyes, the colour and softness of brown pansies, widened in shock.

"I…will?" She straightened. "I mean, yes, I will." She let out a self-conscious laugh as she shook her head. "Sorry, I must sound like an idiot. I'm just…" She blew out a breath. "I've been trying to make a go of this for a while, and frankly, it's been quite hard."

"Starting a small business is just about the hardest thing you can do," Quinn replied seriously. He picked up his cup and took a sip of tea, a drink he was still trying to get used to after years of drinking black coffee, but he figured when in Yorkshire… "Kudos to you for even trying it," he added.

She leaned her elbows on the table, interest lighting her eyes. "So how did you get into the hotel business, if you don't have any experience? What on earth made you buy a manor house in *Mathering* of all places?"

She sounded so incredulous, Quinn would have laughed if he wasn't already starting to wonder that exact same thing himself. "Why not Mathering?" he countered with a smile.

"Well…" She shook her head slowly, her forehead puckered in a frown. "I suppose it *is* a beautiful place, if a bit remote. The moors are certainly beautiful. I'm born and bred, like I said, so I suppose it just feels so familiar to me. I'd rather visit a city like San Francisco."

"Really, one city is mostly like another—skyscrapers, streets, traffic, trash."

"I haven't been to enough cities to know," Harriet replied with a little laugh. "But you sound like someone who isn't crazy about cities."

"I'm not." Not the cities where he'd lived, anyway, the circles he'd travelled in, which had been filled with people whose ambition was rivalled only by their vapidity. He'd been glad to get out, even if in retrospect he wouldn't have chosen the method he'd decided to take. "Trust me," he told Harriet, "you're not missing much. I'd rather live here." Where there was space and sky and room to breathe. To *be*. Here there was no cheap gloss, no fake gilt. People felt real in a way they hadn't back in San Francisco, or growing up in the myriad places he'd never quite been able to call home. Harriet certainly seemed real to him. He felt as if he could see every emotion reflected in her face, which was something of a feat because he wasn't always great at reading people. But he felt like he understood her already.

She raised her eyebrows, her head cocked to one side so that unruly curl sprang forward again, brushing her cheek. Quinn had the urge to tuck it behind her ear, let his fingertips linger. Her skin looked soft, lightly golden, scattered with freckles. The urge was a surprising one, because when he was focused on work, he rarely had the head space, never mind the time or the inclination, for any kind of romance. The few girlfriends he'd had over the years—and there really had only been a few—had been fascinated, then exasperated, then hurt by him. It was a sequence he was well used to, and so he'd mostly stopped trying, although the complaint had generally been that he didn't try enough. Better just to work and not hurt anybody…even if that ended up being a rather lonely life.

"You'd really rather live here?" she asked, as if to check,

shaking her head.

"Wouldn't you?" he replied. "I'd think you must, since you haven't moved."

Something in her closed right up, like a fan snapping shut. He so often had the unfortunate knack of saying exactly the wrong thing. Harriet rose from the table, bustling about although there was no reason to. He watched her wipe an already clean counter, move the sugar bowl two inches to the left. "Anyway, about the cookies," she said, her back to him, and Quinn had to keep himself from wincing.

Ouch. They hadn't really been flirting, not at all in fact, but he'd been engaged and interested, and he'd thought she was, as well—there had been an *energy* between them, or he'd hoped so, anyway—until he'd apparently put his foot right in it...as he often did, because he really wasn't so great at reading people. Computer code, yes, but *people*...too frequently he managed to offend without meaning to, either by saying something rude or not saying anything at all. Either way, he'd found it all exhausting, and yet at the same he craved that sort of connection. Hence the idea behind the hotel...but maybe it wasn't what anyone else wanted? He had yet to meet a single person on board with his vision, but he still believed—or at least hoped—they were out there. He'd find them.

"Yes, about the cookies," he replied, deciding to follow her lead, at least for now. "You might have heard the hotel is opening the week before Christmas. I thought you could supply your wonderful cookies for our opening night. We're having a party—nothing too fancy; that's not what the hotel is about. But your cookies would be perfect as part of the buffet."

"Okay, wow." She turned around to face him, tucking her curls behind her ears. Again. It seemed to be a nervous gesture, but he found it enticing. He found *her* enticing. She was dressed in a corduroy skirt, colourful tights, and an old wool sweater with holes in both elbows, and there was something so relaxed and real and *normal* about her. He loved it.

"Great," she said, tucking her hair back again, even though it was unnecessary. "How many were you thinking?"

Quinn had no idea. The opening night was still more of a vague, formless idea than anything specific or concrete—he wanted music, and food, and wine, and laughter. He wanted it to be relaxed and warm and real. He'd said as much to Perry, who had nodded in understanding, although her expression had been long-suffering; she was well used to his vague ideas, and how to tease them into reality.

"Yes, but what is that in real money?" she'd asked. "Are we talking ball gowns and tuxedoes, orchestras, champagne…?"

"No," Quinn had replied definitively. "None of that." That world had been his childhood, his parents going from party to party, a social whirl of glitz and glamour, power and ambition. He wanted something completely different for this place.

"That's what people expect from a place like this," Perry had warned him, not for the first time. "A manor house hotel—"

"And that's not what they're going to get," he'd replied firmly.

"I'd say a hundred of each?" he guessed now, and Harriet

goggled for a second before she managed to smooth her expression into something more serious. Was that far too many? Could you *have* too many cookies? "Will that be a problem?" he asked seriously.

"No," Harriet replied quickly, and then added, "I mean, no."

Quinn raised his eyebrows. "No?" he returned with a playful smile. "Or no?"

"Sorry." Harriet shook her head, closing her eyes briefly before she gave him a wonderfully wry smile that transformed her lovely face—lighting up her eyes like gold, suffusing her with warmth. "I'm just a bit taken aback by it all. After yesterday, I didn't expect to hear from anyone at the hotel ever again."

"You did leave rather abruptly," Quinn remarked. "Why was that?"

She hesitated before admitting, "I don't really know. I was nervous, I suppose. I'm not used to that type of cold call. And I'm not exactly one for the hard sell, it has to be said."

"Well, your cookies speak for themselves, fortunately," Quinn replied as he stood up. As enjoyable as it was to sit in this homely kitchen and chat, he knew he needed to get a move on. He had a lot of work to do to make this whole thing happen, but he was already looking forward to seeing Harriet Mowbray again, whenever that would be. Soon, he hoped. "So, five kinds of cookies…one hundred of each? The opening is scheduled for the seventeenth of December. Doable?"

"Yes," Harriet replied, and then, with a shy, teasing smile, she added, "I mean, yes."

Quinn grinned. For a second he had the impulse to extend the conversation, maybe even ask her out on a date, but he suspected it would discombobulate her completely, and he'd most likely get it wrong, anyway. Besides, it was probably better not to mix business with pleasure. Not yet, anyway.

But as for what the future might hold…well, that was something worth thinking about.

Chapter Four

FIVE MINUTES AFTER Quinn Taylor had left, Harriet was still standing in the middle of the kitchen, staring into space, one hand pressed to her flushed cheek. Had that—had *any* of that—actually happened? She could hardly credit it, and yet it had. It *had.* Quinn Taylor, enigmatic millionaire American, had burst into her home like a whirlwind and stirred everything up. *Five hundred cookies!*

But more alarming—and exciting—than the prospect of having to bake so many cookies, was the man himself. She'd never met anyone remotely like him—the energy, the attractiveness, the way he just *said* things. The way he'd looked at her, as if she were fascinating and he needed to learn more. The way he'd made her feel…

"Damn it!"

The shout followed by a heavy thud from upstairs had Harriet startling back to the present. Her father was awake, and it didn't sound like it was a good start to the morning. Harriet hurried upstairs, tapping once on her dad's bedroom door before she poked her head in.

"Oh, Dad!" she exclaimed, rushing towards him. He'd fallen from bed and was sprawled on the floor, his pyjamas twisted about his gaunt frame, his eyes flashing temper, his white hair flyaway about his reddened, whiskery face.

"I'm fine," he snapped, even though he clearly wasn't.

"Let me help you up—"

"I'm *fine*," he said again, trying to shrug off the hand she put under his elbow, but not quite managing it. Harriet knew he wouldn't be able to get up by himself, just as she knew his fierce pride and sense of independence made him hate the fact and resent her for knowing it.

"I know you are," she said quietly. "Let's get you back in bed, and then I'll fetch you a cup of tea and some toast. Maybe a fried egg?" As she spoke, she guided him gently upwards, one hand under his elbow, the other holding his arm. She had to heave and heft more than she'd expected, as he helped her less than he might have even a few weeks ago; her father really was becoming frail and physically unstable, just as the doctor had warned them. As the brain tumour progressed, his balance would go, followed by his mobility, and his memory and speech would be affected, too, a slow—or not that slow—and inevitable decline. Eventually—in just a few months, if the medical experts were to be believed—he would be reduced to a vegetative state, unable to speak or move before his organs shut down one by one, and he finally left this earth, like a candle being slowly snuffed out to darkness. It was a terrifying thought to Harriet; it had to be even worse for her father.

"I just tripped on the bedcovers," he said grumpily, the words a little slurred. Harriet managed a smile as she settled him back into bed.

"Easily done," she told him, although she knew it was a fiction. He hadn't tripped on anything; the covers weren't even close to the floor, but it seemed kinder to maintain the pretence, although she wasn't sure how healthy it was. Her dad was dying, and they all knew it. Why couldn't they speak of it, then? Acknowledge it, process it, even lament and grieve together? Because they couldn't. It was as simple as that. Her father had insisted, when he'd first received his diagnosis, that there was nothing to say; he'd made it clear he didn't want to talk about it, or anything emotional, and yet Harriet ached to ask questions that had tortured her for years, even as she dreaded the answers.

Why have you never loved me, Dad?

Did she even want to know the answer to that?

"So," she said once he was back in bed. "Toast and fried egg? Tea?"

He nodded his assent, still seeming grumpy. "Where's Rachel?"

Harriet's heart sank a little at this completely expected question. Her father preferred Rachel to bring him his breakfast, his cups of tea, to help him to dress when it was needed, and assist with the shower, the curtain pulled firmly across to protect his dignity. Never mind that Harriet had been the one who had stayed in Mathering to look after him when their mother had walked out thirteen years ago. Never mind that she'd made his breakfast, and his lunch and dinner, too, and done his laundry and changed his bedsheets and every other blasted thing that needed doing through all those years, without so much as a muttered thank you, or at least not many, while Rachel had gallivanted off to London and stayed there.

Now that her sister was back, her father wanted Rachel.

Not her. Never her.

It was something that really should stop hurting, Harriet reflected, far from the first time, and yet it never seemed to.

"Right, then," she said briskly, turning towards the door. "I'll be back in a few minutes with your breakfast."

"I want Rachel," her dad insisted, sounding as sulky as a child, and Harriet gritted her teeth.

"I'll see if she's back," she told him when she trusted her voice to sound pleasant. She walked downstairs and back to the kitchen, taking several deep breaths as she stared out at the frosty morning, trying to let go of her anger—and her hurt. Her father had always been this way. Admittedly, it was worse now, or at least more obvious, probably because his brain tumour had removed whatever social filter—and there hadn't been much of one to begin with—had kept him from being so painfully blunt.

I want Rachel.

No, he'd never said it like that when she'd been a child, but she'd felt the truth of it in a million different ways. How he'd ask Rachel about her day at school, but never Harriet. He'd go to Rachel's plays and sports days and parent–teacher conferences, but not hers. His gaze had always skated over her and rested on his other daughter, the one he loved. It was so obvious, it felt practically biblical. Jacob and Esau. Cain and Abel. Rachel and Harriet. Not that she intended to *kill* Rachel or anything, of course, but still. It stung. A lot.

Taking another deep breath, Harriet reached for a frying pan and set it on top of the Rayburn. She moved around the kitchen, grateful for the activity that kept her mind blank yet reassuringly occupied. Cooking and baking had always provided this sort of comfort, a respite from reality, the one area of life where she knew what to do and she felt capable and confident.

And she *should* feel confident, she told herself, because she'd just had an order for five *hundred* cookies. She wanted to remember that, not the way her dad made her feel so unnecessary and unimportant. So unloved.

Cookies, Harriet, think about the cookies.

She cracked an egg into the frying pan and cut a thick slice from the loaf of homemade bread she'd baked that morning, just as Rachel came into the kitchen, yanking her earbuds out of her ears as she wiped her forehead with the back of her wrist.

"Dad awake?" she asked, nodding to the egg now bubbling in the pan.

"Yes, he wants you." Harriet hadn't meant to sound quite so pointed, but she knew from the tightening of her sister's lips that she had. Well, so what? Just because they had both acknowledged that their father preferred Rachel didn't make it easier for Harriet to accept—or handle on a day-to-day basis.

"He doesn't mean anything by it, Harriet," Rachel told her quietly.

"Yes, he does." This time she managed to speak matter-of-factly. "What he means is, he'd rather deal with you than with me. That's exactly what he said when I went upstairs to help him back to bed after he'd fallen. 'I want Rachel.'"

Rachel shook her head. "I just meant he's not trying to hurt you. Not deliberately."

"Well, that makes me feel loads better, thank you," Harriet returned sarcastically before she let out a breath and shook her head. "Sorry. I'm not trying to take it out on you. I know it's not your fault. It just…hurts." Still. A fact that annoyed her almost as much as her dad's behaviour. Why did she still have to be so affected by it? She'd accepted it as fact long ago, so why couldn't she move on?

"No, I'm the one who should be sorry," Rachel replied, grimacing. "I can only imagine what it's been like for you. It's not fair, it basically sucks, and I wish I could do something to make it better."

"You can't fix everything," Harriet reminded her, trying to smile. She prodded the bubbling egg as she attempted to stave off the dispiriting sense of failure that interactions with her father inevitably caused.

"I know this isn't easy," Rachel continued, "and the truth is, it's only going to get worse." She lapsed into silence, her forehead furrowed, while Harriet flipped the egg. She knew exactly how her dad liked his fried egg—crisp around the edges, with the yolk a little runny, and a twist of salt and pepper on top. She knew this, and she'd made it for him a thousand times at least, and he still didn't love her.

What was *wrong* with him? What was wrong with *her*? Harriet put the bread in the toaster, pushing down the lever with a bit more force than necessary. She hated having these thoughts—again and again. Why couldn't she just be done with them, with him? It didn't help, of course, that she hadn't had the guts to leave Mathering, make her own life somewhere else, away from all the memories, as well as the man himself.

"The next couple of months are going to be hard," Rachel continued quietly, like a warning, and one Harriet didn't need.

"I know," she replied. They were hard already. Since his diagnosis a month ago, their dad had declined noticeably—in speech, in mobility, in memory. Some days he was more lucid and aware than others; some days he just slept. The mood swings were more noticeable too—the bouts of irascibility, although he'd always been something of an irritable or at least a taciturn man, and, far harder to deal with, his moments of uncertainty or even fear, when he became confused—and realised it. That look of dawning awareness and horror in her father's eyes made Harriet's heart ache for him, even as she struggled to feel anything for him at all. She longed to love him, but it was hard to love someone who was dead set on not loving you.

"Did he come down for a cup of tea?" Rachel asked in surprise, sounding pleased, because their dad hadn't ventured downstairs in a few days, at least.

Harriet turned from the stove to see her sister was glancing at the two mugs left on the table, which she hadn't cleared up yet.

"No, I'm afraid not," she said after a pause, and then decided to leave it there. Of course, that wasn't enough for her sister. Rachel looked up at her, eyebrows raised, eyes narrowed.

"Someone came over," Harriet hedged, although she knew already that her vagueness would only make her sister even more curious, as well as determined to find out what she was hiding. She didn't even know why she was reluctant to tell her about Quinn Taylor's visit, only that it felt like something she still needed to process and decide about, before her sister inevitably weighed in with her own expert opinion.

"Someone?" Rachel repeated, just as Harriet had known she would. "Who?"

A small sigh escaped her as she put the toast and egg on a plate, and then poured her father a cup of tea, giving it a splash of milk and two sugars, just as he liked. "Bring this up to Dad and then I'll tell you," she replied, thrusting plate and cup at her sister.

When Rachel had gone back upstairs, Harriet poured herself a cup of tea and sat down at the table, enjoying the moment's peace, although her mind was still buzzing too much to process Quinn's visit—or how she wanted to frame it to her sister.

Half an hour on from his visit, she was trying to figure out what she'd imagined and what had been real. He'd definitely asked for cookies, a *lot* of cookies, but had he been flirting with her? No, not flirting, but there had been…a *buzz.* In her, anyway, like something deep inside her being pressed. Had he felt it, too? Was she insane to think he might have, pathetic wishful thinking simply because she was so intrigued by him? He was so far from the staid farmers and plodding locals that made up most of Mathering, although perhaps that was a bit unfair, since she was one, too, but *no one* swept into the tiny market town and shook it all up. Malton, Pickering, Harrogate, Hawes, yes. Those places had more of a tourist vibe and were closer to the motorway. But Mathering? Little, out-of-the-way, forgotten Mathering? No. Never.

And yet Quinn Taylor had. What on earth had possessed him to buy a decrepit and crumbling manor house and turn it into a hotel, especially when, by his own admission, he had no experience in the industry? She was longing to know, even as she envied his gumption, his sheer, unwavering nerve. She'd never do something like that. She'd barely had the courage to start her own bakery business, when she'd been baking since she was about eight. What had made Quinn Taylor so confident, so fearless? If she ever got to know him well enough, maybe she'd ask him. Pick up some tips.

Of course, the likelihood was she *wouldn't* get to know him. She'd bake the cookies and probably give them to Ms Pink Hair, and never see Quinn again. He seemed like a busy man; he'd left quite quickly, now that she thought about it. The realisation caused a sinking sensation in her stomach. She'd probably bored him, and that was why he'd left so quickly.

"So, who was your mystery visitor?" Rachel asked as she came back into the kitchen.

"How's Dad?" Harriet returned, as much because she actually wanted to know as a stalling tactic. She was worried about him, even if he couldn't care less about her.

"He's okay. A bit grumpy, but he's managing his breakfast on his own, which is something. But no distractions, Harriet!" Rachel wagged a finger at her. "Who was here?"

"It's not a big mystery," Harriet replied, wishing her sister wouldn't get *quite* so involved in her life. Rachel seemed to be on a mission to Make Harriet Better. Not that her sister would put it like that, but that was how it sometimes felt. It was a bit ironic, considering that just a few months ago, Harriet would have loved for Rachel to show some interest in any aspect of her life. Just maybe not this much.

"It's not?" Rachel prompted, her eyes getting ready to narrow.

"No. It was the owner of the manor house hotel. He tried my samples yesterday, and he came by to ask for an order of five hundred cookies for the hotel's opening night party in December." Harriet had meant to impart this information in a cool, even unimpressed manner, as if she received these kinds of orders every day of the week when her sister knew very well she did not, but the note of triumph in her voice, as well as how it upturned into a squeal by the end, put paid to such blasé aspirations.

"He did not!" Fortunately, Rachel was squealing, too, and Harriet found herself smiling. Why had she been trying to act like it was no big deal when it so obviously was? As usual, she confounded herself. "Hats, that's wonderful!"

"Yeah, I was rather surprised by it," Harriet replied. She reached for the bowl of scone dough she'd been in the middle of mixing before the morning's excitement had overtaken her. "Glad, though. Five hundred cookies! That's a lot."

"Did you give him a price?" Rachel asked. "Did he offer a contract?"

Oh, right, *this* was why she'd been play-acting a little bit, Harriet remembered. Because her sister had a way of pouring cold water all over her burgeoning hopes without even meaning to. Without realising the effect she had. "No, and no," she replied, a touch more firmly than she needed to. "It was just an initial conversation." Quinn hadn't even mentioned such details, she realised. Had he even meant the offer? But why would he come seek her out if he hadn't?

"Oh-kay," Rachel said after a moment, and now she definitely wasn't squealing. She was frowning, like maybe this wasn't the amazing news Harriet had made it out to be, even when she *hadn't.* She hadn't wanted to, because she'd known, on some subconscious level, this would happen. "So, did you arrange some follow-up, to iron out the details?" She sounded sceptical.

"No, actually. He just asked for the cookies and that was it." And she'd been too flabbergasted to think about things like contracts and prices. "I suppose I'll head over to the hotel at some point," she added, "to *iron out the details.*" A prospect that made her nerves flutter and her stomach clench, with both alarm and anticipation.

"Well, you should do that soon," Rachel replied warningly. "Get it all down on paper before he changes his mind."

"Yes, thank you, Rachel. I know how to run a business." Harriet had meant to sound wry, but it came out a bit shrewish. Briefly she closed her eyes. "Sorry. Your enthusiasm is great."

"But my advice isn't?" Rachel filled in, fortunately not sounding too offended. Their relationship was still struggling through some growing pains, something they were both aware of. At least they were both trying, or at least trying to try, and for now it was enough. "Sorry if I come across as pushy, Hats, but I really am excited for you. This could be your big break."

"Yes, maybe." Harriet didn't want to get too excited too soon. She was already well versed in what disappointment felt like, time and time again. And yet she wanted this. A lot. "We'll see," she said, like a warning, and Rachel shook her head slowly.

"Your cookies are amazing," she stated. "The millionaire owner of a hotel came to your *house* to find you, so he could place an order for five *hundred* of them." Her voice dropped to something soft and sad. "Why not believe in yourself, Harriet?"

Because no one else ever has. She didn't say it, thankfully. She wished she hadn't even thought it. She wanted to get *over* these hang-ups. She wanted to move on in all sorts of ways—professionally, personally, romantically, even. Briefly Quinn's easy smile flashed through her mind. *No, don't go there.* Thinking of him that way would just complicate a potential professional relationship, and probably end up being really humiliating.

And yet…

"You're right," Harriet told Rachel, an uplift of confidence in her voice that she was determined to feel…eventually. "It is pretty amazing. I'm going to head over to the hotel tomorrow and seal the deal."

Chapter Five

"WE HAVE A problem."

"Another one?" Quinn did a theatrical double take as he tried his best to smile. Perry was standing in the doorway of his office, arms folded, her expression calm yet grim. "Will wonders never cease, et cetera," he said on a sigh. "What is it this time?" It was the day after he'd gone to see Harriet, and he wasn't as focused on work as he needed to be. In fact, he'd been sitting at his desk, staring out his window, thinking of dark curls and shy smiles and really making a fool of himself, mentally, at least. Never mind. Time to focus on the problem of the day, or really, of the minute.

"I just received an email from the contractor that the bathroom fixtures are on backorder," Perry told him. "They won't arrive until January."

"Really?" Why was he not surprised? It had been one thing after another with this place from the get-go. Everything twice as expensive as originally estimated, more problems than he ever could have imagined, even in his supposedly pragmatic worst-case scenarios, and the hotel still looked like a building site just four weeks from their grand opening, for which they currently had precisely zero bookings. What on earth had he been thinking?

He supposed he hadn't been, not really. When you had silly money burning a hole in your pocket and a sense of the complete vacuousness and loneliness of your current lifestyle, and when you turned your back on that lifestyle in a way that made it pretty impossible ever to return…well, you made bad decisions. Or at least nonsensical ones. Or, he corrected, determined to be positive, ones that seemed nonsensical to other people. A lot of other people.

"So can we get some other ones?" he asked Perry, who shrugged.

"I guess? I'll ask the contractor who's doing the bathrooms."

He gave his friend a frank glance. "Perry, do you think I'm crazy?" He held her gaze, willing her to say it, the memory of his last night in San Francisco clearly dancing through both their minds, the incredulity etched on her face when he'd admitted what he'd done. Perry had stood by him, even when everyone else had deserted him, appalled and disgusted. She'd been a good friend for a long time.

"Crazy?" She raised her eyebrows, her gaze steady on his. "No. Idealistic? Yes."

"Idealistic…" He turned the word over in his mind, musing on it. He was glad she didn't think he was crazy, even if perhaps she should. "How do you mean?"

"Thinking this would be easy—"

He let out an abrupt, genuine laugh. "I never thought this would be easy—"

"Well, then, thinking it would give you something you didn't have already," Perry amended. "Although I don't know if that's idealistic or naïve." She shrugged. "Maybe both. Either way…something motivated you to do this, Quinn, and I'm not sure what it was. But whether you can find your happy in North Yorkshire remains to be seen."

Because he hadn't found it in San Francisco—they both knew that much was for certain. And he hadn't found it at school, or growing up, or at home. But here? "And yet you came with me," he pointed out with what he hoped was a whimsical smile. "Why was that?"

"I came because we've been friends for nearly twenty years," Perry told him bluntly, "as you know. And in the past, your crazy ideas have usually managed to work out." Her tone suggested this one might not. "And truthfully, I was tired of San Francisco, too," she added a bit more quietly. There was too much sympathy in her voice, which had Quinn looking away. So, they were going to talk about that night in a roundabout way, it seemed, yet how his career had gone down in a big, flaming ball of fire was not something he chose to dwell on in any great detail. "But," Perry added, her tone still worryingly gentle, "maybe this is the time to remind you I'm here on a six-month contract?"

Because of course she wouldn't be staying in Mathering forever. Quinn was still amazed she'd come at all; he supposed it was a testament to their friendship, or maybe just her concern over the state he'd been in. Still, he couldn't really blame her for tiring of the charm of life in a North Yorkshire market town.

"Noted," he replied. "And really, Perry, if you want to go sooner, I wouldn't blame you. And I'd be okay," he added firmly. "You don't need to worry about me."

Perry gave him one of her old, raffish smiles, although Quinn could tell it didn't quite meet her eyes. "Who said I'm worried about you?"

She hadn't needed to, he thought. Well, at least *someone* was worried about him, he supposed. For some reason, this made him think of Harriet. He lifted his gaze back to Perry, managing a cheerful smile. "All right, so problem solved then, hopefully, in terms of the fixtures? You'll talk to the contractor?" She gave a shrugging sort of yes. "Keep me updated, on the bathrooms as well as any other potential calamities. Hopefully we'll have fitted bathrooms for the opening. At least the plumbing's fixed, right?" That had been yesterday's headache.

This, at least, resulted in the barest twitch of a smile from his friend. "True. And yes, I will."

As Perry left his study, Quinn slumped back in his chair. Generally speaking, he tried to put a good face on this whole madcap plan, act like it was one huge adventure, which it *was*...but he was starting to have some serious doubts—not just about doing it, but, as Perry had intimated, *why* he was doing it. What had possessed him, to go from designing video games and apps to running a hotel in the middle of nowhere? It was absurd, the sort of headline you'd see on one of those tabloid websites: *Madcap Millionaire Loses All His Money in Renovating Hotel in Rural North Yorkshire. Locals Furious, Colleagues Confused. "I had no idea he was struggling so much," said friend...*

Although of course everyone had. He'd managed to make sure of it. A hefty sigh escaped him as he ran his hands through his unruly hair before springing up from his chair.

He needed to move, to get out of the doom spiral of the thoughts circling inside his head. He grabbed his coat and headed down the hallway to a door that led directly into the back garden, stretching right down to the river.

Once, it had been a glorious patchwork of various landscaped lawns and terraces, as well as possessing a walled garden, a rose garden, a herb garden, and an orchard. He had hired three local landscapers in an attempt to restore it to its former glory, but in November everything looked dead and brown, anyway, right down to the river at the bottom, which was flowing by in a granite-grey stream. The Derwent, just like in that cheerful watercolour in Harriet Mowbray's kitchen.

And there he was, thinking about her again, when he really needed to be thinking about the hotel and how he was going to make it a success…

Quinn had told himself he wasn't bothered by his father's withering scepticism when he'd made the announcement that he'd bought a manor house in Mathering to turn into a hotel. He was used to his father's disdain, so often masked as sorrowful despair, ever since he'd started kindergarten and had *not* been the smartest kid in the class. Far from it. Fast forward to the elite prep school he'd gone to aged eleven and been kicked out of at aged twelve. Then boarding school in Switzerland, where he'd been suspended more times than he could remember, before his father had pulled some serious strings to keep him in and then to get him into college—an old friend of his was a trustee at Stanford—and then Quinn had dropped out just three months before he'd have received his degree.

Hopeless, his father had said, shaking his head, full of disgust he hadn't even managed to cloak as despair, and Quinn had pretended not to care. He figured if he pretended long enough, he'd start to feel it, and for the most part, he had. Sort of, anyway.

He'd been a screw-up all through his childhood; he'd *known* that, and he'd chosen to be one because at least then he had some agency, some control. It wasn't the most mature way to live your life, but then he'd only been a kid. By his early twenties, he thought he'd managed to grow out of that tendency to be both self-destructive and self-protective—the ultimate irony—but then he'd discovered he hadn't.

When he'd made his first million with Q Games, and then his *twentieth* million, he'd thought he would have finally proved something to his dear old dad, not that he acted like he cared, even though he knew, deep down, he did. He always did. Finally, he wouldn't be hopeless.

But his father didn't work that way, or maybe Quinn didn't. Nothing, he knew, had been proved to either of them, except perhaps that he *was* hopeless, or at least this manor house dream of his was.

He stood on the banks of the churning river, his hands thrust into the pockets of his coat, the cutting wind blowing right through him and whipping his hair around his face. So many people looked at him and saw a success story, but Quinn knew what he really was. He was someone who had stumbled on a little luck and had been faking it every day since. The Mathering Manor House Hotel was meant to be the one real thing in his life, a kind of real that hadn't convinced anyone yet, not even Perry, but that Quinn desperately wanted to believe in. A place to connect, to live life the way it was meant to be lived, without the distractions and shallowness of life as he'd known it.

Was that kind of goal a little too ridiculously high-minded for a hotel?

Probably. Maybe he should have bought a campsite, or a spa, or some kind of spiritual retreat centre, not that any of those options appealed at all. He'd seen the photo of the house, and something had twanged to life inside him, a spiritual tuning fork that had insisted *this* was the right note. And absurdly, he'd actually acted on that airy-fairy feeling. With a sigh, Quinn turned back to the house, and all the jobs that waited him there.

He'd just sat down in his chair at his desk when Perry tapped on the door. Quinn tensed, a groan ready to escape from his lips. Another problem *already*?

"Quinn?" She poked her head around the door. "The cookie lady is here again."

Harriet! Quinn felt a smile spread across his face like melting butter. "Send her in, please, Perry," he said. When he saw how surprised she looked at his eager response, he explained, "I spoke to her yesterday about providing cookies for the opening night party."

Perry frowned. "You did?"

"They were delicious, were they not?"

"Yes, but…" His assistant cocked her head and folded her arms. "That's the kind of stuff I'm meant to handle, isn't it?"

"You can't handle absolutely everything," Quinn countered although he feared his friend could see right through him. Perry had witnessed the fallouts of his few previous relationships, not that she'd ever given him advice on any of them. She'd been single for as long as he'd known her, preferring the company of computers to people, but she had enough astuteness to realise something was up when it came to him and Harriet Mowbray. Although, he reminded himself, nothing was, except in his own thoughts.

"Send her in," he repeated firmly, and Perry slipped back through the door.

Quinn rose from his chair, pacing the room, amazed at how energised—and yes, anxious—he felt, just at the prospect of seeing her again. What was it about her that intrigued him so? The vulnerability she couldn't quite hide, or that curvy, generous figure that he couldn't quite keep from noticing? Both, probably, and in equal measure.

"Quinn?"

He turned at the sound of her voice, unable to keep another wide smile from stretching across his face. "Harriet!"

SHE HADN'T EXPECTED such an enthusiastic response. Harriet was glad for it, but she wasn't quite sure what to do with it. It wasn't the way people usually greeted her, especially not in Yorkshire, where a terse and silent nod was the usual method of saying hello.

"Hi," she said, and stepped into the office, closing the door behind her. She glanced around the room in curiosity; on her last visit to the Mathering Manor House Hotel, she hadn't made it past the foyer. This room was clearly

Quinn's. She could tell just from what little she knew of him—it was chaotic, with various papers scattered across the large desk, a huge bulletin board covered in photos ripped from magazines as well as random drawings done in spiky black pen and clothes piled in an armchair in the corner—a pair of trainers, what looked like pyjamas, a scarf.

"Sorry," Quinn said, following her gaze to the chair. He sprang over to it and swept the clothes off it, onto the floor. "Would you like to sit?"

Harriet shook her head slowly, unable to keep from laughing. "What's it like in your brain?" she blurted. Before she could be embarrassed by such a question, Quinn gave her a delighted grin.

"Like this!" he exclaimed, sweeping his arm wide to encompass the room, and this time she did laugh.

"Thank you," she said once she'd subsided, and sat in the chair. Quinn leaned against the front of his desk, long legs stretched out before him, arms folded, his face alight. He was wearing another wrinkled shirt, this one a pale green button-down, and another pair of jeans, looking just as lived in. Harriet had the sense that he probably just threw on whatever clothes were to hand without even noticing what they were, and she realised she liked that about him. There was no pretension, no artifice, no trying to impress or intimidate. He just *was*.

"To what do I owe the pleasure of your company?" he asked, and she wanted to laugh again at how chivalrous he sounded, yet without making the words a mockery. She believed he meant them, and that made her feel all warm and tingly inside.

"I realised we hadn't discussed the finer details about the cookie order," she stated, hoping to sound—and seem—professional, yet also friendly. "That is, when you'd want them, and also, ah…" This was the hard part, for her, at least. "The price."

He raised his eyebrows, a small smile playing about his mobile mouth. "I think you're the one who is meant to quote a price?"

"Right." She swallowed dryly and reached into the bag she'd laid at her feet for the estimate she'd painstakingly put together last night on her laptop. She should have given it to him right away, perhaps, but she'd been too nervous. "I was thinking six hundred pounds, which breaks down to one pound twenty a cookie…"

"One pound twenty!" Quinn exclaimed, sounding so appalled that Harriet nearly dropped the sheet she'd just taken out of her bag.

"Er…if that's too much…" she began in something close to a stammer. She was already starting to blush.

"Too much!" He leaned forward, his eyes practically blazing into hers. His energy had suddenly transformed into intensity, and Harriet felt electrified, everything in her buzzing, although with fear or awareness she couldn't even say. Both, probably. She clutched the paper to her, feeling like a mouse who had just been spied by a cat, and yet also feeling something that was decidedly *not* mouse-to-cat-like, but something far fizzier and nicer.

"It's not enough," Quinn stated firmly. "One pound twenty! That would barely cover the ingredients, never mind the labour." He shook his head, leaning back against the desk once more. "I absolutely insist on paying at least one pound thirty per cookie."

"Oh." She blinked at him, entirely discomfited by this unexpected exchange. "Well, all right, if you insist." She managed a small, tentative smile, and he let out a crack of laughter that made her jump, just a little.

"Do you think I'm crazy, too?"

"Too?" she repeated uncertainly.

"Oh, everyone else does." He waved a hand, sounding positively blithe about the fact. "My father, of course, and my mother, by default, because she always agrees with him, no matter what. My brother, naturally, although I haven't spoken to him in years. Perry—with the pink hair? She's my executive assistant. I'm sure she's ruing the day she agreed to accompany me here. In fact, I'm sure she is, although she did tell me she didn't think I was crazy, although maybe she should." He let out a sigh, and for a second the laughing, lively lines of his face collapsed into something sad and drawn, startling Harriet because it was such a striking difference; it was almost as if he'd taken off a mask. She had a sudden, strong urge to bring back the Quinn she'd seen only seconds ago, the one that had made her feel energised and alive.

"That's not that many people, actually," she ventured. "I think if you want a proper pity party, you're going to have come up with a few more." He looked so shocked that she worried he hadn't realised she was joking. Why on earth had she talked like that to the one person who was hoping to employ her? Something of Quinn's irrepressible confidence had seeped into her, emboldened her to be light and laughing in a way she usually never was. "I'm sorry, I didn't mean—" she began, only to be cut off by his delighted laughter.

"You're absolutely right—that's not nearly enough, but I'm afraid I haven't even gotten started," he told her. "There are my former colleagues, my associates in the gaming industry—"

"You were in the gaming industry?" Somehow it made sense, even though she knew next to nothing about the gaming industry. But he was so energetic and eccentric and *interesting*. Of course he had a job doing something extremely cool like that. Whatever 'gaming industry' actually meant.

He looked tense for a second, as if he hadn't meant to let that slip out. "For my sins," he agreed, smiling. "Or really, for my stupidity. I couldn't hack school, so I ended up making games." He sounds careless, but determinedly so, and Harriet wondered if there was a story there, a scar. He leaned forward again before she could form the question to ask. "Tell me, what do the locals think of this place? Of me?"

"I don't know that anyone knows you," Harriet replied honestly. "You've kept us guessing, certainly. There's been some talk about who you might be, but that's all."

"I did come to the ceilidh," he reminded her, and although his tone was matter-of-fact, just the mention of their dance together had Harriet blushing again. Since seeing Quinn Taylor again, she'd managed to remember exactly how his hand, so large and dry, had felt encasing hers. How he'd put both those hands on her waist and lifted her up during one of the reels. How, for a second, she'd felt lighter than air, weightless, as if she could fly around the room and right out the window. How when he'd slipped through the crowds, a genuine man of mystery, she'd had the urge to run after him, call him back, or at least ask him his name.

"And you left without saying a word," she reminded him now. "No one knew who you were, I don't think. You didn't introduce yourself." At least he hadn't to her.

He raised his eyebrows, which were dark and peaked; they hardly needed raising. "Surely in a place the size of Mathering," he remarked, "locals could guess the identity of the one stranger in town? That he was Mr Mystery Millionaire? I might change my name to that, you know. It sounds pretty catchy."

She smiled before pretending to be affronted—did that count as that flirting? "It's not *that* small."

"Isn't it?" He let out another laugh, careless and easy. "Does it have any good coffee shops?"

She hesitated, a little startled by the change in conversation. "A few." That was, two.

"Well, in that case," he suggested, pushing up from the desk, "why don't we go to one and hammer out the rest of this deal? And I can pump you for information, as well. If I want to make a success of this hotel, I need to get to know the local residents, what makes them tick."

Which had to be the only reason he was asking her out for coffee, Harriet told herself quickly, like a warning. No need to get excited about the invitation, although in fact she was more nervous than excited. Coffee…in town. Everyone in Mathering would talk, because, yes, it was actually that small.

"All right," she said, standing up, trying to seem if not

actually feel brave. "That sounds like a plan." Like she went out to coffee with handsome millionaire hotel tycoons every day of the week—not a big deal at all, oh no.

"Wonderful." He paused, simply to look at her, an expectant smile on his face that made Harriet wonder if she was meant to say something more. Or did she have dirt on her nose? Or worse, far worse, a bogey peeking out from a nostril? She resisted the urge to put her hand up to her face and check, or at least hide anything incriminating.

Quinn, however, just nodded as he smiled. "Wonderful," he said again, like a pronouncement, and then he reached for his coat.

Chapter Six

THE TWO COFFEE shops in Mathering were technically tea rooms. There had once been a hipster sort of café that did soy lattes and the like, but it had only lasted for about six months before it closed up shop. Farmers didn't do specialty coffees, it seemed. Yorkshire farmers certainly didn't pay close to four pounds for one.

As Quinn and Harriet strolled down the hotel's drive towards the town, she tried desperately to think of something to say. Preferably something witty or clever, but she'd settle for anything at all. Unfortunately, her mind was a complete, buzzing sort of blank. Quinn asking her to go for a coffee had taken her completely by surprise; she was still processing the fact that they were strolling down the drive, almost like a…like a *couple*. Not, of course, that they were anything close to that, but it felt invigorating to be walking next to a handsome man who seemed interested in what she had to say. Interested in *her*, if just for her cookies.

She pulled her coat more tightly around her; the sky was the colour of pewter, the air possessing the sharpness that promised icy rain later, maybe even snow.

"So how long have you actually been in Mathering?" she finally asked, glad to have thought of something to say at last. They'd reached the wrought-iron gates at the end of the drive, and stepped through them, onto the street.

"Since September," Quinn replied, "about two and a half months, but they'd been doing work before then for a while."

"I'm amazed there wasn't more gossip about you," Harriet replied, trying to tease, or maybe even—gasp—flirt. "Mysterious millionaire sweeps into Mathering—you should be the talk of the town!"

He gave her a laughing, glinting glance. "I thought Mathering wasn't that small?"

"We-ell..." She made a face, and he laughed his acknowledgement. They turned left, towards the town's high street, basically the only one with any shops. Population four thousand, Mathering comprised only a handful of streets, most of them of terraced houses and then a few outlying farms. Besides a couple of pubs and the two tea rooms, along with a handful of takeaway places, there was a primary school and a petrol station, a feed store and a hardware, and that was pretty much it.

"Like I said before," Quinn told her as Harriet led him towards the nicer of the town's two tea rooms—Agatha's, little more than the front room of a house, but quaintly decorated with mismatched cups and little round tables of wrought iron. "I've been trying to keep something of a low profile here. The ceilidh was the only time I ventured out, besides the occasional pint at the pub, but I got the sense that the bartender there was pretty tight-lipped."

"Toby at the Tickled Trout?" Harriet guessed. "Yes, it's something of a local contest to see how many words you can get him to say."

"I think I got three. 'What'll you have?' to be precise."

She laughed, and he grinned, which gave her insides a funny, tickling sensation. "That sounds about right."

"Well, at least I'm batting average, then, I suppose."

They turned down a narrow side street off the high street, towards Agatha's. Terraced houses with neat stoops and wrought-iron railings lined both sides of the streets; a grey cat stalked along a fence, tail waving high in the air.

"Are you sure we're going in the right direction?" Quinn asked her, peaked eyebrows raised. "Although I'm sure you must know Mathering like the back of your hand."

"Indeed, I do," Harriet agreed. And then some, not that he'd meant it as a barb, and she was determined not to take it as one. "We're going to Agatha's. It's a little tea room that she runs out of her sitting room, really. I'm afraid there aren't any Costas or Starbucks in town, or anywhere nearby, really. You'd have to go to York or Harrogate for one of those."

"Out of her sitting room?" Quinn beamed, seeming delighting by the notion. "That sounds absolutely magnificent. Who wants a Starbucks when you can be in someone's house?"

"Well, I don't know about magnificent," Harriet replied with a laugh. "But quaint, yes." His enthusiasm and zest for life was kind of catching, she thought. Already she found herself walking with a swing in her step, a bounce to her feet. The self-deprecating thoughts that usually circled her brain she could bat away like harmless flies. In just a matter of moments, life was starting to feel more promising, as if the sun had come out from behind the clouds even though the sky remained the colour of stone.

"So why have you been keeping a low profile?" she asked curiously as they continued to walk down the street, Quinn inspecting every wrought-iron railing and wheelie bin with his usual air of lively interest. "Do you want to maintain an aura of mystery until the hotel opens?" Was she trying to flirt again? Harriet wondered. Did she even know how?

"An aura of mystery," Quinn replied musingly. "Now that might have been a good idea, but no, I'm afraid not. The truth is far more mundane." He paused and then stated matter-of-factly, "I'm just not always that good with people."

"Really?" Harriet couldn't keep the surprise from her voice. She thought he seemed good with people, far better than she was. He was so energetic and enthusiastic, delighting in everything, finding humour and even joy everywhere, or so it seemed. How could he not be good with people when he had that kind of infectious energy?

"Really," he confirmed. "I give a fairly good first impression, but the more you get to know me, the more you'll realise it's true."

Which sounded like he was warning her off, Harriet thought with a ripple of alarm. Was that what he was doing? The verbal equivalent of a 'do not enter'? She had no idea how to respond, but fortunately they'd reached Agatha's, and so she opened the door with a cheery jingle of bells, while Quinn did the gentlemanly thing of letting her go in first, which meant they had an awkward dance as she tried to hold open the door for him *and* go first, while he sprang to grab the door before it swung shut and they nearly collided.

"Sorry," Harriet said a bit breathlessly when they were both through the door. "The more you get to know me, the more you'll realise I can be a bit awkward." She'd meant it as something of a joke, but it came across like a confession, which made the moment even more awkward. Oh, dear. She clearly couldn't do banter.

"Not at all," Quinn replied smoothly. "I don't find you remotely awkward. Now let's look at this place!" He gazed around the room with something like wonder, taking in its tiny tables, a Welsh dresser on one side crammed with old bits of china, the flowered wallpaper clashing with the flowered tablecloths clashing with the geometric pattern of the carpet, which was straight out of the 1970s. Agatha's took a little getting used to, Harriet realised. Maybe she should have taken him to the other tea room, which was more of a standard café, with Formica tables and plastic chairs, watery tea, and rock-hard scones. Agatha was a much better cook.

"Marvellous," Quinn murmured as he completed his inspection of the room. "Marvellous."

Just then Agatha herself bustled out from the back, looking beadily between Harriet and Quinn. "Haven't seen you in some time, Harriet Mowbray," she said, sounding as if she was scolding her but Harriet knew from experience that was Agatha's way of being affectionate. She'd been coming to this tea room since she could remember; her mother had taken her after dentist appointments, for a treat—cream buns and a shared pot of tea, just the two of them—a memory tucked deep into her subconscious and usually left there because it hurt too much to think about.

"Sorry, Agatha, I've been busy," she replied, like an apology.

"Are you still trying to bake a better scone than me?" Agatha demanded, and Harriet smiled wryly, one hand pressed to her heart.

"Agatha, you know I could never do that. It's impossible."

"Harrumph." The older woman sounded annoyed, but she was smiling. She planted one scrawny hand on her hip as she glanced up at Quinn, who, at well over six feet, was almost a foot and a half taller than her. "And you must be Mr Fancy Hotel."

Quinn gave Harriet a theatrical look of alarmed astonishment. "Word *has* gotten out!"

"Of course it has," Agatha replied before Harriet could say anything. "Nothing happens in this town that I don't know about. I hope you got those bathroom fixtures sorted. Can't be running a hotel without proper plumbing, especially not a fancy one!"

Quinn's jaw dropped in a look of comical amazement; there was nothing theatrical or put on about his shock now. "How on earth did you know that?" he asked.

Agatha smiled rather smugly. "Billy Walker is your contractor, isn't he, and his sister does my hair on a Tuesday. She told me yesterday afternoon while I was having my perm." She patted her tight, blue-rinsed curls.

Quinn shook his head in wonder. "I'm amazed you don't know more about my business," he said. "Harriet here was saying she'd expected more gossip about me."

"Oh, we don't gossip in Mathering," Agatha replied.

"We just know."

"That's true, I suppose," Harriet added. "A Yorkshireman or woman knows how to keep their own counsel." She gave Quinn a laughing look. "So maybe I was the only one who didn't know anything about you, because everyone else was keeping mum!"

"Well, you do now," he replied with a lingering smile that seemed warm and almost intimate, so Harriet felt snagged by his gleaming grey gaze even as part of her longed to look away, to break the intensity because it felt like too much, and all under the beady and very astute eye of Agatha.

"Well, are you going to sit down and stay awhile?" Agatha demanded. "Full cream tea for two." It was not a question so much as a demand.

"Maybe we could see a menu," Harriet suggested, striving for some normalcy.

Agatha shook her head firmly. "Heavens, child, you know I don't do menus."

"I don't, either, so cream teas it is, then," Quinn replied cheerfully.

Agatha went back to the kitchen while they took a table by the window. They were the only people in the place, and Harriet wondered if she'd made a big mistake in coming here. It really did feel like hanging out in someone's living room, and while Agatha might be in the kitchen, Harriet had no doubts that she would be able to hear every word they spoke.

"This place is unlike anywhere I've been before," Quinn pronounced. "I love it."

"She does do a very nice cream tea," Harriet allowed.

"But you must have been to Mathering before you bought the hotel?"

"Yes, but only briefly. I saw an advert for it in a magazine—*Country Life*? The one with the big glossy photo spreads."

"Yes, that would be the one." Sometimes, when she came across the magazine at the hairdresser's, she flicked through it for a good old-fashioned gawp of all the amazing properties—castles in Scotland, Tudor piles in Buckinghamshire, thatched cottages in Cornwall. A girl could dream, after all.

"There was something about the house," Quinn mused. "Maybe it's higgledy-piggledyness, for lack of a better word. An honest to goodness turret, and that awful sixties addition out back. I don't know why, but that monstrosity was part of the reason I fell in love with it, can you believe?"

"No, I can't actually," Harriet replied, shaking her head. "I'm amazed that someone got planning permission for it, but I think there was some scandal at the time—money changed hands, even?"

"John Telford was a crook," Agatha called out from the kitchen. "He gave the planning permission for a bribe in 1967. It was back when the place was a nursing home."

A giggle escaped Harriet and she clapped her hand over her mouth. "Sorry," she whispered.

But Agatha called out tartly: "I can hear you, you know. I may be old, but I have the ears of a bat."

Quinn shook his head slowly, his eyes dancing, making Harriet think, rather whimsically, of sunlight on puddles. "Well, I'm glad for it, because that sealed the deal for me, I think. It made me think of the house as a kind of underdog, and I've always been a sucker for an underdog."

"I hope you don't think I'm an underdog," Harriet replied in mock affront. She'd expected Quinn to laughingly assure he didn't, but his smile dropped away as he gazed at her seriously, and her stomach hollowed out.

"I don't," he replied, "but I wonder if you do."

Well, she'd walked right smack into that one, hadn't she? And she had no idea what to say about it. She glanced down at the table, reaching for her napkin and putting it in her lap, for want of anything better to do, and after an unsteady beat, Quinn continued, "Sorry, I tend to say whatever comes into my head."

"It's fine," Harriet half mumbled, flushing.

He was making it worse, and he seemed to realise it, for after another pause, he said, "In any case, I called the realtor right away, and came up here directly. I bought it on the same day, and then headed back again, until the sale came through in September. So, I haven't really seen Mathering at all. Maybe you can show me the sights?"

Was that an olive branch for his underdog remark, Harriet wondered, or something more? "You came all the way from America?" she asked, deciding to focus on the first part of his statement rather than the latter.

"No, I was in the country already. In Norfolk, actually." Quinn stopped abruptly, as if he wasn't going to say anything more. He'd sounded uncharacteristically cagey, Harriet thought, and she wondered what he was choosing not to say. There had to be more to this story than he was telling her. "After I sold my business," he explained, seeming to choose his words with both care and reluctance, "I went backpacking for a couple of months, all through Europe. I ended up in England, and then I found this place." He smiled and shrugged, like he'd explained it all when Harriet was left with only more questions.

Backpacking? When he'd said he'd travelled through Europe, she'd pictured private jets and five-star hotels. But then again, she didn't really know how millionaires lived. "You sold your business? What was it, exactly?" she asked. "Something in the gaming industry, you said…?"

He paused as if weighing up how much to tell her. He really did like to keep a low profile. "Q Games, it was called," he said finally, as if coming to a decision. "I was a games developer, for online games, you know, the really geeky kind that involve elves and orcs and finding treasure." He grimaced a little, but Harriet was only impressed.

"That's so cool," she exclaimed. "Did you love it?" She could see how it could be someone's passion.

"For a while," Quinn replied. "I loved the games, the world you could lose yourself in, ever since I was a little kid. I started out with the really retro classic games that were based in MS-DOS. Seriously old-school, the kind of thing a third grader could do in an after-school IT club these days. Then, as a teenager, I moved on to *Myst*—do you know it? The first of its kind, a fabulous adventure story, started in the nineties. It was retro by the time I came to it but I was genuinely obsessed, for a while."

"And then you developed your own games?" Harriet surmised. "Would I know any?"

He gave a modest little shrug. "Only if you're a gamer, I'd guess. *Wilderwood* was my biggest one—a multiplayer fantasy game with a *Hunger Games*-like survival element. So, you battle orcs and elves but the other players are out to get you, as well, which means you need to band together, make alliances, share your loot, et cetera."

"I haven't heard of it," Harriet confessed. "But it sounds really cool." She might be tempted to do some cheeky Google searches later today.

"Well." He picked up a coaster off the table and rotated it between his fingers. He had beautiful hands—elegant yet strong, with long, tapered fingers. "I guess, if you like that sort of thing." He sounded dismissive, which she didn't understand. He'd clearly had some major success in his life—designing a game thousands, maybe even millions, of people had played.

"So why did you sell it?" Harriet asked. "Q Games?"

He shrugged, his expression darkening, his gaze on the coaster that he was rotating rapidly through his fingers, now no more than a blur of cardboard. "I got tired of it all. Not the gaming, or at least not just the gaming, but the world around it. The industry. The shallowness of everything in San Francisco, as well as the snobbery—the whole tech world. It's all so superficial, and yet everyone acts so elitist, as if they're cooler and smarter and more sophisticated than everyone else. And then there's relentless chasing after pleasure or status—I don't know which one was worse, actually. The posing and posturing, the constant one-upmanship, the subtle sneers and digs… It all felt so *fake*." The words came out in laconic bursts, and as he finished, he let out a slightly shamefaced smile. "Sorry. Far more information than you needed. The short answer is, I needed a change."

"Well, you certainly got that," Harriet told him, and he laughed, the sound of genuine amusement, that moment of darkness banished, at least for now.

"That I did."

QUINN HADN'T MEANT to say all that. He wished he hadn't, even as part of him was glad he'd been at least that honest. Still, as much as he liked Harriet and enjoyed her company, he really didn't want to open the door to his kind of crazy for her to see and study, analyse like some specimen. Although she could do that anyway, easily enough, with a little digging. It was all online, if she searched hard enough. The video of him losing it at that party back in San Francisco had been posted online and briefly gone viral, at least in the gaming world, although six months on, it had subsided into the nether reaches of YouTube, thankfully, to be replaced by the latest scandal or TikTok trend. Still, all it would take was a search of 'Quinn Taylor' and a click through several pages to get to the threads on Reddit speculating just how bonkers he was and where he was hiding, and a lot more besides.

The fact that she was sitting here opposite him asking normal, interested questions most likely meant she hadn't done such a search yet, but he supposed it was only a matter of time. They had internet out here in rural North Yorkshire, after all. Maybe dear old Agatha already knew everything about him. If she'd learned about the bathroom fixtures, she'd probably done a Google search and learned a lot more besides. She looked like the kind of octogenarian who knew her way around an iPad. At least, as Harriet said, Yorkshiremen and women knew how to keep their counsel. He wasn't particularly looking forward to having his name splashed about here, along with all the rumours and gossip, which was all part of the reason he'd been keeping a low profile. He wanted the hotel, and the ideas behind it, to be the attraction, not him acting like a grandstanding idiot, but he knew the word would get out eventually. It always did. He hoped by that time he'd be prepared for it.

"Here we are," Agatha announced, coming out of the kitchen with a tea tray loaded up with all sorts of goodies. She set it down on the adjacent table with a flourish; the tray was as big as the table itself.

"This looks incredible," Quinn told her sincerely as Agatha began to place various dishes from the tray onto their table. There was a teapot, two cups, cream, and little lumps of brown sugar, and a three-tiered cake plate that had cucumber sandwiches, currant-studded scones, and delicate little petit fours, iced to pink perfection. There were also bowls for clotted cream and jam, each with its own tiny silver spoon.

"Agatha certainly knows how to do a cream tea," Harriet told him with a smile.

"You've been coming in here since you were naught but a bairn," Agatha replied. "I remember you and your mam sharing a cream tea between you. You used to eat the clotted cream with a spoon."

Harriet's laughing expression dropped away, and she glanced down at the table of tea things.

"Ah well," Agatha said softly, and with a sympathetic

smile for Harriet, who wasn't looking at her, she went back into the kitchen.

Well, clearly there was some history there. "Did you come here a lot with your mother?" Quinn asked, curious as to the nature of that exchange, and Harriet gave a rather terse nod.

"Yes, a long time ago," she replied, and it was as clear as could be that she didn't want to talk any more about it. He could read that much about a person, at least. She began to pour the tea, her head bowed, not meeting his speculative gaze.

Well, *that* really was interesting, Quinn mused. Clearly, he wasn't the only one with secrets. And he'd respect Harriet's, as she hopefully would respect his.

"So," he said once the tea things had been poured and they'd both put a sandwich on their plates. "What got you into baking?" He noticed the look of relief that passed over her face at the fact that he wasn't going to press about her mother.

"I've just always liked it," Harriet replied. She took a nibble of her sandwich before putting it back on her plate. "Ever since I was little. Baking is comfort, to me, and it's also love." She blushed and ducked her head. "That sounds sappy, I'm sure, but I just mean the care that goes into it, as well as the experience of eating. Together, I mean. I used to make cookies for my sister and parents..." She trailed off, looking down at her plate. "Anyway. That's why. I don't know if I made any sense."

"You did," he assured her. "I don't bake, but I certainly love to eat what other people have baked, and I can see how it encompasses both comfort and love." He pictured Harriet in her kitchen, hands deep in dough, a smudge of flour on her face, baking treats for the family she so clearly loved. He liked the image; it was so different from his own sterile home life, where he'd barely seen his parents, and when he had, he wished he hadn't. As for his brother, well, they certainly hadn't baked cookies together. They'd been in competition ever since Rupert realised he could take Quinn's place as the chosen child, and he had.

"But what made you think you wanted to do it as a business?" he asked Harriet. He was genuinely curious, but if he thought his question would encourage her to tell him all about it, he was mistaken.

"Well, I don't know that it's actually a business," she said in little more than a mutter. "I mean, I've only done a couple of things so far."

"Isn't that how every business starts? I've only developed three games, and one of them bombed."

"Did it?" She glanced up, smiling, although she still looked uncertain. "Which one?"

He grimaced. "It was called *Vampires Versus Aliens*. A gorefest that I was talked into producing by some investors. I hated it." And yet he'd done it, because he'd wanted to impress the people he thought mattered and succeed in something when his father had always told him he'd do nothing but fail. Well, in the end, his father had basically been right, because once again he'd pulled off an impressive act of self-sabotage. He was not going to do that again, ever. Or so he kept telling himself.

"*Vampires Versus Aliens*," Harriet repeated. "Well, it

sounds…" She let out a little bubble of laughter and then shook her head. "I don't even know what it sounds like. But anyway, that's completely different."

He cocked his head. "Is it?"

"Your gaming business versus my little bakery-that-isn't?" She raised her eyebrows in challenge. "You had employees, didn't you? And an office space? You probably had one of those tech offices I've read about that has pinball machines and a masseuse and, I don't know, a bowling alley."

"Pinball machines, yes," he replied, grimacing at the memory. For a while, he'd fallen in with the whole tech crowd—the guys in narrow-legged suits and white sneakers, intentionally goofy, smarmy in their arrogance, picking up beautiful women just because they had money and thinking it was because of their personalities. He'd been such a fool, in so many ways, because, for a little while, he'd felt like he fit in somewhere. "But I didn't bring them in," he told her. "I was convinced by an investor."

"Like with the alien game?" She wrinkled her nose. "Well, you had other stuff. A website, and more importantly, a profit. I haven't had either."

A profit he was frittering away on this hotel. "Businesses come in all shapes and sizes," he replied mildly. "If you don't need any of the above, why bother with them? Although I could get you a pinball machine, if you wanted. They ended up being quite a nice form of stress relief." She rewarded him with a small smile, and he continued earnestly, "But really, all of that is just added overheads." He cocked his head, his gaze sweeping over her, trying to figure out what was holding her back. Did she have the same hang-ups he had? Who had told her she wasn't good enough, when she so obviously was? "Why do yourself down?" he asked quietly, and she grimaced good-naturedly.

"Now you sound like my sister."

"Do I?" He was glad someone in her life was telling her not to be so hard on herself. "How so?"

Harriet shrugged. "Oh, she's always giving me little motivational speeches. It's completely unnecessary, because I give them to myself all the time." She cast her eyes towards the ceiling. "Opportunities don't happen; you create them. It's never too late to be what you might have been. Triumph is 'try' with the added 'umph'. Et cetera." She lowered her gaze to glance at him wryly. "I have a thing about quotes," she admitted, like it was a guilty secret. "I keep looking them up, hoping they'll inspire me, and you know what? They never do."

"No," Quinn agreed after a moment. He understood the need to give yourself a talking-to; he tried it all the time, much good it did him. "It's sort of like a quick fix that doesn't actually work."

She let out a laugh. "Exactly."

He paused before suggesting, "I'm a great believer in luck and I find the harder I work, the more I have of it." He raised his eyebrows. "Do you know that one?"

"Thomas Jefferson," she retorted, smiling. "Of course. Trust me, I've got most of the Brainy Quote website memorised. You are not going to catch me out when it comes to pithy sayings."

He laughed, enjoying her humour. "I'm not sure I actually believe that one, though. Hard work didn't get me all that far in life, but luck did." He realised he'd let a little bitterness slip out and he tried to moderate his tone. "Not that I didn't work hard, but it wouldn't have come to much without the luck. It wouldn't have come to anything."

She cocked her head, looking intrigued. "You mean with that *Wild* game?"

"*Wilderwood.* Yes. It happened to take off and make me a lot of money. Nothing, really, to do with me." But he hadn't actually been talking about that, Quinn realised. He'd been thinking about his childhood, about the hours he'd spent studying, to no avail, until he decided trying was for losers and if he couldn't earn his father's approval, he'd rather not try to gain it at all.

"Can you really say that, though?" Harriet argued, smiling. "The game must have been pretty good, otherwise people wouldn't have played it."

"*Dungeon Keeper* was a terrible game and yet lots of people played it," he countered. "One doesn't necessarily equal the other."

"Now who is doing themselves down?" Harriet exclaimed, and he laughed his acknowledgement.

"You're right," he admitted. He didn't usually reveal quite so much of his own insecurity; he preferred to present the light and laughing Quinn Taylor to the world, until he found he couldn't. "I guess it's a good thing I'm out of the industry."

"And into the hospitality one," Harriet replied with another smile. He found he really liked her smile—the wide warmth of it, its easy openness. She was someone who gave of herself willingly and generously, although he wondered if she realised that. "I still don't understand how you got from point A to point B," she told him. "What made you buy Mathering Manor, exactly, besides its ugly 1960s addition?"

Exactly? It wasn't a question whose answer he could fully articulate, but he decided, for Harriet's sake as well his own, that he'd try. "I don't know that I have a precise reason," he told her slowly, "except that it felt like a gut instinct. I have a vision for the kind of place I want it to be. The kind of person I want to be in it." And in case that sounded a bit too kooky, he added, "I know that sounds a bit vague, but maybe it's better if I explain it to you in person. After we have our tea, I'll take you back to the hotel and give you a tour. What do you say?"

Chapter Seven

"ALL RIGHT," HARRIET replied after a startled pause. "I'd love to."

"Great." Quinn's smile was swift, almost fierce, his gaze lighting on hers. The quick business meeting she'd envisioned this morning was turning into a whole-day affair…not that she minded. At all, in fact. She'd loved talking to him, hearing about his life, feeling herself unfurl under the warmth of his gaze. She wasn't so naïve or deluded to think anything would actually come of it, but a little masculine interest felt good after the decided drought of the last few years. And, in truth, she'd love to have a nose about the hotel, as well as hear of Quinn's vision for it, which sounded more than a little bit intriguing.

He was intriguing, in all sorts of ways. Full of laughing lightness, yet with the occasional flash of intensity, like streaks of lightning. Relaxed and confident, yet sometimes surprisingly dismissive of his own success, doing himself down the way he'd said she was.

And then there was the physical side to think of—dark, brooding looks suitable for an alternative action hero or a character in a gothic novel, and yet with that wide, ready smile and easy laugh, both of which made Harriet want to smile and laugh, too—and she'd done a fair bit of both since she'd met him. It had felt good, to enjoy someone's company, to let the tightly held parts of herself loosen, and even roll away. She found she didn't miss them—not the anxiety, not the insecurity, not the indecisiveness. When she was with Quinn, she felt herself becoming someone she hadn't known she could be…and she'd only just met him!

Maybe that made her pathetic, or, she decided, maybe it made her interesting. He certainly was.

"We haven't even had our tea yet, though," she pointed out as she reached for the teapot. "Shall I be mother?"

Quinn raised his eyebrows, looking amused. "I'm trying to figure out a meaning for that phrase that isn't disturbing, but I haven't come up with one yet."

Harriet couldn't keep a carefree giggle from escaping her as she started to pour. "It just means I'll pour the tea," she told him. "I don't even want to think about what the disturbing meanings were that you might have been thinking of!" She gave a mockingly stern shake of her head.

"Well, put it this way," Quinn said as he took a cucumber sandwich and put it on his plate. "I don't want to think of *you* as my mother."

For a spine-tingling second Harriet nearly dropped the teapot. She didn't think she could possibly mistake the intent of his words, the deliberate way he'd said them, or the way he kept his gaze resting on hers, waiting for her response, until she felt forced to break it, looking down at their cups of tea.

"Well, that's good to hear," she finally replied a bit shakily as she replaced the teapot on its caddy. "Because I'm not nearly old enough to be your mother."

She glanced up to gauge his response and saw something flicker in his eyes that Harriet was afraid looked like disappointment. She hadn't meant her remark as some kind of set-down, far from it, but as confident as she'd been feeling, she'd had no idea how else to respond. *What do you want to think of me as, then?* With a bat of her eyelashes, a teasing smile? That would have felt far too flirtatious, as well as cringingly forward. She simply couldn't have managed it. Not well, anyway, and probably not at all. Not yet.

She smiled again, trying to lighten the mood, as she reached for a sandwich. "In any case, I look forward to the tour. I've always wanted to have a nose around that big old place. It's been abandoned for years."

"Yes, and trust me, it looked it, before I started forking out the money for renovations." He sighed as he poured milk into his tea and then stirred. "Money pit doesn't even begin to cover it, I'm afraid."

"Do you think you will be ready to open for Christmas?" Harriet asked as she nibbled her sandwich.

"I certainly hope so. Our website goes live next week, and Perry has organised all sorts of articles and interviews online. She's very good that way, so hopefully we'll get some custom. I've hired about two dozen people I don't even remember what for, and I wouldn't want them to be out of jobs." He gave a slight grimace before taking a bite of his own sandwich. "This is delicious," he exclaimed through a mouthful. "And I don't even like cucumber all that much."

"What you need," Agatha stated as she came into the sitting room, clearly having listened to their entire conversation, "is to get the word out."

Quinn looked at her with startled interest. "I thought that was what Perry—that is, my assistant—was doing."

"I know who your assistant is," Agatha replied with a slightly haughty sniff. "And I'm not talking about magazines and the like." Another sniff. "Word of mouth is how we do things here."

Quinn rested his elbow on the table, his expression arrested, giving Harriet a sneaky opportunity to study to him—the angled planes of his face, the straight nose, the full lips. Long, dark lashes, those silvery-grey eyes... He really was an incredibly handsome man.

"And yet I thought Yorkshiremen—and women—kept their counsel!" he protested, with a smile for Harriet. She looked away quickly, embarrassed to have been caught practically ogling him.

Agatha straightened, angling her head so she was looking down her nose at him, which was quite a feat considering she barely topped five feet, and even sitting Quinn was taller than her. "When they need to," she informed him loftily.

"Of course, of course," Quinn murmured. "So, what do you suggest? How should I get the word out?"

Agatha tapped the side of her nose. "You can leave that to me," she told him before she refilled both their already full teacups. As she retreated back into the kitchen, Quinn whispered so quietly he was little more than mouthing the words "She is absolutely incredible."

"I heard that!" Agatha called, and both Quinn and Harriet burst into smothered giggles before they reached for their teacups at the same time, fingertips brushing in a way that made Harriet's arm tingle. She tried not to notice, even as she felt her whole body hum. She had never met a man like Quinn—so exciting, interesting, full of vigour and zest. When she was with him, she felt as if she were interesting, and who knew, maybe she was.

Even with the bat-eared Agatha bustling around them, the mood between them had eased into something relaxed and friendly, as if they truly knew and understood each other, even when Harriet reminded herself that they didn't. Still, it was a nice feeling, to feel so at ease with another person…and even more than that, although Harriet was trying not to think about that too much. She didn't want to get her hopes up, to start dreaming crazy dreams when that clearly wasn't what was happening here. It couldn't be. A man like Quinn, a millionaire who had been places, done things, had loads of wonderful ideas, could not be interested in her—a woman who had gone nowhere, done nothing, and had one very shaky idea she was only barely managing to put into action. It simply wouldn't happen, and she needed to remember that. Frequently.

They chatted inconsequentially for the next twenty minutes or so, keeping to movies and books and even the weather, conscious of Agatha listening to every word. When they'd polished off all the sandwiches and cakes as well as two scones apiece, Quinn finally rose from the table.

"Let me guess," he said, aiming the words for Agatha, "the proprietor of this establishment takes cash only?"

"Of course I take card," Agatha retorted indignantly, and came out with a card reader already in the palm of her hand.

Quinn grinned as he took out his credit card. "I thought

you might," he murmured. "I bet you're on Snapchat, even."

Agatha wrinkled her nose. "That's for the youngsters. But I do like a good TikTok video." She smiled and processed his card, while Harriet reached for her coat.

"Thank you for tea," she said once they'd left Agatha's tea shop. "It was very kind of you."

"My pleasure, truly." He glanced at his watch, one with a battered face and a worn leather strap that seemed to suit him. "Are you sure you have time for a tour?"

Harriet hesitated, wondering if he was trying to put her off. She'd had a lovely time, but maybe he'd changed his mind, or decided he'd had enough of her. They'd spent over an hour together, already, after all.

"Only if you do," she replied after a second, trying to sound like she didn't mind much either way.

"I do, I definitely do," he replied with alacrity, and relief poured through her in a sweet rush. "I want to show you everything."

QUINN HAD NO idea what Harriet would think of the hotel, and more importantly, his plan for the hotel. He hadn't actually articulated it to anyone, not properly, although he'd tried to explain it to Perry, who seemed accepting if sceptical, especially about the technology elements, or lack thereof. But Harriet was a different matter entirely. He wanted her to understand, to *get* it. Maybe even to get *him*. Because, he knew, his vision for the Mathering Manor House Hotel was as much of him as anything else was, if not more. Telling

Harriet about it would be basically telling her about himself…something he was usually reluctant to do.

The air nipped at their cheeks as they walked back up towards the manor, their hands buried in their pockets, their faces lowered against the icy wind that had picked up since they'd gone into the tea shop and kept them from being able to have a conversation until they'd climbed the drive and reached the house, stepping into the front hall with gusty sighs of relief.

"I'm freezing," Harriet confessed as she took off her bobble hat, dark curls springing to life and surrounding her face, which was rosy from the cold. "On a day like today, you really can believe Christmas is little over a month away."

"Don't say that," Quinn replied, dramatically clutching his chest. "Or you'll send me into a panic."

Harriet gave him a teasing smile. "I can't actually imagine you panicking, but maybe that would be a good thing…?"

He laughed and dropped his hand. "Maybe," he agreed. He certainly needed to get in gear, which was what he usually depended on Perry for, but he knew she didn't feel as passionately about this project as he did. "Anyway." He shed his coat, hanging it on the hat stand in the hall before taking Harriet's from her, which gave him the opportunity to step a little closer, slide it from her shoulders. He felt the warmth of her even through her layers of clothing—she was wearing a denim pinafore dress with a wool sweater and colourfully striped tights. The effect was a bit Pippi Longstocking crossed with Raggedy Ann, but somehow it worked and Quinn liked it. He liked *her*.

The more time he spent with Harriet Mowbray, the more time he wanted to. She was utterly without artifice or pretence, as real as they came, and unable to hide her feelings, although he suspected she was trying. When he'd made that remark about not wanting to think of her as his mother, she'd looked shocked, a blush pinkening her cheeks, but he didn't think she'd been displeased. He hoped she hadn't been, because more and more he was thinking about mixing business with pleasure—in a very pleasurable way. Whether that was sensible or not was moot—he was in the habit of making nonsensical decisions, after all.

"So where do we start?" she asked, tucking her curls behind her ears; they inevitably sprang forward again, but she didn't seem to notice.

"Why not right here?" Quinn replied. "This is the front hall."

A smile quirked her full mouth. "I'd noticed."

Quinn glanced around the space—the original, well-worn slate slabs that he'd wanted to keep, because he loved their history, the way they had been worn down by centuries of footfalls, the ancient stone moulded into the shape of actual footprints.

"I like the grey," Harriet remarked, nodding at the walls. "It's a nice, calming sort of colour."

"Thanks," he replied with a wry smile. He hoped she didn't think he was expecting non-stop flattery; what he really wanted was her honesty, her understanding. "I wanted it to feel like a home, but a nice one. A place where you immediately feel welcomed and comfortable, without having to impress anyone or be something you're not."

"Grey walls definitely do that," she replied, so straight-faced that for a second Quinn didn't realise she was joking. When a tiny smile quirked her mouth, he burst out laughing.

"How pretentious do I sound?" he asked. "Seriously?"

"Well…" She pretended to think.

"I've been in San Francisco too long," he told her regretfully. "Everyone there is so absurdly earnest, while trying to be cool."

Harriet cocked her head, her eyes alight even as she frowned slightly. "Where are you from, originally?"

He gave a shrug. "Everywhere and nowhere. My family moved around, following my father's career—London, Geneva, Abu Dhabi, Dubai. When I was seven, I was sent to boarding school for some stability."

"Only seven!" Harriet looked horrified. "That's so young."

He shrugged again. "I didn't mind." Which was enough said about all that.

Harriet must have understood that, because she didn't ask anything more about his childhood. "Is not having to impress someone part of your vision?" she asked instead, sounding interested rather than dubious, the way Perry—or really, anyone else—might have.

"It's the beginning of it," he admitted. "But let me show you." He beckoned to her to come into the first reception room the hall opened into, with its imposing double doors, long, sashed windows, and a fireplace big enough to lie down in. "This is the drawing room," he told her. Right now, it was covered in drop cloths and scattered with stepladders, but he definitely had a vision for this room. "Picture lots of squashy sofas and armchairs, comfortable ones, the kind you can sink into, curl up in. A thousand-piece puzzle on the coffee table guests can work on if they wish, one piece at a time. Watercolours and oils on the walls, but nothing too pretentious or arty, for lack of a better of word. Pictures like the one you have your kitchen—that make you think, I *like* that. And that's all."

He paused to take a breath. "A roaring fire on cold days. A friendly face bringing you afternoon tea or maybe a sherry. Drinks before dinner, where all the guests gather to chat through their day, get to know one another. No one has to stand on ceremony or put on airs. No one needs to pretend they're smarter or more sophisticated than they are."

Harriet wrinkled her nose, thinking it through, before she smiled, her eyes alight. "It sounds like an Agatha Christie novel, the kind that takes place at a house party."

"Exactly," Quinn replied with an enthusiastic nod, thrilled she'd picked up on the vibe so quickly. "Minus the murder, of course."

"Of course."

They smiled at each other in a rather silly way, and Quinn's heart felt as if it were singing. He almost asked her out right then and there, a proper date, but they were talking about the hotel, and there was so much more to say.

"Next door is the library," he told her as they wandered into a slightly smaller but no less imposing wood-panelled room, with glass-fronted bookshelves and a smaller stone fireplace. "Guests can take out any book they like, and they're welcome to leave one, too—"

"Let me guess," Harriet interjected, flinging out one hand, clearly getting into the spirit of the thing, which delighted him. "Leather club chairs, a snifter of brandy on the side table for guests to help themselves. As for the books, an eclectic mix of contemporary commercial fiction and your not-so-run-of-the-mill classics. Maybe a few bespoke collections—the complete works of Agatha Christie or Zane Grey, perhaps?"

He let out a laugh of pure delight. He hadn't thought of all those details, not yet anyway, but he loved them. "Can I hire you?"

She laughed right back at him. "You already have."

He almost grabbed her hand to take her into the next room, but thought better of it at the last moment, so his hand just sort of twitched by his side. "This is the games room," he told her, beckoning her forward to a room adjoining the library by a set of wood-panelled doors. "We're going to have lots of board games, card games, the works. A couple of tables—you know the kind I mean? Green felt on top."

"Yes." She nodded, looking around as if she could see it already. "You could fit three in here, at a pinch."

"I'm thinking tournaments for guests, as well. Chess, bridge, pinochle, running scores, every night at eight."

"After dinner?" She nodded. "What about Monopoly? For the children? Or is this an adults-only venue?"

Quinn stared at her, thunderstruck. "I haven't even thought about children!" he said, shaking his head slowly, amazed at his ignorance. Perry hadn't thought about them, either, but then he wouldn't have expected her to. They'd both lived completely child-free lives. "But yes, family friendly," he stated, "absolutely. Always." He sounded so fervent he could tell he'd piqued her curiosity. Why did he feel so strongly about including families when his had been so dire? Well, maybe that was why.

"You haven't thought of that?" she echoed uncertainly. "Because that's kind of a big one, you know, to plan for? You'd need family rooms, adjoining ones, I mean; a children's teatime; kid-friendly menus; a play area outside…"

"That might be stage two," Quinn allowed. "Once we're up and running with what we have. Do parents even *want* to take kids to a manor house hotel?"

Harriet lifted her shoulders in a shrug. "Honestly? I have no idea."

"Let me show you the rest." This time he did take her hand, loosely, like a friend, or sort of. Her fingers convulsed in his, a twitch of surprise, but she didn't pull away, and so, holding her hand, Quinn headed into the hallway that led to the other wing of the house.

"The dining room," he announced as they came into a large room with a set of six sashed windows facing the front. "We knocked through a wall to make it bigger. Breakfasts will be a full fry-up with a cold buffet of cereal, fruit, et cetera. Lunch will be either pack-a-picnic if you're going out for the day, or something moderate—soup and sandwiches, cold meats. Dinner is the grand affair—three courses, a dessert cart, a carvery. Just the one table to seat twenty-four—we have twelve bedrooms—and everyone eats family style, together. Again, with the house party vibe." He was still holding her hand, swinging it a little, as they strolled along. "What do you think?"

"It sounds absolutely lovely," she told him sincerely. "Old-fashioned, but in an entirely nice way."

"The way hotels used to be, before it was all beauty spas and health centres and guests needing to be spoiled half to death," Quinn agreed. "But I haven't told you the most old-fashioned part." He paused for dramatic effect. "No technology."

Harriet raised her eyebrows, lips parting in surprise. "None?"

"None," Quinn confirmed. He was very conscious of her hand clasped in his, their fingers almost, but not quite, entwined, the warmth of her palm pressed against his. "No TVs, no internet, no screens at all. And definitely, *definitely* no phones."

Her eyebrows inched higher. "No phones? Really?"

"People surrender them when they arrive. They'll be kept in a locked box."

She looked impressed, but also hesitant, which he understood. It was a bold move, certainly. "But what about emergencies?" she asked.

"We managed without smartphones for millennia," Quinn replied. "I think people can survive for a couple of days. And in any case, if there is a proper emergency, the person in question can call the hotel itself. The point is, people can escape the endless doom scrolling—"

"Do you doom scroll?" she asked, sounding surprised, and he smiled, brushing off her question.

"Of course, doesn't everyone? The point is, no distractions. No fobbing people off or hiding behind a screen. No endless scrolling and clicking instead of talking, reading, dreaming, *being.*" He heard the throb of passion in his voice and wasn't embarrassed. He meant this absolutely.

"I'm finding it hard to believe you were a video game designer," she teased. "Although maybe that's why you've gone in the other direction? Because you've seen the effect of a screen-heavy life?"

"Exactly." And then some. He'd felt the shallowness of his childhood, his whole existence, the way he'd had to try to fit himself into a mould first for his father and family, then his friends, then his colleagues, always play-acting, always hiding. It wasn't just about screens, of course, it was about the whole environment. The whole *world,* everyone trying to show their best self, while hiding their real one. But this place would be different. He would be different.

"And you think people will be on board with the idea?" She tugged her hand from his, gently enough that it didn't feel like a rejection, but Quinn still missed the warmth of it, the feeling of her closeness. Harriet walked to the window to look out at the front terrace, the sunlight that was now peeking from behind a bank of grey clouds gilding her dark hair in gold.

"There are plenty of other hotels if they aren't," he replied with a shrug. "If you can't offer something different, what's the point?"

"That's true." She turned back to face him, a thoughtful look on her face. With the sunlight still touching her hair, Quinn thought he'd never seen someone so appealing. She wasn't beautiful in the glossy, airbrushed, stick-thin way of the women he'd known back in San Francisco, but in a way he much preferred—an honest way, real and warm. The personification, he thought whimsically, of his hotel.

"I like it," she told him. "Every bit of it. It's a wonderful idea, Quinn."

He thought it was the first time she'd actually used his name, and it was enough to have him blurting, "Have dinner with me."

Harriet's eyes widened, their irises darkening to a deep, velvety brown, her lips parting soundlessly before she repeated wonderingly, "Dinner..."

"As in a date." Always best to be clear.

She stared at him for a few agonising seconds, and for the first time he realised he had no idea what she was thinking. Her eyes were still wide, her lips slightly parted, her head cocked to one side, bouncy curls framing her flushed face. He waited, holding her gaze, his heart starting to thud. It had been an impulsive invitation, and yet one he meant utterly. It amazed him, really, just how much he wanted her to say yes.

A small smile curved Harriet's generous mouth. Her eyes glinted gold. Quinn's heart turned over.

"Yes," she said simply.

Chapter Eight

A DATE. SHE'D actually been asked out on an honest-to-goodness date. Harriet couldn't keep from grinning in an entirely silly way as she tottered down Mathering Manor's drive to her car, her mind full of vague yet wonderful possibilities of candlelit dinners and dancing under the stars.

After she'd agreed to their date—in a haze of incredulity—Quinn had suggested tomorrow night. *Tomorrow!* Harriet had felt as if her head were spinning like a top, everything was happening so quickly. Quinn had seemed so very sure, so purposeful and confident, as if he had absolutely no doubts or qualms about asking her out. As if it was very much what he wanted.

It was a prospect that filled Harriet with wonder and hope, as well as a cringing little sense of her own pathos that she was doing her best to banish. It felt so *nice* to be wanted, for once, and while that realisation might be a little sad, it was also okay. So what if she hadn't had the best of luck with boyfriends, or parents, or really anything so far? Things could change. *She* could change. She already was.

In fact, she felt so buoyed by her afternoon with Quinn that on impulse she pulled into the hardware on the edge of town and bought a tin of slate-blue paint for the front hall. If

Quinn could have a vision for an entire hotel, she could manage a hallway. It was ridiculous, that she'd let it go on for weeks, with nothing but bits of old paste on the bare, ugly walls. She was going to change that. Immediately.

She marched out of the shop with her tin of paint, feeling more confident and purposeful than she had in a long time. Yes, it was only paint, and it was also only a hallway, but so what? *So what?* It felt like her battle cry, her new motto, worthy of a meme or a mug. Forget cringeworthy sayings about nothing being impossible or opportunities being created, not found. Her new words to live by were *so what.*

"So what!" she said aloud, the words snatched away by the wind, which was kicking up properly now, a wintry wave rolling over the moors.

As Harriet drove back to Embthwaite Farm, vague notions of helping Quinn do up the hotel paraded through her mind in a romcom-worthy montage, involving smiling over stepladders and getting hopelessly tangled together in ropes of fairy lights.

They hadn't even talked about decorating for Christmas, but she could picture it already…trees in every reception room, loads of fresh greenery festooned with red velvet bows—small ones, mind, nothing too showy. An old-fashioned nutcracker, a bowl of burnished walnuts, hot chocolate with lashing of whipped cream and of course her Christmas cookies offered in the afternoons, when the evening closed in, and they drew the thick velvet curtains across the windows as the first snowflakes started to drift down…

All right, maybe it was a mashup of every Christmas-set romance novel or film she'd read or seen *ever*, but she was still smiling as she turned onto the farmhouse's long drive, past the turn-off for the Mackeys' farm, its low, whitewashed house just visible over the brow of a low hill as twilight settled on it, the valley already lost in shadow. The fizzy feeling didn't leave her as she stepped into the darkened hallway, smiling at the sight of the bare walls, knowing they'd be transformed soon enough, as her life was being transformed. Was it too twee to think that way? She didn't care.

On the kitchen table, she found a hastily scrawled note from Rachel, her irritation detectable in every decidedly bold stroke of the pen.

> *H, where are you?! You were only supposed to be going out for an hour or so? I had to run to the supermarket for something for dinner. Dad's sleeping, but you should check on him. I was hoping he'd come down for supper—Ben is coming, if you remember. —R.*
>
> *P.S. Turn on your phone!!!*

A sigh escaped Harriet as she reached for her phone left forgotten in her bag and duly turned it on; she'd switched it off when she'd headed into Mathering Manor, not wanting the distraction. Three text messages and two voicemails popped up from her sister, a glaring indictment right there on the screen. She'd forgotten Ben was coming to dinner tonight. Not a huge deal, really, but she understood Rachel's annoyance—sort of—about her absence. They weren't really meant to leave their dad alone, although he'd always insisted he would be perfectly fine by himself.

Harriet couldn't keep herself from feeling a needling of guilt that she'd left Rachel holding the bag all day…but then she'd been holding it for over a decade. Not that she'd ever say that to her sister, of course. She wanted to be moving past even feeling that, but sometimes it was hard, especially when Rachel left her a note with the word 'supposed' underlined twice in heavy pen.

She pushed the paper away from her and shucked off her coat before steeling herself to head upstairs and check on her father. As she went, she flicked on a few lights; night had drawn in, and the house felt cold and dark and unwelcoming.

Upstairs, she tapped on her father's door. "Dad?" she called softly and received only silence as her reply.

Unease rippled through her as she pushed open the door. The room was as dark as the rest of the house, so she could barely make out the shadowy forms of the furniture—a heavy wardrobe, an old bureau, the bed with its rumpled covers and her father's huddled form beneath them.

"Dad?" she called again, and he made a harrumphing noise.

"What is it?"

Hello to you, too. "Just checking you're all right."

"Why wouldn't I be all right?" he demanded, as grumpy as ever.

Maybe because you have a brain tumour? "I just wanted to make sure," Harriet replied as lightly as she could. "I just got back. Would you like something? A cup of tea, or a scone? It's gone chilly, hasn't it?"

"Where's Rachel?" he demanded in a surly voice, and Harriet stiffened.

She was used to this, of course, but his blatantly obvious preference for Rachel stung a bit more now, coming off an afternoon with someone who had been interested in what she had to say, who had chosen to be in her company for an extended period of time. This was her *father*. She'd never, as far as she'd known, done anything to warrant this kind of lack of interest, even dislike. How could she have?

"Why don't you like me, Dad?" Harriet asked abruptly. Even with him huddled under the covers, she saw the shock blaze across her father's weathered face, or at least what she could glimpse of it peeking from above the duvet. He'd never expected her to ask the question that had been boiling beneath the surface for so long. She'd never expected to be brave enough to ask it, but spending time with Quinn had made her think, and here was another motto—why not?

Why not?

"Well?" she demanded, and now her voice rang out, hard and sure.

Her dad didn't reply for a long moment. He didn't even move, and when he did, it was only to draw the bedcover further over his hunched shoulders, and then huddle beneath it.

"Are you sure you want to know the answer to that question?" he asked, his voice muffled by the covers.

For a second or two, Harriet simply stood there, the words reverberating through her. *Are you sure…?*

No, she realised sickly, she wasn't. She wasn't at all, when he put it as plainly as that. Without saying a word, she turned and walked out of the room, closing the door behind her with a firm click. She felt numb and yet raging as she went back to the kitchen, started banging pots around for no good reason. Rachel had said she would make dinner, but Harriet supposed a pot of boiling water on the stove couldn't hurt, and in any case, she needed something to do. Anything to do.

Are you sure you want to know the answer to that question?

No, she really didn't think she did. For a single, liberating second, she'd been glad she'd asked it. She'd felt recklessly powerful, taking control of the narrative, being the one who decided, who said 'so what?' to the world.

Not anymore.

The doorbell rang, and a gusty sigh escaped her before she turned and walked resolutely to the front door.

"Harriet!" Ben Mackey stood there, smiling easily, dressed in a dark green flannel shirt and a pair of jeans, his dress-up clothes, or so Rachel liked to tease.

"Hey, Ben." Her voice, she knew, sounded a little flat, and he frowned, picking up on it immediately.

"Everything okay?"

She found she couldn't pretend, the way she once might have at least tried to. The lovely, fizzy feeling she'd had from being with Quinn had evaporated completely, as if she'd never felt it at all, as if she'd never even known what it felt like. "Not really," she replied, and she turned to walk back into the kitchen.

Ben followed her, standing in the doorway of the kitchen while she uselessly banged a few more pots around. Fred lifted his head from where he was lying in front of the

Rayburn, blinked at her in silent reproval at the noise, and then retreated to safety under the table.

"What's going on?" Ben asked quietly.

Harriet lowered a pot lid as she took a deep breath. Did she really want to say…?

Why not? So what?

The sentiments felt like a mockery, and yet she *felt* them.

"I asked my father why he's never liked me, and he replied, 'Are you sure you want to know the answer to that question?'" she stated flatly.

Resounding silence from Ben. Harriet resisted the urge to bang a few more pots around. Instead, she put both hands on the Rayburn's railing, curling her fingers around it as she took a steadying breath.

Then: "I'm so sorry, Harriet." Ben's voice was quiet and heartfelt and, to her surprise, he stepped towards her, and his arms closed around her in a hug. She turned towards him, burying her face in his chest as he tightened the embrace. There had been nothing ever remotely romantic between her and Ben; he'd always been, absolutely and in every way, Rachel's.

And yet, after Rachel had gone, they'd become friends in their own right, the two who had stayed. It felt good to be hugged, but even as she put her arms around him, Harriet realised it wasn't Ben she wanted to be hugging. It wasn't Ben's shoulder she wanted to cry on, as a pressure built in her chest and behind her eyes and she struggled to contain the urge not just to cry, but to sob outright.

Briefly she thought of Quinn, but they were in the fun-and-fizzy stage, if they were even *in* a stage, not the let-me-tell-you-about-my-lonely-childhood one. She didn't want to burden him with this. She didn't even want to reveal it. And yet she wanted someone's arms around her, someone who cared, who could offer comfort…

And there was no one, she realised. No one in her life to give that freely.

She pulled away from Ben, wiping her eyes. "Sorry," she mumbled.

"You don't need to be sorry."

"Just having a moment," she told him, trying for a smile, and not quite managing to hang on to it. "Anyway." She turned back to the stove, although there was nothing there but a pot of simmering water. *Where* was Rachel?

"Harriet…" Ben began, and she tensed. Oh, no. Here it came, whatever it was. "He might not have meant it, you know."

Really? "What do you mean by that?" she asked, finding she was genuinely curious, as well as deeply exasperated. She knew Ben had a certain fondness for her dad, two Yorkshiremen and farmers, to boot. They had the same taciturnity, yet Ben's was moderated by gentleness. Her father's wasn't. "I mean, he *said* it, Ben," she continued flatly. "I think he meant it."

"He has a brain tumour."

"I'm aware."

Ben sighed, raking a hand through his hair before it flopped back onto his forehead. "I'm just saying…he doesn't always say stuff that makes sense anymore. Stuff that means anything. It might have just been a snappy sort of comeback, or his version of it, in his current mental state."

"Okay." She didn't say anything else, because she didn't trust herself to. Ben was basically telling her to excuse her father for saying she didn't want to know the reason he didn't like her? He'd basically admitted he didn't like her, she realised afresh, with a wave of something like grief. And if he didn't like her, he obviously didn't love her. It was something she'd always known, in an academic way, but hadn't let herself accept on a heart level, even as she'd sensed it, felt it, *lived* it. Every single day.

"I'm sorry," Ben said. "I'm crap at this. I'm not trying to dismiss what you're feeling, honestly. I'm just trying to think of a reason why that's more…bearable."

Harriet let out a hollow laugh. "Are you taking emo lessons from Rachel or something?" Not that her sister was the most emotionally sensitive person on the planet, but this was not how Ben Mackey, Yorkshire farmer through and through, tended to talk.

"Maybe," he admitted, a small smile tugging at his mouth. "Is it working?"

"I don't know." She drew a deep breath and let it out slowly. "The fact is, he said it, Ben. He didn't deny that he didn't like me. He didn't pretend not to understand, or even not to hear me."

"Like I said, a snappy comeback—"

"No." She spoke firmly, quietly, with a certainty she didn't normally possess. "I appreciate you're trying to help, to make me feel better, but the reality is I've known all my life that my dad didn't like me. I've felt it in a thousand different ways, some little, some big, and having him confirm it—without yet knowing the reason—is really just the unfortunate cherry on top of the whole wretched cake. I believe he meant what he said. I just don't know yet if I want to tell him that I do actually want to know the answer."

Ben nodded slowly, his expression solemn. "Fair enough."

Harriet managed a smile. Surprisingly, she felt a little lighter for having said that all aloud, although there was still a heaviness inside, a grief. Her father didn't love her. Well, lots of children grew up with fathers who didn't love them, or with any fathers at all. It may have affected her, but it didn't have to define her. It felt like another motto, something to say but harder to believe. To feel.

"And now," she told Ben in a voice that was only a little bit brittle, "I'm going to bring the dad who doesn't like me a cup of tea."

Upstairs in the darkened bedroom, her father had fallen asleep. Harriet set the cup of tea on the bedside table and gazed down at him, her heart twisting within her at the sight. His jaw was slack, his cheeks white and whiskered. His hands had become too shaky to shave, and Harriet realised Rachel must have been shaving him most mornings, because when she'd seen him, he'd usually been clean-shaven. The thought didn't bring the usual painful twist of resentment or bitterness that he allowed Rachel to do something he never would her, just sorrow.

Time was running out. All she'd wanted for her whole childhood—her whole life, really—was for her dad to love her, and soon it would be too late. Maybe it already was. Because, after having absorbed the shock of his admission that he really didn't like her, Harriet was coming to the creeping realisation that there was, according to her father, a *reason*, something real and concrete and specific he must have been thinking of, for why he didn't. Something he'd known about but had never said. Was she too boring? Too stupid? Or maybe she reminded him of her mother—but no, that couldn't be it, because her mother had left when she was seventeen, and her father hadn't liked her basically since she'd been born.

What could the reason be?

That creeping sense of realisation was beginning to coalesce inside her, into something hard and cold and very unwelcome. Harriet turned away from her father, tiptoed out of the bedroom, and quietly but firmly shut the door.

As she came into the kitchen, she saw that Rachel had arrived, and was now unpacking a couple of bags of groceries for what looked to be a very complicated curry. Ben was leaning against the table, a bottle of bitter in one hand. He smiled when he saw Harriet, and she managed a somewhat tight-lipped smile back.

"Harriet!" Rachel turned to face her, brushing a wisp of dark hair from her eyes. "You were gone a long time. How did the meeting with your millionaire go?"

Ben straightened, looking startled. "What millionaire?"

"Quinn Taylor, the owner of the Mathering Manor House Hotel," Rachel filled in.

Harriet saw how avidly both Ben and Rachel were staring at her, waiting for her to dish the details on her day, and she only felt tired. A short while ago, she might have been excited to tell Rachel about her big date, but not now.

Now she didn't think she could stomach whatever response her sister gave. The slightly pitying enthusiasm: *Oh well done, Harriet!* Or the sisterly words of caution: *But do you really know him? Can you trust him?*

"It was fine," she said, managing to sound casual and even dismissive only because she felt so very weary. "We sorted it all out."

Rachel looked both disappointed and a bit suspicious at this response. "But what took so long, then?"

"He gave me a tour of the hotel."

"Did he? What's it like?"

"Like a big manor house in need of a lot of work," Harriet replied frankly. "But he's got the enthusiasm and the vision, I think. Hopefully the time, too, although the opening night is coming up rather fast." She glanced at the ingredients Rachel had put on the countertop—lemongrass, chilli powder, coconut milk, coriander. "So, what are you making?" she asked brightly.

Rachel's gaze narrowed. She looked like she wanted to ask more questions, to press and press, and Harriet really wasn't in the mood. Then her sister glanced at Ben, and thankfully she seemed to change her mind.

"Red Thai curry. Do you want to slice the peppers?"

"Yes," Harriet replied with a grateful smile, glad her sister was going to let it go, and she reached for a sweet pepper, ready to slice the life out of it.

Chapter Nine

"I'VE GOT FRIES! Or chips, as they say in merry olde England."

After a perfunctory tap on Quinn's door, Perry pushed it open, a Styrofoam tray of chips in her hands, and a bag of what smelled like burgers in the other. She stopped as she took in the sight of him standing in front of the mirror, wearing a pair of dark blue jeans and a button-down shirt that was actually ironed for once, a tube of hair gel in his hand, as he debated the merits of whether to use it, or if he even knew how. He was generally not one for styling products, but he felt the need to make an effort.

"Are you going out?" Perry asked, sounding both incredulous and suspicious.

"I have a date," Quinn told her. He hadn't mentioned it before, because...well, he just hadn't. There had been so much to do, as there always was, and he hadn't really wanted to get into a conversation about his love life, or lack thereof. He'd had a feeling Perry wouldn't approve, although he wasn't sure why. Now, as he saw the surprise cross her face, he thought he probably should have mentioned it at some point.

"A date?" Perry set down the burgers and chips on top of

his bureau. "With who? No, let me guess." Her mouth firmed, eyes narrowing. "Cookie Lady." She definitely sounded disapproving.

"Her name is Harriet," Quinn replied mildly, putting down the hair gel, deciding it was too risky a proposition. "But yes."

Perry planted her hands on her hips as she shook her head slowly. "Are you sure you want to do that?" she asked.

"Er, yes? Since I have?"

"Quinn, you know you're not great with relationships at the best of times. When you're busy and stressed, you're even worse. There is a lot riding on this hotel, and you're…" She paused. "You're still recovering, a bit, aren't you?"

Recovering. It made him sound like an addict or something, rather than someone who had, only briefly, lost the plot. "I'm fine, Perry," he told her, the very slightest of edges to his voice.

"I'm not trying to criticise, but in the past—"

"Harriet is different," he said, cutting her off, although he realised what he meant was that he was different with her. Being with Harriet didn't stress him out. He wasn't worried that she looked at him and saw someone who would eventually disappoint her. He had yet to sabotage their friendship, the way he'd done with so many others. He hoped he never would with Harriet.

Perry's eyes narrowed. "Different? How?"

Quinn turned away from Perry's assessing gaze to study his own reflection. "I can be myself with her."

"Does she know about San Francisco?"

"If you mean that I had a meltdown at a party, then no.

It's not like I have to air my dirty laundry the very *second* I become interested in someone." He knew he sounded annoyed, and he couldn't help it. Perry was making it sound like he had a criminal conviction or something, and he didn't. It had only been a reprimand and a warning.

"I'm not saying that," Perry replied quietly. "I'm just…" She blew out a breath. "Oh, I don't even know. I'm concerned for you, Quinn. You were in a really bad place—"

"It wasn't *that* bad," he tried to scoff. "And frankly, I don't regret it. I was tired of that whole scene—"

Perry looked understandably sceptical. "So, you're cool with being blacklisted from the tech industry for the foreseeable?"

He shrugged. "Maybe."

"Fine." Perry gave a little shrug as she scooped up the tray of chips and the bag of burgers. "I guess I'll have to eat this all by myself while watching an entire season of *Ice Road Truckers.*"

Perry did love a random reality TV show. As she started to turn from his room, Quinn felt a pang of guilt, an urge to apologise—although for what? He'd already apologised to Perry, and his whole team at Q Games, for the way he'd behaved, what he'd done. He'd spent three months backpacking around Europe, trying to forget, or really, to make peace with the way things had gone, his own part in it. And he had…mostly.

This was his new start, his chance to do something he felt passionate about, without any of the emotional baggage from before. He wasn't going to sabotage it. And he didn't want Perry to, either, with her well-meaning warnings.

"Perry," he called, and she poked her head through the doorway, eyebrows raised in query. "I appreciate your concern," he told her. "Thanks."

Perry nodded before turning towards her own room across the hall, to watch TV. They'd moved from a nearby farm cottage to two refurbished rooms on the top floor of the hotel, mainly to save money. There wasn't a lot to do in the evenings, and Quinn had watched his fair share of *Ice Road Truckers* and other shows, with Perry providing an acerbic running commentary. They hadn't made plans for this evening in particular, and he didn't think he'd needed to tell his assistant *all* of his movements…except maybe he should have?

"Sorry," he called as he heard her opening her door. He felt bad for leaving her alone. "Tomorrow night?"

"Don't worry about me, Quinn," Perry replied from the hall, her tone turning a little sharp. "I'm fine."

Quinn let out a little sigh. He didn't want to fall out with Perry; she'd had his back for nearly twenty years. She was the one person who understood his tendency to self-sabotage, even when he didn't always understand it himself. He appreciated her concern and even her warning, but he really wanted to look forwards now…with Harriet.

From Perry's room down the hall, he heard the hard rock opening to *Ice Road Truckers.* He glanced again in the mirror, ran a hand through his hair with a slight grimace for his reflection, and then turned away.

HE'D INSISTED ON picking Harriet up from Embthwaite Farm, and as he drove down the lane in the twilit darkness, he wondered about her family. She hadn't said much, besides that she had a sister and a mother, although she hadn't wanted to talk too much about the mother part. Did her father farm the land here? Had she ever moved away from Mathering? Did her sister live with her?

He was still mulling over these questions when he knocked on the front door, only to have it thrown open after about a millisecond.

"You must be Quinn," a woman said whom he surmised had to be her sister. She was very similar to Harriet in her colouring—dark hair and eyes, a scattering of freckles—but different in every other aspect. Where Harriet was warm and curvy, this woman was hard and angular. Where Harriet's hair sprung about her face in a riot of wild curls, this woman's hair hung poker straight, brushing her high cheekbones.

"I am," he replied with an easy smile. "But I'm afraid I don't know who you are."

"Rachel, Harriet's sister," she replied, looking slightly put out that he hadn't known. "Come in."

"Actually, I'm ready." A bit breathlessly, Harriet slipped by her sister and outside before Quinn had been able to put so much as a foot over the threshold. Clearly, she didn't want them interacting, but he wasn't going to mind. It meant he could spend more time with her, and she looked, he saw, absolutely gorgeous. She was wearing a dark green wrap dress in some stretchy material that made the most of her curves, including an intoxicating peek of cleavage. She'd left her hair loose and wild, a riot of dark curls about her flushed face, her freckles standing out like a spattering of gold dust on her nose. Unlike the last times he'd seen her, she was wearing a bit of make-up, too—something about her eyes that made them look large and dark, and her lips were a deep, berry red that made Quinn think about kissing her.

"So nice to meet you," he called to Rachel, who was watching them from the doorway with slightly narrowed eyes.

"And you," she replied. "Hats, when will you be back?"

Quinn had to stifle a laugh. How old was Harriet? Maybe thirty? And her sister was asking curfew kinds of questions?

"I don't know," Harriet replied a bit tartly, and then added, like a concession, "Not too late."

Quinn decided he was determined to keep her out until midnight, at least.

"This is your car?" she asked in surprise when he opened the passenger door to the beat-up and decidedly unimpressive Toyota he'd bought second-hand.

"Yes, I've never been one for flashy cars, I'm afraid." Or flashy anything. It reminded him too much of his childhood, of the way his parents had thrown money around like it meant something, gave them a sense of their own importance and dignity, simply because they were rich. "I just never saw the point."

"No, me, neither," Harriet replied. "A car is just a way to get from point A to point B as far as I am concerned."

"Me, too," Quinn replied, beaming, as if the way they both viewed cars was conclusive of something. Maybe it was. "Your sister seems a bit protective of you," he remarked as he did a three-point turn in the drive. "I only say that because I can still see her standing behind the front door, glaring at us."

Harriet peered out the window, letting out a sound that was part groan and part laugh as she sank back into the seat, shaking her head. "She's making up for lost time, I suppose, or else she's just nosy."

"Making up for lost time?" He started down the track, leaving Embthwaite Farm and the curious Rachel behind.

"Yes, she wasn't around for quite a few years," Harriet replied, pursing her lips as she glanced out the window. "I mean, I wasn't a child at the time, so I can't really blame her. We're only fifteen months apart, but you'd think it was years sometimes."

"Why wasn't she around?"

She glanced him, a hint of laughter lurking about her mouth although he thought her eyes looked sad. "Are you sure you want to do the whole let-me-tell-you-about-my-family-trauma thing thirty seconds into our evening?"

"Oh, is that what this is?" He slapped his hand on his forehead, smiling, grateful for the way she'd addressed the issue. "Well, we could just get it out of the way. You tell me your trauma and I'll tell you mine." He grimaced wryly. "Sorry, that sounded a little dirty."

She let out a huff of laughter. "All right, then, here it is in a nutshell. My mum walked out on us when I was seventeen, in my last year of school. Rachel had left for university a few months before. I asked her to come back to help out, and she refused. I mean, she had exams, so I sort of got it. But she came back less and less, until it was years between visits, and so it was just me and my dad, which might have been okay if my dad actually liked me, but he didn't. Doesn't. And now he has a terminal brain tumour, and is going to die in about three months, so…"

She trailed off like she'd run out of steam, and the only thing Quinn could think to say was: "Is that all?"

HARRIET STARED AT him in startled affront before she, suddenly and noisily, burst into guffaws of laughter. Yes, her laugh was more bray than trill, but right now she didn't care. She realised that was *exactly* what she'd wanted him to say, even if she never could have articulated it to herself. She didn't want his pity; she had enough trouble dealing with her own. His dry humour had been absolutely perfect.

He grinned at her, clearly delighted by her response. "Although to be fair, I have to admit your story might beat mine."

"All right, then," Harriet replied, wiping her eyes, feeling the wonderful, freeing release of that laughter reverberating through her, of being *able* to laugh at something that had so often hurt her. "Let's hear it, then." She leaned back, arms folded, eyebrows raised, a slightly silly smile curving her lips. Quinn smiled back at her before turning to face the winding road.

"Well, it's pretty basic," he replied, "now that I think about it. Unhappy rich family, more money than anybody should have, snobby, snobby, snobby, travelling around, parties, yachts, the whole expat lifestyle. Elder son is meant to inherit the empire, pass the baton on, et cetera, but it turns out he's hopeless and so a major disappointment—capital M, capital D—to his parents, especially after he was chucked out of several schools and then dropped out of college three months before graduation simply because he couldn't see the point of it anymore." He glanced at her, smiling, clearly wanting to continue the banter vibe, but Harriet was too curious to keep up the pretence that it was all sweetness and light.

"How was the elder son hopeless?" she asked quietly.

Quinn turned back to look at the road, his lips pursed. "Oh, let me count the ways. Not sporty, not academic, not interested in fast cars or designer watches or golf or tennis or the stock market. Not willing to play the game, whatever it was—suck up to the right people, ignore the wrong ones, attend the schmooze fests and brag about his condo in the Caribbean, the week skiing in Switzerland, et cetera."

"That doesn't sound all that hopeless to me," Harriet replied. "In fact, it sounds eminently sensible."

For a second, his eyes lit up with warmth, maybe even hope, but then he shrugged. "Well, you know, it was pretty hopeless to my father." He turned back to her, eyebrows raised. "So, who wins the woe-is-me stakes, do you think?"

"I think it's a tie," Harriet replied, deciding she wouldn't ask any more questions right now, since he didn't seem to want to give the answers. "Until I know more information, anyway."

"All right, we'll have to keep a running score. I've got a few more zingers to share when the time is right."

"So do I," she replied, smiling, and he laughed.

"Sounds like it's going to be a fun evening."

"I'd actually rather not talk about any of it," she confessed as he turned onto a country road, heading away from Mathering. She was amazed she'd said as much as she had already, when she didn't usually. "I feel as if I've let it affect me far more than I should have over the years, made me resentful even when I didn't want to be." She paused and then admitted, feeling both reckless and shy, "I'm trying not to let it now, but sometimes it's hard."

"Good for you," he said sincerely. "That is hard, especially when it's not always possible to see how it's affecting you. At least that's what I find. Why am I the way that I am? Why do I do the things I do?" He shook his head ruefully. "Can anyone answer that, really? Can anyone truly know?"

"Maybe not," Harriet replied, thinking she hadn't had so philosophical a conversation since, well, just about ever. "Although I suppose we can but try," she added in a pseudo-noble voice, lifting her chin, and he grinned.

"Indeed, indeed. We shall try. But if we're not going to talk about our families, what are we going to talk about?"

"The hotel?" she suggested. "I was wondering how you might decorate it for Christmas."

Once again his eyes lit up, with both humour and hope. "It sounds as if you have ideas?"

"Well…" She ducked her head, suddenly too shy to admit she did, that she'd been thinking about it quite a lot.

"I hope you do, because I need them," Quinn told her. "I need as many ideas as I can get. I collect them like stamps or—I don't know—postcards." He put on a stentorian voice. "Friends, Romans, countrymen…give me your ideas!"

She laughed, loving that he was just a little bit bonkers about everything. It was so different from her own quiet and cautious approach to life, and yet they seemed to have similar stories, growing up. He'd felt he was a disappointment to his father, just as she had been to hers, and yet they'd responded in entirely different ways—Quinn seeming not to care, determined to get the most enjoyment and interest out of life, while she'd retreated into her shell, hidden away from the world, too scared to try. Maybe she'd learn to be more like Quinn.

"Wait till we're settled in the restaurant," Quinn advised as he turned into the car park of an old timbered gastropub bedecked with fairy lights; Harriet had driven by it before, but she'd never been inside as it was too expensive. "And then you can tell me every last idea that you have."

As they walked into the pub, a tantalising aroma of good food and woodsmoke from the open fire washed over Harriet in a comforting wave. It was the kind of place with snug booths and low lighting, menus written by hand and food served in artisanal, stylised portions on boards of slate.

As they were led to a deep, cosy booth and handed menus, Quinn waved his away. "Just tell me the specials," he told the waitress, who looked a little startled by his action. "I always have one of those."

She duly reeled them off, while Harriet studied the offerings on her own menu.

"Wonderful," Quinn said, once the waitress had gone. "I think I'll have the halibut." He reached for the wine menu that had been left on the table and handed it to Harriet. "Would you like to choose the wine? That is, if you want any?"

"Oh, all right." Harriet took the heavy menu, flipping it open with an attempt at insouciance. "I'm afraid I'm not much of a connoisseur."

"I like a good Cabernet or Sauvignon Blanc, if we're going to go with a white," Quinn replied, "but really, I don't mind. You choose."

She glanced at him over the top of the menu. "You really have a thing about menus, don't you?" she remarked, meaning to tease. "You didn't want one at Agatha's, either."

"True." The smile he gave her seemed just a little too quick, slotting in place and not reaching his eyes. "The truth is, I'm somewhat dyslexic, as it happens. Fortunately, only with letters, and not numbers, otherwise I'd struggle with computer code. Menus are my Waterloo."

"Oh." Harriet felt herself start to blush. "I'm sorry, I didn't realise—"

"Why would you?" Quinn countered easily enough. "There's no way you could have known without me telling you, and I've become pretty adept at hiding it over the years. Not that I'm ashamed of being dyslexic, not anymore. It is what it is. But trying to decipher a menu when it feels as if it might as well be written in Sanskrit, especially while on a date, is an experience I prefer to avoid."

Harriet put down the wine list. "That must have been hard, growing up," she observed quietly.

"Hence the major disappointment aspect of my childhood," he agreed with a nod and a smile. "My father went to Oxford, and to London School of Economics. He put me on the list for his boarding school—a swanky one in Switzerland—when I was six months old. To say his academic aspirations for me were high is, unfortunately, something of a massive understatement."

"Capital M, capital U?" she dared to tease gently, and he chuckled.

"Indeed."

"I'm sorry." She certainly knew what it was like to feel like a disappointment, and she thought Quinn seemed to have handled his wonderfully well. Better than she had, certainly.

He shrugged, seeming unconcerned. "I'm used to it now. It doesn't bother me anymore. I don't let it."

"Lucky you, then." She wished she had his insouciance, his ability to get over things by sheer force of will. She felt as if she were constantly snagging herself on the thorns of the past, letting them scrape and hurt her, never free of them the way she wanted to be, while Quinn seemed to have figured out how to walk away, free and clear, navigating his new life with success and joy.

"Well, you know what they say," he replied with a grin. "You make your own luck."

"Luck is preparation meeting opportunity," she quoted back at him.

"Exactly." He lapsed into a musing silence before he gave a little shake of his head. "But I thought we weren't going to talk about our families. Tell me about your Christmas ideas instead."

"All right." Shyly at first, and then with growing confidence, Harriet told him about the initial ideas she'd had, when she'd lost herself in something of a daydream—as she spoke, she started to worry they were all a bit basic and obvious. Christmas trees? Check. Red velvet and fresh evergreen? Check. Twee nutcracker? Check. All of it could be found on a single Pinterest page, probably, and yet Quinn was nodding with such interest and enthusiasm that somehow it didn't even matter.

"I love it all," he declared. "You have to help make it happen."

"I'm sure you have people already—" she began to protest.

"I don't," he assured her. "Perry is very good at organising things, and making sure the plumbers and electricians do what they're meant to, but she's not particularly interested in home décor, and frankly, neither am I. I know what I want, and I even know what I want it to look like, but somehow, I can't put into words—or motion." He raised his eyebrows whimsically. "A kind of decoration dyslexia?"

Harriet laughed and shook her head. "I don't think that's actually a thing."

"Isn't it?" He pretended to look disappointed. "Oh, well."

The waitress came to take their order, and after she'd gone again, Quinn leaned back in his booth, arms folded. Harriet had the sense he was going to ask something personal, and she tensed instinctively, even as excitement flared. It was both scary and exciting, this process of becoming known by another person. It was like a peeling away of layers, an unveiling, but also an exposure. She was left feeling both revealed and understood; each sensation warred with the other, one wonderfully comforting, the other intensely uncomfortable.

"So," Quinn said, and she tensed all the more, her heart starting to beat harder. What was he going to ask?

"Yes?" She fought the urge to clear her throat, tried to look interested and light-hearted, the way he did.

Before he could continue, the waitress returned with the bottle of Cabernet Harriet had ordered and poured them both large glasses. Harriet resisted the urge to reach for her wine and gulp half of it down in one go.

"What," Quinn asked in a thoughtful pronouncement, once the waitress had left, "do you want most out of life, Harriet?"

"Most…?" she repeated, mainly as a stalling tactic. She'd known he was going to ask something big, but this felt all-encompassing. How on earth could she answer that?

"Yes, most. If you could have anything—and I'm not talking about just money or something like that—but about something deeper, bigger, something for your whole life, your whole *self*, what would you want?" He leaned forward, his eyes alight, his expression focused and intent. "What's your *dream*?"

Chapter Ten

QUINN GAZED AT Harriet in growing alarm as she stared back at him without saying a word, her mouth slightly parted, her eyes suddenly filling with tears. What had he done? He'd meant it as a way to get to know her, nothing more than an innocent, innocuous question, but right now it seemed anything but. She was looking at him like he'd just kicked her puppy right in front of her, or worse. Maybe it had been a bit too personal, he realised belatedly.

"Harriet…" he began, only to have her shake her head and sniff.

"No…" Her voice wobbled alarmingly.

"*Harriet…*" He reached over to her, flinging out one hand, meaning to—what? Touch her hand? Her shoulder? Some gesture of comfort, but what he did instead was accidentally knock over her very full wine glass, and send it flying right into her lap.

"Oh!" Harriet jumped up, aghast, her lovely green dress now covered in red wine. She was sodden, dripping.

Quinn stared at her in mute horror for a few seconds before he finally found his tongue. "Harriet…I am *so* sorry…" He didn't know what else to say. This wasn't a drip or drab of wine; it was a full, large glass, poured all over her. She was *soaked.* He handed her his napkin, and she took it, dabbing at the stain uselessly for a moment before she shook her head.

"I don't think…" She took a quick breath. "I'm sorry, but I think I need to change my clothes."

"Don't be sorry," Quinn replied quickly. "If anyone should be sorry…" He shook his head, realising afresh what a complete disaster this was. He'd just gone and ruined their date before it had even begun! Not just with the wine, he knew, although that was certainly a major factor, but with asking that question, even if he still didn't understand why it had upset Harriet so. The fact was it had, and he should have anticipated that. Somehow. He'd sabotaged their date, and the frustrating thing was, he hadn't even meant to.

"Look," he said, "what if we go back to the house? The hotel, I mean. You can borrow some of my clothes and we can take our food away with us and eat it there. Unless you'd just rather call it quits and go home." He couldn't keep from sounding rather pitifully abject at the thought. He didn't want to end things already, a failure.

Harriet, Quinn thought, looked torn between the two. If he were her, he'd probably want to go home, crawl under a duvet, and never see him again. What an idiot he'd been. What an idiot he so often was. Maybe he should have heeded Perry's warning; maybe he wasn't ready for this.

"That sounds fun," Harriet said finally. She did not sound entirely convinced, but he decided he'd take it.

"And I'll pay for your dress, of course," Quinn continued quickly. "Let me just sort out our meals." He hurried to find their waitress, wanting to spare Harriet as much further embarrassment as he possibly could, although it was challenging when she was soaked through, the stained dress clinging to her.

Fortunately, the waitress was able to sort their meals out quickly, and within a few minutes Quinn was carrying two foil containers out to the car, shepherding Harriet as he went.

"I really am so sorry about this," he said for the fourth or fifth time as he unlocked the car.

"Quinn, it's all right." Harriet managed a smile. "It was an accident."

"I know, but what an accident. Well, I told you I wasn't athletic, right? I'm actually pretty clumsy. There's a word for it, you know." He put the food in the back before hurrying round to open her door. She slid in with a smile of thanks.

"A word for it?"

"For a tall, awkward person, of which I am one." He paused for dramatic effect as he climbed into the driver's side. "It's a looby."

Harriet let out a choked laugh. "A looby?" He nodded solemnly and started the car. "What a word."

"I know, right? My English teacher called me it once, so I looked it up. Apologies again for being such a looby."

"Again, apologies accepted, and we don't need to talk about it anymore, I promise."

"Even though you smell like a winery, and look like one, too?" he dared to tease.

She laughed, which filled him with equal parts relief and joy. She'd managed to get past that wobbly moment, and so would he. "Even so," she assured him with a small smile.

It was only a few minutes' drive to the manor house, and as Quinn pulled up around the back, he had a moment's qualm because Perry, almost undoubtedly, would still be in her room eating chips and watching *Ice Road Truckers*. It was somewhat unlikely that she would gate-crash his date, but it was possible, and he definitely did not want her to give him any more warnings, or heaven forbid, make any innuendoes about his past, in Harriet's presence. Hopefully she'd keep to her room.

"Now for some clothes," he told Harriet as he opened her door and they then headed inside, straight back to the kitchen, an enormous room fitted with industrial-sized equipment. It had been renovated early on, at least, and was fully functional, which meant he could heat up their meals. "I'll zap these in the microwave and get you something to wear. Won't be two ticks."

He hurried upstairs, his mind on what clothes were clean and serviceable for Harriet to wear, when Perry poked her head out of her room.

"Back so early?" she surmised, sounding not entirely displeased.

"Bit of a mishap," Quinn replied as he went into his room. "I spilled wine all over Harriet and so we've come back here to eat. I'm just finding her something to wear." He poked his head out of his room. "You don't have anything, do you?"

"No," Perry said rather flatly. To be fair, she and Harriet weren't the same size, but Quinn registered her almost hostile tone and once again, he felt a frisson of unease. Was she just worried about him…or was something else going on?

"Fair enough," he told her. He paused and then asked cautiously, "You don't have anything...*against* Harriet, Perry, do you?"

He saw her prickle. "Why on earth would I?"

"I don't know," he replied honestly. "I'm just asking because you seem a little...hostile."

"I'm not hostile," Perry snapped in a tone that certainly *sounded* hostile.

"I know you're worried about me," Quinn said. "But it's not anything else, is it?"

"No," Perry replied, sounding disgruntled. "Of course not."

He decided to leave it for now. He had Harriet waiting downstairs, still covered in wine, and he really wasn't in the right frame of mind to hash it out—whatever it was—with Perry.

"All right, then," he said, and ducked back into his room to grab a clean(ish) T-shirt and a pair of sweatpants with a drawstring that would hopefully mean they didn't pool around Harriet's ankles as soon as she put them on, although that wasn't an entirely unwelcome possibility.

Back downstairs, he found Harriet sitting on a stool at the enormous metal island, her chin in her hand as she looked around. Her dress, now probably permanently stained, was still clinging to her and Quinn had to avert his eyes even though he didn't want to.

"This is quite the kitchen," she remarked as he came into the room. "You're just waiting for an army of cooks and sous chefs."

"And the guests for them to cook for." He made a face as he handed her the clothes. "I'm afraid this is the best I could do. I hope it's okay."

"They look comfortable," Harriet replied with a small smile as she slid off the stool. "Where should I change?"

Right here. Quinn suppressed the entirely inappropriate thought. "There's a bathroom around the corner," he told her, gesturing to the doorway. "But don't get lost—it's a maze of little rooms back there, all the old sculleries and laundries and boot rooms and things like that."

"Sounds like an episode of *Upstairs, Downstairs.*"

"Exactly. I'll get our meals ready and then we can find somewhere comfortable to eat them, amidst all this chaos." There was a small room in the back he'd turned into a sitting room for the duration of the renovation. If he laid a fire, it could be cosy enough.

"All right," Harriet replied with a mock salute. "Be back in a moment."

HARRIET WANDERED DOWN several dark, slate-floored corridors, peeking in various small and shadowy rooms before she came upon the bathroom. She felt calmer now, despite her dress, after having a few moments alone in the kitchen, basically telling herself not to be such a ninny. It wasn't the spilled wine that was upsetting her, although basically destroying one of her best dresses was a bit of a blow. It was the question Quinn had asked her, and more importantly, her reaction to it.

If you could have anything, what would you want?

It was, Harriet knew, meant to have been a playful question, a way for him to get to know her, classic icebreaker, nothing more. And yet the image that had come into her head, slotting in as if falling from the sky, had been enough to make her eyes fill with tears and she'd very nearly started blubbering right there at the table. What an awful humiliation *that* would have been, and yet what had happened had been bad enough.

Quinn had clearly seen how upset she was and had wanted to help her…hence the knocked-over wine.

Harriet peeled the dress off herself, considered rinsing it in the sink, and then decided it was pretty pointless. She pulled on the sweatpants and T-shirt; the sweatpants hung off her hips, but the drawstring seemed to work, and the T-shirt smelled of him—a hint of woodsy cologne, of Quinn. She hadn't realised he had a smell, or more unsettlingly, that she recognised it, until she'd put the T-shirt on.

Leaving the dress hanging on the towel railing, she went back in search of Quinn. He was standing in the doorway of the kitchen, two plates held aloft.

"Ah, perfect fit," he told her with a grin. "You look far better in my clothes than I do." His gaze lingered for a second, making a heat bloom in Harriet, work its way upwards, and pinken her cheeks. "I thought we'd go into a little sitting room in the back. I'll put a fire on."

"Sounds lovely," she murmured, still blushing. She followed him down several narrow corridors as he wended his way through the huge house. "What are you going to do with all these rooms?" she exclaimed, glancing into several of them. They'd gone past the rooms she'd passed on the way to the bathroom and were now deep in the bowels of the house.

"I don't actually know," Quinn admitted over his shoulder. "I'm sure some of them will be useful for storage and staffrooms and the like, but there are more and more times when I am reminded that I really don't know what I am doing here."

"Well," Harriet replied philosophically, "better to have too many rooms than too few?"

"I like your attitude."

They'd reached the sitting room, little more than an alcove overlooking the back gardens that were now cloaked in darkness, dark green velvet curtains drawn against the night, with a small fireplace, a sofa, and a couple of armchairs.

"I think this used to be the housekeeper's office," Quinn told her as he handed her a plate and put his own down on a coffee table before kneeling in front of the fireplace to lay kindling. "For when she needed to cook the books over a glass of sherry?"

"Now that sounds more like *Midsomer Murders*," Harriet teased. She curled up on one end of the sofa, tucking her feet beneath her. This had to be the strangest date she'd ever been on, not that she'd been on all that many. Tucked away in this tiny room in the back of the house, wearing Quinn's T-shirt and sweatpants, a paper plate balanced on her lap…well, it could have been worse, certainly. She was grateful for Quinn's easy understanding.

"There we are," he said once he'd got a cheery blaze going. He reached for his own plate. "Sorry about all this."

"No more apologies, remember? And the food is delicious." She'd ordered a chicken and ham pie, and the pastry was melting in her mouth. "Besides," Harriet continued once she'd swallowed, feeling it had to be said, "it was as much my fault as yours. You asked a perfectly innocent question and I weirdly overreacted to it. Sorry about that. I guess it took me by surprise."

"Well, I wasn't going to say," Quinn replied after a moment, his tone thoughtful. "I mean, you're right in that I meant it just as a…I don't know, a get-to-know-you sort of thing. Why *was* it such a hard question?" The gaze he gave her was startlingly direct, his eyes clear and very grey, so Harriet found that she couldn't look away, as much as she wanted to.

"I thought we weren't going to talk about all the family stuff," she reminded him, clearly hedging.

Quinn cocked his head, his gaze never leaving hers. "That wasn't a hard and fast rule, though, was it?"

"Okay, well." She glanced down, toying with her fork, shredding a bit of chicken with its tines before she made a decision, and looked up. "When you asked that question, the notion that dropped into my head as if it had fallen from the sky was that I wanted my mother back. My mum." Help, but a lump was already forming in her throat! How could this be happening? Why was she getting emotional about this *now*?

Maybe because her dad's illness—and his honesty—was stirring all sorts of things up inside her. Maybe because she'd never truly made peace with the past, because she'd never actually understood why her mother had left the way she did.

Maybe because no matter how hard she tried not to, she still felt like the little girl who had been left behind, inside.

"You said your mother left?" Quinn recalled. "When you were seventeen?"

"Yes." Did she really want to talk about all this with him? She'd mentioned it somewhat insouciantly—as insouciantly as she could—earlier, but now, in order to properly explain, she'd have to dredge it all up from the dregs of her consciousness. She realised, somewhat to her surprise, that she did actually want to do it. Sort of, anyway. "I think what really hurt was how she just walked out one day, with no warning, no explanation at all."

Quinn's eyebrows rose. "Ever?"

"Ever," Harriet replied, although she recognised that wasn't quite true. About four months after her mother had left, she'd called Harriet. The conversation had been brief, painful, and entirely unsatisfactory.

"I wanted to say I'm sorry," her mother had said, the words halting and slow, like she had trouble forming them. *Feeling* them. "But I had no choice."

No choice? Really? Harriet had been furious, but also still too hurt, too wounded, to reply in the way her mother clearly wanted her to. *That's okay, Mum, I understand.*

Except she didn't understand. She hadn't then, and she didn't now. And so, she'd hung up on her mother, something she'd semi-regretted immediately afterwards, even if the slam of the receiver had been satisfying in the moment. Her mother hadn't called back, and Harriet hadn't had any way to contact her.

"There was one time," she explained to Quinn, feeling

she needed to be honest. She explained about her mother's phone call, and he nodded slowly in understanding.

"That must have been very tough," he stated quietly, sounding like he meant it, which she appreciated. "Do you have any idea why she would have left like that?"

No, none. The words were ready to burst out of Harriet, as they always were, because she'd felt them so deeply for so long. The wound was still there, unhealed, festering. And yet this time those words wouldn't come. Rachel had insisted that their mother must have been in a really bad way, to walk out without a word, but Harriet hadn't wanted to believe it. She hadn't been able to forgive, not when her mother hadn't even left her a *note.* Not when she'd spent her whole childhood adoring her mother, doing her absolute utmost to make her feel better, because, yes, their mother *had* been in a bad way—Harriet could admit that to herself if not to her sister—but she'd had *Harriet.*

Harriet, always ready to hug her, cuddle, kiss, listen, care. Harriet snuggled up to her mother's side as she wept. Harriet leaving cups of tea by her bedroom door while her mother slept. Harriet doing anything and everything to make her mother love her the way her father wouldn't, and she'd *still* left her behind.

"My father couldn't have been the easiest man to live with," she told Quinn carefully. "He's a typical Yorkshire farmer—ornery and taciturn. They didn't fight because he's not the type to raise his voice, but he'd go silent a lot, I think. Still does." She paused and then continued stiltedly, "My mum cried a lot—I remember that. She'd try to hide it, but we—my sister and I—knew. I tried to make her feel better, sometimes, and sometimes I felt like I did, when I brought her a cup of tea or gave her a hug. But she…" Her throat had gone too thick; she found she couldn't say it.

"She still left," Quinn completed softly. He reached across the sofa to put his hand, large and warm and solid, over hers. "I'm so sorry, Harriet."

She sniffed, a little too audibly. His understanding was going to be her undoing, she thought. It felt almost as painful as the original hurt, although in an entirely different way. "I really thought we weren't doing the family trauma thing," she tried to joke.

Quinn's voice was serious as he replied, "We don't have to anymore, if you don't want to."

"I wouldn't think you'd want to," Harriet countered as she tried to wipe her eyes as discreetly as she could with her free hand. His hand was still covering hers, and it felt comforting. "I've haven't been a very fun date," she told him. "We should be laughing and chatting and making jokes, not raking through all this old history."

"I don't know that I had any expectations of what we would talk about." His gaze, when she dared to lift her eyes to meet his, was kind and steady. "But I've had a wonderful evening, my bumbling mishap with wine aside."

Harriet felt as if she could sink into his warm gaze the way you would into a deep featherbed. Let herself fall, float, forever. "When you asked that question," she told him unsteadily, "about what my dream was, and the idea that came into my head right away was wanting my mum back… The truth is, I've never let myself think that way before. Not remotely. I've always told myself I'm better off without her, that I wouldn't want her back even if she asked, if she came *begging*, and so it was a shock, a big one, to realise how much I've really wanted it all along."

His hand tightened briefly on hers. "And what will you do to get it?" he asked. "Are you in contact now?"

"No, not really." Harriet gazed down at his hand resting on top of hers, the long fingers, neat square nails. "I mean, not at all. I haven't spoken to her or anything, but she sends me emails occasionally. Short ones, just to let me know I'm on her mind. I've never responded." She admitted this guiltily, a confession. She'd known she hadn't had the emotional capacity to engage with her mother through pithy emails, but sometimes she sort of wished she'd had.

"Maybe you should now," Quinn suggested gently, and Harriet kept staring down at their hands.

Contact her mother? Open that can of emotional worms and let them crawl out, all over her, go where they would? She couldn't. At least, she couldn't have in the past. But already, after just a few days of knowing Quinn, she felt changed. Things felt possible that never had before, simply from knowing him.

"Maybe I should," she agreed, and he squeezed her hand once more.

Chapter Eleven

HARRIET SHIFTED IN the hard plastic seat as she and Rachel waited for her father's name to be called by the nurse at the neurology unit in Middlesbrough. It had been over a week since her date with Quinn, and she felt as if she were seesawing between two existences—her time at the hotel, which was fun and flirty and exciting—and her time at home, which felt like a slow descent into darkness.

All right, she told herself, maybe that was a *bit* melodramatic, but there could be no denying that their father was continuing to decline, which was why they were here at the hospital. Rachel had phoned two days ago, when their dad's slurred speech had become not just incomprehensible, but positive gibberish. The look of panic on her father's face as he'd realised he wasn't making sense had been heartbreaking to see, and yet when Harriet and Rachel had tried to help him, he'd wheeled away, stumbling a bit, hiding his confusion with the usual anger.

"Peter Mowbray?" the nurse called, and Rachel bolted upright. Harriet turned to her father.

"Dad, that's you," she said gently, to which her father replied, his tone rough and the words so garbled she almost couldn't make them out.

"I know it's me, girl."

Girl? When had she become just girl, rather than Harriet? She had to bite her tongue to keep from making some unhelpful retort. *Your father has a brain tumour*, she reminded herself as she and Rachel helped him up from his seat. *Show him some grace.* Even if he wasn't showing her any, and never had.

In the doctor's office, it turned out there wasn't much that could be done, which Harriet had anticipated but Rachel had refused to believe.

"What about another MRI?" she demanded, sounding querulous, which Harriet suspected was simply to hide her fear. Rachel had always been close to their dad—closer than Harriet, anyway—although she'd still wanted more from him.

Just like their mother had wanted more?

Ever since her date with Quinn, Harriet found herself thinking about her mum. Wondering what her story truly had been, instead of just filling in the bits she hadn't been sure about herself. Wondering if she had it in her to extend the same sort of grace to her mother that she was trying to, to her father.

Even if she didn't feel they'd extended all that much to her. Maybe that didn't actually matter so much.

"At this stage, an MRI would simply tell us what is already evident," the GP replied in a gentle tone. "That the tumour is progressing as we expected it to. There isn't anything more we can do."

"I told you that," their dad said irritably, although it took Harriet a few seconds to make out the words. Not only was his speech becoming more garbled, but his Yorkshire accent more pronounced.

"Still…" Rachel persisted, with uncharacteristic feebleness.

"Is there any medication we could try?" Harriet asked. "Not to shrink the tumour, necessarily, but to alleviate some of the symptoms?"

Looking regretful, the doctor shook his head. "I'm afraid not. As time goes on, we can talk about medication for pain management and palliative care."

That was where this was headed, Harriet reminded herself. It shouldn't come as a shock or a surprise, not anymore. They'd been living with the truth of it for nearly a month, the suspicion of it for well before that. And yet she realised she couldn't imagine Embthwaite Farm without her father. His heavy tread on the stair, his solid form in the armchair by the fire, the *Farmer's Almanac* held between his gnarled fingers. Even now, she still had the urge, like Rachel, to insist that something be done. That they have more time.

And yet, time for what? For her dad to realise he loved her, after all? Harriet already knew that wasn't going to happen. But time enough, maybe, for her to discover why he didn't.

"I told you," their dad said again, grumpily, as they helped him back to the car. "A wasted trip."

No one spoke on the way home, and once they'd reached the farm, Rachel helped their father to bed while Harriet did what any good British person did in this situation and made tea. She laid out a few scones that were extras from the latest batch she'd baked for the tea room as well as a dish of her raspberry jam, deciding both she and Rachel probably needed the hit of sugar.

"At least he isn't in too much pain," Rachel said on a sigh as she came into the kitchen. "That's something, isn't it?"

"I suppose." Harriet began pouring the tea.

"I haven't talked to him about his funeral arrangements," Rachel mused, her chin propped in her hand. "I know he was never much of a churchgoer, but he might want certain hymns or something."

A visceral shudder went through Harriet as she suddenly pictured her father's coffin in the parish church in Mathering, and hot tea splashed onto her wrist. She put the pot down hurriedly and ran her wrist under cold water. "Let's not talk about all that quite yet," she told Rachel as she stood at the sink, her back to her sister, her gaze on the frosty ground outside, the hills rolling upwards to a wintry sky.

"We'll need to, though, soon. If his speech is going, he might not be able to communicate what he wants soon enough." Rachel's voice hitched. "I can't believe we're talking like this, and yet we have to."

"It could be months, Rachel—"

"That's not that long. It's been taking months for the sale of the herd—"

"That's in process, anyway." They'd agreed the sale of all dairy cows and equipment a while back, but it was taking some time to arrange. Meanwhile they were taking turns, along with Ben, to milk the herd and organise the milk deliveries. They still hadn't talked about the farm itself, or what would happen to it once their father died. Had he made a will, and if so, what was in it? Harriet had no idea, but she realised, with an unpleasant, lurching sensation, that there was no real reason to think he would have split the property or its contents fifty-fifty, as on some level, she had assumed he would, simply because that was what was expected and fair.

What, really, had been fair about their childhood? About the different way her father had treated his two daughters—bestowing his attention, such as it had been, on Rachel, and basically ignoring Harriet?

Are you sure you want to know the answer to that question?

Slowly Harriet turned around. She leaned against the sink, wrapping her arms around her middle, as if to hold herself upright. "Has Dad made a will?" she asked Rachel. "Do you know?"

Rachel's gaze narrowed. "I assume he has. He's usually pretty solid about paperwork, but I haven't seen it. Why?"

"Just wondering." Harriet glanced out the window again at the slate-coloured sky. "I don't know that he'll have left me anything," she stated as matter-of-factly as she could, even though the possibility hurt, like a tearing inside, and not because of possessions or money, but simply because her father wouldn't have wanted her to have anything.

"Come on, Harriet." Rachel sounded sympathetic but also a tiny bit impatient. "You don't know that."

"Maybe we should find out, then," Harriet replied levelly. She realised no matter what she wanted, she actually needed to know. If Embthwaite Farm and all its belongings was going to go to Rachel, she needed to make some plans of her own. Maybe, she told herself, wanting to find some of

Quinn's positivity, this would be the spur she needed to move out, make her own way.

Rachel shook her head slowly. "How can we? I don't think his lawyer would tell us, would he?"

"There has to be a copy of the will somewhere, if it exists," Harriet replied. "Probably up in the spare bedroom with all those other files."

Rachel frowned. "You haven't seen it, though, have you?"

"No, but I didn't look through all the papers. I just shoved them in boxes."

Her sister was silent, and Harriet tightened her arms around her waist, as if she needed to hold herself together. She felt fragile all of a sudden, like she could splinter into a thousand pieces, but also strangely strong. She was facing this at last, and maybe she'd needed to.

"All right, let's look," Rachel replied finally, and they both turned towards the hall.

They didn't speak as they headed upstairs to the spare bedroom, which was packed from floor to ceiling with boxes of junk. This was not going to be a quick job. Harriet reached for the first box of files and placed it on the bed.

"Should we do this systematically?" Rachel suggested, and Harriet shrugged, not really wanting to get into one of Rachel's management consulting type ideas. Soon she'd be having them make a spreadsheet or something.

"One box at a time?" she replied. "You start over there and I'll start over here?"

Rachel let out a little sigh of acceptance. "Fine."

They worked in silence for about ten minutes; the only

sound was their father's gentle snores from across the hall and the snick and flick of papers as they sifted through them. Most of it, Harriet discovered, could go straight into the recycling—old mail flyers, bills or statements long out of date, *Farmer's Almanacs* that were ten or even twenty years old. The pile of to-be-filed-in-the-bin grew steadily larger.

Occasionally, though, there were bittersweet flashes of a life Harriet had half forgotten. A photo of the four of them on holiday in Scarborough—a day trip to the beach, all the time her father could afford away from the farm. She and Rachel were in matching swimming costumes, holding drippy ice creams and squinting into the sunlight. Their father was unsmiling under his flat cap, and their mother seemed to be smiling too brightly, her grin stretched across her face like a crack in a plate.

Harriet had only the haziest memory of that day, like wisps of a dream that evaporated as soon as she tried to hold on to them, turn them into something more solid.

"What are you looking at?" Rachel asked, coming to peer over her shoulder. She gazed silently at the photo for a moment, her face drawn into thoughtful lines. "I remember that day," she remarked quietly. "We built the most epic sandcastle. I did the towers, and you did the moat. It took all afternoon and then the tide washed it away."

There was a metaphor lurking in there somewhere, Harriet thought. She recalled, distantly, that Rachel had been like an army captain or perhaps a drill sergeant, organising the whole thing. She'd been the deputy, the skivvy, who had been happy enough simply to do what she was told. She also remembered her dad complimenting Rachel on her work, but not Harriet. Or was she layering her current feelings of resentment and hurt over what had actually been a happy memory?

And what about her mother? She peered at the photo more closely, as if its faded image might reveal more clues. "What do you think Mum is feeling in this photo?" she asked Rachel, who glanced at it again before turning back to the box of papers she'd been going through.

"I don't know."

"Guess."

Rachel sighed. "What do you want me to say, Harriet? I think she was unhappy. I know you don't think she was—"

"I don't know about that," Harriet interjected. She put the photo to the side, deciding she'd keep it. She wouldn't frame it or anything like that, but she thought she might want to look at it again.

"I thought that's what you said before—"

"It's what I told you, but I think I knew she wasn't happy. I was always trying to make her feel better."

"I remember that," Rachel replied quietly. "I might have been Dad's favourite, but you were always Mum's."

Harriet let out a ragged laugh. "And yet she still left."

Rachel frowned. "I don't know that that had anything to do with you—"

"Exactly. She didn't think about me at all." Harriet shook her head, her emotions too jumbled up to untangle, and yet for the first time, she wanted to try. "I was so angry with her for leaving, for so long, that it was easier to blame her. To let myself believe there couldn't have been a reason and she was just selfish and horrible, but I don't think I ever really convinced myself, truly."

Rachel was silent for a few seconds, the papers in her hand forgotten. "And now?"

Harriet let out a long, slow breath. "I know that there must have been a reason for her to leave, a pretty good one even, but I'm still not sure if it would be enough for me."

Rachel nodded slowly. "I suppose that's fair." She glanced down at the papers in her hand. "You know, we should tell Mum," she said quietly. "She doesn't know about Dad."

"Do you think she'd care?"

"I don't know, but she deserves to know, surely? She was married to him for twenty years."

Harriet's stomach tightened at the thought. She'd been thinking about her mum lately, yes, and even toying with the very vague and hazy idea of somehow contacting her, but her imaginings had never gone beyond that. She wasn't at all sure she was ready for the reality of talking to her again, maybe even seeing her again. Would their mother come to their father's funeral? The thought gave Harriet a rush of longing, a judder of anxiety.

"Harriet." Rachel's voice was sharp, and Harriet came to herself.

"Sorry, I was daydreaming for a moment." She reached for some more papers, stared down at them blindly, the black type dancing before her eyes.

"No, look." Rachel touched her shoulder. "I've found it."

Harriet glanced down at the bound sheaf of papers in her sister's hand—the last will and testament of Peter Mowbray.

"It's dated thirteen years ago," Rachel said quietly.

"Right after Mum left."

"I suppose she was his beneficiary, originally," Harriet replied. She felt shaky all of a sudden, half wishing she hadn't asked about the will, that Rachel hadn't found it. "Well, what does it say?"

Rachel hesitated, the document resting in her hand. "I'm sure it will just be standard," she said, as if trying to convince herself. "Split equally between us."

Harriet gave a jerky nod. "Well, let's find out."

Rachel pressed her lips together, and then started flicking through the pages. Harriet clenched her hands, nails digging into her palms, before she forced herself to unclench them, take a steadying breath. Whatever was in that will, it didn't actually change anything, but it might confirm it.

Rachel drew her breath in sharply, and that was all it took for Harriet to know. "He's left it all to you, hasn't he?" she stated quietly. She realised she wasn't surprised, or angry, or even hurt, at least not in this moment. Maybe on some level she had always known, or at least suspected. She absorbed the truth of it, let it trickle slowly through her.

Rachel looked up, her face pale, her eyes wide and dark. "I didn't know—"

"I know you didn't. Let's see it?" She took the document from Rachel's slack clasp and started to skim-read all the legalese. It didn't take long to find the relevant portion—it was right there, in black and white. *I leave all my assets and belongings, including the property of Embthwaite Farm, to my daughter Rachel Mowbray, save for a bequest to Harriet Mowbray of ten thousand pounds.*

"Well." She let out a laugh that sounded harder than

she'd meant it to. "At least he gave me something."

"I can't believe this." Rachel sounded dazed. "I really thought it would be fair."

"I think I knew it wouldn't be, because it never has been." The words sounded bitter, but her tone was matter-of-fact. It was, Harriet knew, simply the truth.

"We'll split it, anyway," Rachel insisted. "Whatever there is. Fifty-fifty—"

Harriet shook her head, but she couldn't quite make herself say she didn't want to. It was too much money to refuse simply out of pride. "We'll see," she said instead.

"I'm sorry, Harriet," Rachel told her quietly. "I don't think I entirely believed you when you said I was Dad's favourite. I didn't see it, growing up."

"I know you didn't."

"And I didn't feel like the favourite, because he was always so quiet, so hard to impress. So unemotional."

"He had his moments." For Rachel, anyway. She remembered them—the way he'd rest his hand on Rachel's shoulder as he left the dinner table. The smile he gave her, his eyes twinkling briefly, when she mentioned some success at school.

"Yes, he did," Rachel agreed quietly. "I suppose I just always wanted more of them."

They were both silent, absorbing the import of what they'd learned. *Are you sure you want to know the answer to that question?*

When her father had asked, Harriet hadn't been sure of her answer, but now she thought she was. And with time running out ever faster, she'd need the courage to get it soon.

Chapter Twelve

"ANOTHER BOOKING!"

Perry sounded both triumphant and proud as she came into Quinn's study, brandishing her laptop with the bookings page up for his perusal. The website had gone live three days ago, and Perry had done a blitz of online marketing to raise the hotel's profile. Several local magazines and even one national one was coming in the next week to do an interview; they would be talking to Perry, not him. He wasn't going to do another interview ever again, not after the San Francisco debacle.

Still, the marketing blitz seemed to have done the trick, because the hotel's twenty-four rooms were now half filled. Pretty good for having only been taking bookings for three days.

"That's great," Quinn enthused. More than the bookings, relief though they were, he was glad to see his number-one assistant looking a bit more cheerful, because she'd been quite terse the last week, ever since his date with Harriet. Even he could put two and two together and come up with the requisite four on occasion, and the only conclusion he could draw was that Perry was worried about him, and thought he was going to do something stupid—again—

which he wasn't. He was determined not to; he didn't even feel tempted…and maybe that was because of Harriet herself.

They'd seen each other a few more times since their date, but only really in the context of working on the hotel. Harriet had offered to pitch in and help, and Quinn had accepted with alacrity, both because he needed it and he wanted to spend more time with her. Still, he suspected Harriet's involvement had put Perry's nose a bit out of joint. She'd been more or less in charge of everything, and he'd taken away a substantial part of her responsibility, but only because she obviously had too much to do, and they had to get this thing done.

And, he conceded, because he really did want to spend more time with Harriet.

He hadn't kissed her at the end of their date, although he'd wanted to. Thought about it quite a lot, and even made a clumsy attempt that had ended in the awkward should-we-or-shouldn't-we that had led them to a hug, with them both laughing self-consciously as they'd stepped away. But that was fine. They could take it slow. He wasn't going anywhere, and neither was she. Better they get to know each other, learn to trust each other. Although the danger was, of course, that the more time he had, the more likely he would be to mess something up, because he seemed to be so good at that.

And of course, there was the very real possibility that he had messed things up already, before he'd even met Harriet. If she searched for him online, what would she think?

But he didn't want to think about that. She might discover it all eventually, or he might work up the courage to tell her, but meanwhile he just wanted to enjoy being in her company.

"That's amazing, Perry," he told his assistant warmly. "Your marketing must have really worked."

"Ye-es…" Perry frowned. "Although in the section where they can tell us where they've heard about us, a bunch of guests have put 'Agatha' for some reason. I have no idea what that means. I don't know any Agathas."

Quinn smothered a startled laugh and Perry's frown deepened. She looked up from her laptop to pin him with a pointed stare. "Do *you* know an Agatha?"

"There *is* an Agatha who runs a little tea room in town," he admitted, because he felt he had no choice but to admit the truth. He didn't think Perry was going to be pleased about it, though. "Harriet and I went there about a week ago."

"Surely that wouldn't account for all these bookings," Perry exclaimed, her tone wavering between incredulity and something close to disgust. She was a great believer in all things online; she'd been extremely dubious about the hotel being screen-free. She certainly wouldn't want to believe word of mouth could be more successful than her online marketing wizardry.

"It might," Quinn replied, smiling, hoping Perry could see the funny side of it. "Agatha seemed to know a lot of people. And they do things differently in Yorkshire, it seems."

Perry slammed her laptop shut. "What *is* this place?" she exclaimed, and now there was no hiding her disgust. She started to stalk out of the office.

"Perry," Quinn called. "It's a good thing, right? The bookings—"

"Whatever," she snapped over her shoulder, and he sighed.

He didn't mean for Perry's toes to be stepped on, but somehow it seemed to be happening, anyway, in all sorts of ways, with first Harriet and now the bookings. Back in San Francisco, Perry had been his executive assistant, his cheerleader, and his security guard all rolled into one. He'd assumed she'd appreciate a bit of a break from the intensity of the role, but now he wondered. Her protectiveness of him was starting to feel like smothering.

At least, he told himself, the hotel was coming together. The plumbing was fixed, the bathrooms had been fitted—with new fixtures—and the receptions rooms were freshly painted and at least partially furnished. Next week the kitchen would be inspected, and after that the fire and health and safety regulations would be assessed. It was all finally happening, and just in time.

There was still more work to do, *way* more work to do, but the to-do list was starting to feel manageable. Mostly. It was just three more weeks till the opening night party. His stomach clenched at the thought of the party…the first one he would have been to since San Francisco. A lot was riding on it; a lot was riding on this whole enterprise working. He'd sunk pretty much all the money he'd made from Q Games into the hotel. Was he crazy, the way so many people thought he was?

The way his father did?

But he didn't want to think about his father. He didn't

want to think about the last time he'd talked to him properly, telling him about the successful sale of Q Games, only to have his father dismiss it all as utterly unimportant, as usual.

Games, Quinn? What a total waste of your life...not that I'd expect anything else.

Quinn could picture the sneering curl of his father's lip, the way he'd glanced away. He could even picture the smug smile of his younger brother, Rupert, although he hadn't been in the room, but Rupert had always been pleased to see Quinn taken down yet another notch. He loved being his father's favourite, the one he'd chosen after Quinn, the alleged heir, had been such a disappointment.

He drummed his fingers against his desk, that old restlessness overtaking him once more, leaving him feeling edgy, wanting something he couldn't name. He thought, very briefly, about calling his father to update him on the hotel, then dismissed the notion. His father wouldn't be impressed by anything Quinn said or did; in fact, he'd make a point of being *un*impressed, as he always did. Why Quinn kept trying with the man, if only in his own head, he didn't know. Maybe that was just how children were wired; you couldn't *not* try with your parents, because they were parents. Their default setting was to love and support you, and when they didn't, you felt you were the one who had malfunctioned.

That was how Harriet felt, he suspected, with her parents. Funny how they were alike in that way, even if they hadn't made the comparison out loud. They hadn't talked about family stuff since their date-turned-disaster, and that was okay. Quinn had simply enjoyed spending time with her, but he hoped she'd trust him with her secrets one day.

And would he trust her with his? Not that they were all that secret. He sighed and raked his hands through his hair, just as there was a tap at the door.

"Quinn?"

"Harriet!" He jumped up from his chair as she slipped into the room with a small smile that definitely didn't reach her eyes. She looked subdued; even her curls seemed less wild, tucked behind her ears and staying there, and her face lacked its usual vivid liveliness. "What's wrong?" he asked immediately, and she frowned.

"How do you know something is wrong?"

"So, something is," he surmised. "Anyway, I could just tell." Because already he knew her, could gauge her mood by the light in her eyes.

She shrugged, hugging her arms around herself for a second before she dropped them.

"Just one of those days," she replied, not meeting his gaze. "Winter blues, maybe." The weather had turned—frosty mornings, everything brown and bare, dark now by half past three in the afternoon. They definitely could use a little Christmas cheer, and hopefully they would get it soon, once they started decorating the hotel. "It's fine," she stated, then raised her eyebrows and tried to smile. "What shall I tackle today?"

Quinn decided he wouldn't push, even though he was tempted to. What had she meant, *one of those days*? "What do you feel like tackling?" he asked.

Harriet had come over a few times in the last week to help out wherever she could; she was the kind of person who happily put her hand to whatever was needed and was never too precious about anything. She'd painted a pantry, and scrubbed out cupboards in the kitchen; she'd advised on where to get fresh Christmas trees, and the best place to source local jams and chutneys, as well as where to place the sofas in the sitting room. Yesterday she'd had the brilliant idea of naming all the rooms after Yorkshire dales, just the kind of nice, homely touch Quinn wanted, and had even recommended a local artist to paint the signs for each room, a rush job that the artist had been willing to do.

"I don't mind," Harriet told him. "I just want to be useful."

"You are *beyond* useful," Quinn assured her, although it struck him as a somewhat odd and even sad thing to say. Was 'useful' a synonym for something else? For being valued, even loved? Without even meaning to, Harriet had dropped a few clues in their conversation about the nature of her life; Quinn knew she'd basically been taking care of her father since her mother left thirteen years ago. He also knew, or at least suspected, that her father had not appreciated his daughter's self-sacrificing support one iota.

"You don't need to be useful, Harriet, you know," he said, and the hesitant smile on her face faltered and then vanished as she stared at him in confusion and growing dismay.

"You…you don't want my help anymore?"

"No, no, I don't mean that," he said quickly. "I just…" Here he was, mired in another conversational quagmire. It seemed to be a special talent of his. "It's just," he tried to explain, "I don't want you to feel like you have to earn your keep or something like that."

"My keep?" Her expression had turned watchful. "I'm not living here, though."

"Not your keep, then. My respect, maybe. Or…something." He was so not good at this. "All I meant," he finished a bit desperately, "is that I like you as you are. You don't need to be useful to me."

A blush crept over her cheeks and washed her throat in a dull red. She glanced down at her feet as she shook her head. "Do I seem that pathetic?" she asked in a low voice.

"No, *no*, not at all," Quinn said quickly. He knew he was only making things worse. "I get the feeling that I maybe shouldn't have said anything," he remarked, trying for wry. "It would have been better that way. It often is. Remember what I said about how I make a good first impression and then you get to know me…?" He tried for a laugh, didn't quite manage it.

Harriet was silent. "You're right, though," she said at last. "I do like being useful. I've been trying to be useful all my life. Indispensable, even." She paused and then added, a bitter note entering her voice like a jagged splinter of sound, "For all the good it's done me."

Quinn heard the throb of pain in her voice, and he desperately wanted to assuage it. The trouble was, as ever, he wasn't sure how. "Well, you don't need to be useful to me," he assured her after a moment. "In all honesty, I've never been a big proponent of usefulness."

She let out a huff of laughter, which pleased him. At least he could make her laugh. "No?" she asked teasingly. "You prefer to be useless?"

"Absolutely," he replied with a smile. It was so much easier to make light of his failures, turn them into strange successes. "I tried my hardest to be as useless as possible when I was growing up. It took effort, mind you, but it seemed to work for me." It always amazed him, how he could talk about the hurts of his childhood as if they didn't pain him anymore at all. It was like a costume he put on, a full, latex bodysuit that fit like a second skin. He simply slipped into it and inhabited it, and everyone believed in who they saw: light, laughing Quinn, so funny and smart and whimsical and wry. *What a great guy! So fun to be around. A bit eccentric, it's true, but that's just part of his charm.* Until he slipped up and showed his true colours.

"It didn't really work for you all that well," Harriet pointed out in a reasonable tone, "if you were expelled from two schools and dropped out of college before you graduated."

And just like that, she peeled away that safe suit he thought hid him so well, left him vulnerable and revealed in a way he both craved and hated. She raised her eyebrows. "Did it?"

"I forgot I'd told you about that," Quinn admitted. "I suppose it depends how you define success."

"Not by being expelled, I should think." She paused, cocked her head. "I wonder if you did the exact opposite of what I've done, Quinn. I've tried to be useful to make people, well, love me, or if not love me, then at least need me. You made yourself useless so that people *wouldn't* love you." She gazed at him openly, her dark eyes wide and searching. "Why was that, do you think? Was it to give them a reason because you were scared they wouldn't, anyway?"

Ouch. How on earth had she seen all that? Said it? He'd thought he'd been so much better at hiding his feelings, he supposed, when he obviously wasn't. He opened his mouth, closed it again.

Harriet shook her head. "Sorry, I'm probably projecting onto you, and I shouldn't. I've just…" She closed her eyes for a brief moment, then snapped them open. "I've had a confirmation that everything I had believed is actually true, and the truth is, knowing that feels *horrible*." Her lips trembled before she pressed them together. "You'd think I'd feel a little validated, at least, but I don't. I feel…*violated*." She cast her eyes to the ceiling, blinking her eyes rapidly to keep the tears pooling there from falling.

"What did you believe was true?" Quinn asked. He was concerned on her behalf, and he ached to take her in his arms. He was also really, really glad they weren't talking about him anymore, because he didn't think he'd have been able to cope with any more of her honesty right now.

"That my dad didn't love me. And he doesn't. It really is that simple." She lowered her head to look at him, and a single tear tracked down her cheek. She dashed it away quickly. "Sorry," she mumbled, and Quinn decided this was in fact the moment for a hug.

He stepped towards her, reaching out to draw her slowly to him. When his hands hit her shoulders, she tensed for a second, but then she came, willingly, stepping into the shelter of his embrace so her cheek was pressed against his chest, his chin resting on her head.

Quinn had forgotten how *nice* a hug felt. Better than a kiss, in some ways. He certainly appreciated the feel of her warm, curvy body in his arms, but he also enjoyed the simple act of hugging—the comfort of it, the humanity, the connection.

"Do you want to tell me about it?" he asked.

"We found my father's will," she said, her voice muffled against his chest, her springy curls brushing his lips. "He left everything to my sister—the farm, the house, all his possessions. He gave me a bequest for ten thousand pounds."

Quinn tightened the embrace. He had no idea what to say.

"It's not about the money," Harriet continued quickly. "It really isn't. It's just about the…the *meanness* of it, I suppose. What has he had against me all these years? I mean, *what*?"

"Have you asked him?"

"Yes, last week. And he asked me in return if I really wanted to know the answer. I didn't reply then because I was too shocked that he'd answered at all. And I keep wanting to tell him I do want to know, but the truth is, I'm not sure about that at all." Her words were coming faster and faster, wobbling all over the place, while Quinn kept his arms around her, her body snuggled against his. "I thought I did, and when I found the will, I was just…numb, really. I thought, fine, that's it; I knew it all along, anyway, so it doesn't have to hurt. It was only later that I realised how hurt I was—*not* because of the money—"

"I know," he said gently.

"Anyway." A shudder went through her. "I need to ask him. I need to know. Maybe I'll have some peace about it, then. But we don't have much time left—his health has really started to fail. He's already losing his speech. Sometimes he tries to speak, and it just comes out as gibberish.

One day soon he won't be able to tell me anything at all, and I'll have lost my chance to know." She pulled away to gaze up at him, her eyes filling once more with tears. "I keep thinking, 'Why did it have to be this way?' Why couldn't he have loved me just a little? It's not," she continued in that quick way of hers, "that he was cruel or even unkind. He wasn't, actually. He was just…indifferent. Like I didn't matter to him either way, he could take or leave me that easily."

"That's its own kind of cruelty, especially when coming from a parent," Quinn replied quietly. He knew the feeling, although his own father's indifference had perhaps been a bit more pointed, a bit more deliberate.

"I suppose it is. Anyway." She stepped back from his embrace, forcing him to drop his arms. "Sorry to have such a wobble I'm still processing it all, I guess." She wiped her eyes again, shaking her head. "Gosh, I'm a nightmare, aren't I? Plus, I got mascara on your shirt. I guess we're even in the clothing stakes."

"Hardly. I am still going to buy you a dress, and in any case, I didn't notice about my shirt." Quinn gazed at Harriet, aching for her, for the way she was so obviously trying to pull herself together and failing. "I suggest we have a Useless Day," he pronounced suddenly, and she blinked at him.

"A what?"

"An Entirely and Wonderfully Useless Day," he reiterated firmly, warming to the idea. "Forget the hotel and all that needs doing here." Briefly he thought of Perry, working so hard, and then he pushed the thought away. She might appreciate a day where no one was getting up in her business.

"Forget baking cookies or scones or what have you. Let's go somewhere—do something—entirely useless."

Harriet's eyes narrowed in thought. "Such as?"

"What is the most useless thing you can think of doing?"

She shrugged, bemused now, as well as uncertain. "Sleep?"

"Sleep is very useful," he admonished with a playful wag of his finger. "You can't survive without it! No, I am talking properly useless. No health benefits at all. No work involved."

Harriet gave a little shrug. "I don't know, then. Go somewhere, maybe. Somewhere that's just…fun."

"Okay, let's do that, then," Quinn said with alacrity. "Where would you like to go?"

Her eyes widened as she laughed softly. "Quinn, you have a hotel that is set to open with a grand party in just three weeks, and your bedrooms still don't have any furniture in them."

"It's on order."

"The sitting room—"

"Coffee tables coming tomorrow."

"The Christmas decorations—"

"We can't really decorate until the rooms are furnished," Quinn pointed out reasonably. "Really, there's nothing to do today *but* be useless." He was choosing to forget the dozens of emails he had to reply to, the health and safety checklists he'd promised to run over with Perry, the food hygiene certificate they needed to be given next week, the staff contracts that needed to be reviewed, and on and on and on. Right now, none of it mattered in comparison to being with

Harriet and making her happy.

She let out a little huff of laughter. "You're crazy—you know that?"

For a second he tensed; had she seen the video? Read the rumours on Reddit? Did she know what he'd done, how he'd wrecked his whole life on purpose? But then he saw how guileless her expression was, and he relaxed. No, she hadn't. Not yet, anyway, and maybe she never would. It would take some digging, after all, and if she hadn't done it already…well, he could hope, at least, that she wouldn't find out until he worked up the courage to tell her himself. "Certifiable," he assured her cheerfully, and she smiled.

"All right, then. Let's go somewhere."

"All you need to do is choose where."

She hesitated and then said shyly, "How about York? The Christmas markets are running and I've always thought they were wonderful. But it's almost an hour away—"

"No problem," Quinn assured her. An hour in the car with Harriet was not an unappealing prospect. "Let's go."

She looked startled. "Right now?"

"Why not? What's stopping us?" A million different things, but he had no intention of pointing any of them out. He willed her to let go of her inhibitions, her uncertainties, her sense of deficiencies, and just be…with him.

"All right," Harriet said, and Quinn couldn't keep from letting out a whoop of joy.

Chapter Thirteen

HARRIET FOUGHT AGAINST a sense of unreality as she and Quinn slipped out of the hotel like thieves on the run and headed to his car. She didn't do stuff like this, ever, except since meeting Quinn she sort of did. Her life had become something of an adventure with him, every twist and turn unexpected, joyous, in a way it had never been before. She found she was looking forward to their day in York—another date, even?—with more than a little excitement. Quite a lot of excitement, actually. She loved feeling like this, free and a little bit wild.

"Are you sure there aren't a million and one things for you to do back at the hotel?" she asked as he started down the drive. "Or even a million and two?"

"More like a million and three," he replied easily, "but nothing is as important as this."

"As important as being useless?" she teased. "Really?"

"Really," he assured her, and now he sounded serious.

"Are you trying to teach me a lesson?" she asked, not sure how she felt about the notion. She appreciated his thoughtfulness, but she didn't want to be some sort of project, like another room in the hotel, in need of a lick of paint, some new plumbing. "Something along the lines of that I'm valuable as I am, and I don't need to be useful to be liked, that kind of thing?"

He let out a laugh as he slid her a playful glance. "And if I am?"

It was like a mix between a self-help book and a rom com, she thought. At the end of the afternoon, she'd thank him for opening up the world while they sipped hot chocolate and he teasingly dabbed whipped cream on her nose or something ridiculous like that. As much as she liked to imagine those sorts of movie montages, and as much as she appreciated what Quinn had already shown and taught her, she definitely didn't want to be his pity project, a work in progress. "That's very kind of you," she told him, "but I've kind of done enough self-psychoanalysis already." She turned to look out the window at the frost-tipped moors blurring by, under a pale blue sky. "It's kind of like with the Brainy Quotes. You can say as many of them as you want, but it doesn't mean you believe them, or that they can make a difference."

Quinn was silent for so long that she turned her head to look at him; his expression was inscrutable, his lips pursed into a thoughtful frown. "And what if I said," he finally asked, "that having a useless day is actually just an excuse to spend time with you? That I'd rather go to York, or anywhere with you, than do the million and three things back in Mathering?"

He was still looking at the road, but Harriet felt as if he'd stared right into her soul. Reached right down into it and squeezed. *That* made her feel far more valuable, and liked, than anything else possibly could have.

"I suppose," she said when she trusted herself to speak, "I'd say I like the sound of that much more."

"Good." He turned to glance at her, grey eyes glinting. "Because it's true."

Was it? Why did she have so much trouble believing that a man like Quinn could actually like her? She'd so enjoyed spending time with him this last week, but she'd had to keep warning herself that it didn't necessarily mean anything. He hadn't asked her out on a second date, after all, and he hadn't kissed her on the first one. Maybe she was just amusing him for a short time. It was a painful notion, but a necessary one, she'd thought…until now.

Now she was starting to believe he really did like her…useful or not.

YORK WAS DECKED out in full Christmas regalia as they drove into the city, parking on the outskirts of the city walls. Every tree and building was festooned with fairy lights, and the York Minster was lit up like a firework, with a brass band merrily playing Christmas carols in front. Quaint wooden market stalls selling every kind of Christmas ornament and delicacy were set up in the square, and Quinn, being Quinn, had to stop every second or so, to take it all in, study and examine absolutely everything with alacrity and interest.

"Amazing," he exclaimed when they came to a glassblower's stall. "You actually *blow* into it? And they're beautiful. Just fantastic." He bought something at nearly every stall, insisting it was for the hotel—delicate glass-blown ornaments, wicker reindeer, hand-stitched Santas made of felt. They had to go back to the car twice for all his purchases; he was like a child in a candy store, dipping his hand into absolutely every jar of sweets.

"This day isn't turning out to be useless at all," he told her mock-severely, when they'd stopped their retail therapy for hot chocolate and hot, cinnamon-dusted doughnuts that had been meltingly delicious, burning their tongues. They were sitting in a wooden booth, hands cradled around their paper cups of cocoa. "Considering all the stuff I'm buying for the hotel, this is seeming a very useful day, indeed."

"Well, maybe being useless is overrated," Harriet teased, "even if you swore by it."

"Maybe," he agreed, and she decided to be daring and press for just a bit more information. She'd certainly shared a lot of her emotional stuff; she wanted to know more about his.

"So why did you feel you were such a major disappointment to your parents?" she asked. "Capital M, capital D? Was it because of your dyslexia, or something else? Something more?"

He tensed a little, the laughing lines of his face turning wary, guarded, before he deliberately relaxed. "The dyslexia was part of it, certainly," he agreed. "I was pretty hopeless at school, unless it involved computers. But it wasn't just the academics; it was the whole package, really. I was a pretty odd kid, to tell you the truth. The kind who asks awkward questions and doesn't get social cues and spends recess by himself, reading comic books."

Harriet could imagine it, and it made her feel sad. Yes,

Quinn was quirky, and maybe he'd been even quirkier as a child, but he was also lovely and warm and full of enthusiasm. Had the kids in his class not been able to see it? Had his family?

"And your parents didn't like that?" she surmised.

"They had a particular vision of what they expected Quinn Latham Taylor the Third to be like—that's my full name, by the way. Quinn after my great-great-great-grandfather, who built a railroad, and Latham after my great-great-great-grandmother, who was some kind of aristocracy." He sighed, raking a hand through his hair before he took a sip of his hot chocolate. "It was a lot to live up to."

"What was their vision?" Harriet asked. She was curious, simply because she wanted to know more about him, but also because his life seemed so different from hers, even as they shared some surprising and striking similarities. Quinn Latham Taylor the Third. It certainly was a mouthful.

"Oh, you know. Rich, successful, sporty, academic, entitled. The kind of guy who pops the collars of his Polo shirts, wears a monogrammed gold Rolex—I have one, by the way, that I got for my thirteenth birthday—and talks stocks and golf." He let out a laugh that managed to sound both bitter and genuine. "I failed on *so* many fronts."

"You might not have been what they expected," Harriet allowed, "but you succeeded in your own right. I mean, designing a super popular game…making so much money…? Not that I know how much money you made, but…"

He shook his head, the movement decisive. "A silly amount, frankly, but it simply was not good enough, I'm afraid."

"With a capital N, G, and E?" she dared to tease, and he smiled faintly.

"Absolutely."

"I'm sorry, Quinn." Emboldened by the depth of her emotion, Harriet reached over to cover his hand with hers. "I know what it feels like to not earn your parents' approval."

He twined his fingers with hers, making her gesture more intimate, and causing lovely little sparks to shoot all the way up her arm. "Especially when you shouldn't have to earn their approval at all."

"Yes, exactly."

"I struggled with that for a long time," he admitted. He was gazing down at their hands, seeming lost in thought. Surely he wasn't aware that he was stroking her palm in a way that made her insides melt and her toes curl with pleasure? "And you were right, what you said earlier. I did act out and fail on purpose—although trust me, it wasn't that hard—because I was sick to death of trying and failing, of never being good enough. It felt easier to act like I didn't care. Eventually I really didn't."

"Didn't you?" Harriet asked softly. He sounded like he still cared, at least a little.

"Well, I tried. Sometimes..." He paused, and she had the sense that he was going to reveal some secret before he continued, "Sometimes I failed in that. But anyway," he finished, squeezing her fingers, "this hotel is me trying in a totally different way. I hated my parents' whole world—the utter shallowness of it. I saw more of the same when Q Games became successful—everyone I encountered was so stuck on image, on success. I thought at first it was a haven for goofy guys like me, because everyone in tech is a little on the eccentric side, you know? But I found out it doesn't keep people from being smarmy, arrogant jerks." He blew out a breath. "I'm afraid, in the end, I didn't handle any of it very well."

Harriet was just about to ask him what that meant when he stood up from the table rather abruptly. "We haven't actually done anything useless yet today," he announced. "And I know you think uselessness is overrated, but I'm still a fan. What can we do in York that has no purpose but having fun?"

Harriet glanced up at him, deciding to let go of asking to clarify whatever he'd meant. He clearly didn't want to talk about it, and she understood his reticence.

"There's a fun fair around the corner," she told him. "With a Santa's grotto, a merry-go-round, and a helter-skelter. We could go there?"

"Excellent." Quinn beamed at her. "Let's go."

HE'D COME ALARMINGLY close to telling her about his little breakdown, Quinn thought as he took Harriet's hand in his—it felt easy now—and they walked towards the fun fair. He'd almost told her about the party, how he'd completely lost his cool, along with his job, and embarrassed himself rather unbearably, as well as being blacklisted from the tech world for probably forever. Not that he cared about any of that, at least not much, but Harriet might. She might not want to date someone who seemed not just a touch quirky, but utterly unstable.

He released a shuddery breath, mentally shaking his head. She'd find out soon enough, if she became curious, which she probably would. And then he'd just have to deal with the fallout—probably by walking away, just as he did before. Self-sabotage at the highest level. He wanted things to be different this time; *he* wanted to be different. He just hoped he could.

"Here we are," Harriet said as they rounded the corner from the Minster and came to another square that was set up as a mini amusement park—with the requisite rides she had mentioned, as well as the Santa's grotto and a few game stalls and arcades.

"I didn't know what a helter-skelter was," Quinn told her, nodding towards the tower with its twisting slide that was the centrepiece of the little park, "but now I do. Shall we go on?"

Harriet let out a surprised laugh. "I think it's for children—"

"Surely not." He tugged her towards the slide. "Let's ask."

Sure enough, adults were allowed on the slide as well; they were given a burlap bag to sit on and Quinn kept hold of Harriet's hand as they climbed the narrow, twisting steps to the top of the slide. "I hope you're not scared of heights," he remarked as they reached the top.

"It's a little late to ask now," Harriet replied, but she was smiling.

"Right, then." He positioned himself on the burlap bag, legs splayed out front. "You sit in front."

"We're going together?" She sounded startled.

"What's the point otherwise?" He grinned at her. He was quite looking forward to snugging his arms around her waist, having her fit close to his body.

"Um, okay." Tucking her hair behind her ears, she manoeuvred herself to between his outstretched legs and sat down gingerly. Quinn put his arms around her waist—she felt exactly as he thought she would, warm and soft—and tucked her in firmly against his chest, his fingers laced across her middle.

"This all right?" he murmured, because the last thing he wanted to do was make her feel uncomfortable.

"Um, yeah. Fine." She sounded breathless. He *felt* breathless, holding her so close. Her hair was brushing his cheek and he could smell the scent of her—cinnamon and something light and floral. Intoxicating.

"Are you ready?" he asked, and she nodded, so her hair tickled his lips. He pushed off and they started sliding down—slowly at first, and then faster as they picked up speed, zipping round the curves in the slide. All Quinn could hear was Harriet's squeak of slightly scared laughter; all he could feel was the warmth of her body against him. The Christmas lights of York swirled around them in a blur of colour, and he felt as if he were almost flying.

Then they reached the bottom in a thud, his feet hitting the ground, his arms instinctively tightening around Harriet. She twisted to look up at him, her face alight, and all rational thought left him completely as he bent his head to kiss her.

The feel of her lips on his was exactly what he'd expected, exactly right. Warm, soft, willing, generous. Her mouth opened under his and he deepened the kiss, bringing one hand to the back of her head to anchor her to him. The whole world fell away, and his mind spun and spun as the kiss went on and on.

"Hate to break it up," a voice called, startling him back into his senses, "but we need the slide back, guys."

Harriet broke the kiss first, laughing self-consciously, looking dazed. She scrambled up from the slide and then Quinn heaved himself up, a bit awkwardly, being so tall, his limbs splayed akimbo before he righted himself. He handed the burlap bag back to the ride operator, who grinned and winked at him. Quinn felt too shaken by that simple kiss to smile back.

It felt as if it had changed everything. It had just been a kiss, and yet he knew he'd never felt like that before. Like he'd found himself—no, not just found, but *discovered. This is who I am meant to be.* He hadn't realised he hadn't known that, until now.

Harriet was waiting a few feet away, still looking dazed, and—he thought—a little cautious, like she didn't quite know what to make of their kiss. He felt too happy to be cautious himself, too sure of his own feelings.

"Well, *that* was fun," he said with a deliberately raffish smile that fortunately had her laughing.

"Yes, it was."

"What shall we do now?" He reached for her hand and swung it as they walked along.

Harriet glanced at the darkening sky, looking a little worried. "I'm afraid I should probably get back soon. Rachel's been with my dad all day, and I don't like to leave her holding the fort for too long."

The same dad who didn't seem to care about her at all? Quinn felt an unreasonable needling of annoyance and even outrage on Harriet's behalf. It was her choice, of course, how she spent her time, but he didn't want their day to end. He was also uncomfortably aware that while he'd basically said 'screw you' to his own father, living that out day by day, she was diligent in her care and responsibility towards her own.

"All right," he replied, knowing there was no point saying otherwise. "I had a really good time today."

"So did I." She turned to him, looking troubled, and Quinn stopped right there in the street.

"What is it?" he asked, lifting his hand to brush a strand of hair away from her cheek, letting his fingertips linger.

"I don't know." She smiled, although she still looked troubled, or at least uncertain. "I don't get kissed a lot," she blurted, and then ducked her head, flushing. "That came out wrong," she half mumbled, and then she shook her head. "Actually, no, it didn't. It's the truth. I haven't…well, this is something you are probably realising as I speak, but I haven't had a lot of romance in my life. A couple of guys I went on dates with over the years, but it never really went anywhere. I mean, rural Yorkshire is not exactly teeming with prospects, if you know what I mean." She let out a huff of laughter. "I don't even know why I'm telling you this, only that I feel like I have to, because…well, I just do." She looked up at him then, her eyes so wide and clear, every emotion reflected in their soft, brown depths.

Quinn knew what she was trying to say without her having to form the words. *Don't break my heart.* So often he didn't get what people were trying to say, misread the social cues, the subtext, but with Harriet he felt he understood her completely, because he felt exactly the same. This was the first time his heart had ever truly been involved, and already it was in her hands, resting there, vulnerable and exposed.

"I won't," he promised softly, and her forehead furrowed.

"You won't...what?"

All right, so maybe he didn't know exactly what she was thinking. But he *felt* it all the same. "I just meant...this is pretty new for me, too."

She rolled her eyes, managing a laugh. "You must have had girlfriends before, Quinn, in your jet-setting life—" Her eyes widened. "Not that I'm your girlfriend. I mean, I don't—I wouldn't—"

"It wasn't all that jet-setting," he cut off her abject stammering with a smile, adding, "And yes, I've had relationships, although not that many, and they weren't very serious. They ended pretty quickly, as a matter of fact, mainly because I didn't care enough to put the effort in, which makes me look bad, but I'm being honest." He paused. "I've never felt this way about someone before."

She gave a little shake of her head, but he thought he saw a yearning in her eyes. He certainly felt it in himself. "Can you really say that? We barely know each other."

"I feel like we know each other pretty well," he countered. "Think of all the family trauma we've shared, after all." She smiled faintly, and emboldened, he continued, "I mean it, Harriet. This is new for me, too." He brushed a stray curl that had sprung forward again away from her face, and then, because he so desperately wanted to, he kissed her again.

He brushed his lips against hers like a question, one she answered by sighing softly and settling into him. His arms came around her and he drew her more snugly against him, deepening the kiss. Her head fell back, and his heart sang.

He really had never felt this way with anyone before. And already he felt he knew Harriet better than he'd known anyone, better than he even knew himself.

Except, he realised as he drew back, smiling down at her, she didn't know him in the same way. And when she did...?

Maybe this would all go up in flames...just as it had before, because he'd not just let it...he'd lit the match.

Chapter Fourteen

SHE HAD A *boyfriend*. Harriet kept trying out the word, seeing if it fit. Over the last ten or so years, she'd had a handful of dates; with one guy, she'd managed four or five before they'd drifted apart, both seeming grateful that they no longer had to try. No one had really stuck…not until Quinn.

And, of course, it was very early days for her to think about anything *sticking* at all. They'd had two dates, two kisses. That was it…and yet it felt like so much. It was so much more than she'd ever had before.

She'd come home from York a week ago, feeling as if she were floating on air. Rachel had noticed the silly grin on her face right away, of course, and demanded answers…answers Harriet had, for once, been more than willing to give, dreamily telling her about their day in York.

"So, this thing with you and Mr Millionaire…it's serious?" Rachel had asked, hands on her hips, sounding cautious, even sceptical.

Some sibling dynamics never changed, Harriet had reflected as she'd floated about the kitchen, getting things ready for supper. Fortunately, she no longer minded so much, not when she had Quinn to daydream about. "I don't know if I would use the word 'serious' yet," she told her sister, "since we've only gone on two dates. But it feels...special. And important."

Rachel frowned. "Is he going to stick around Mathering, do you think? Won't he want to go back to California or wherever?" Harriet had already told her he had come from San Francisco.

"Do you think," she had replied, keeping her voice mild, "you could just be happy for me? Say 'That's great, Hats; I'm so happy you're happy'—that sort of thing? Without any warnings or caveats?"

Rachel had had the grace to look abashed. "Sorry," she said. "I am happy for you. I'm just in older sister protective mode, I suppose." She'd paused and then added, "Making up for lost time, maybe."

Harriet had softened a little at that. "You don't have to feel guilty, Rachel. It's all water under the bridge now, and I know I was as much to blame for how we drifted apart as you were."

Rachel had made a face. "I don't know about that. I was older—"

"Barely. I'm not having you pull rank on me anymore," she'd teased, wagging her finger. "Water under the bridge. Seriously." And for the first time, she'd known she actually meant it, right down from the depths of her being. She was ready to move on from those old hurts.

It had felt good to finally make peace with her fractured relationship with her sister, fully and completely. Their relationship would always have cracks, scars, but in some ways that made what they had now feel stronger. It was like *kintsugi*—the Japanese art of putting broken pottery pieces back together with pure gold. The fractured lines made it look only more beautiful.

But not every relationship was like that, Harriet knew. A week on from her day in York with Quinn, and she still hadn't worked up the nerve to ask her father what he'd meant. To be fair, she'd been busy at the hotel; now just two weeks from the opening party, and it really was all hands on deck. Every day, things came together just a little bit more—the reception rooms were almost finished, the bedrooms were being decorated, the handcrafted signs Harriet had suggested hung on each door—Mossdale, Coverdale, Bishopdale, Fossdale.

Staff had started appearing, some moving into the rooms on the top floor—maids, cooks, bellboys, housekeeper. Perry was run off her feet managing the HR side of things, which was just as well because Harriet had had the distinct feeling the other woman didn't like her. When they'd crossed paths, Perry was polite, but coolly so. Harriet couldn't tell if she was possessive of the hotel, or Quinn, or both. In any case, she seemed to resent Harriet's interference.

As for her father…Harriet knew that as every day slipped like a pearl off a string, the window of opportunity to ask her father what he'd meant grew smaller and smaller. He'd been sleeping more, speaking less, having more headaches, and generally just seeming *less than.* It was heartbreaking to witness, not because of what she was losing in terms of her relationship with him, but because of what she'd never had, and now never would. All that was left was the chance to know why.

November had slipped into December quietly, the higher moors dusted with snow, the lower ones rimmed with frost. Chunks of ice bobbed in the Derwent, and the nights drew in before four o'clock, fathomlessly dark by five. Mathering had decked itself out for Christmas, with festive lights strung along the streetlamps, and a large Christmas tree in the town's small market square. Toby of the Tickled Trout dressed up as Father Christmas every year and gave the children presents at the lighting of the tree; it was generally considered the only time he said more than three words at once.

Rachel, in a heroic and perhaps misguided effort to include their father in some of the festivities, decided they should take him out to the tree lighting in early December.

"Are you serious?" Harriet asked. "He hasn't been out of the house in weeks, Rach, since we took him to the GP. And it will be so dark and cold—"

"But he loves the outdoors," Rachel protested, "and I think it must get a bit depressing, to be in your bedroom all the time, just staring at the walls. It's short, anyway—switch the lights on, have a cup of mulled wine, head home." She waggled her eyebrows hopefully. "Don't you want to feel like a family again, Harriet, just a little bit?"

Did she even know what that felt like? Harriet wondered. Sometimes she wasn't sure. Since they'd found their father's will, she'd looked at that photo of their beach day in Scarborough, studying it like historical document or sacred text, as if trying to determine its authenticity. She wished she could remember what she'd felt in that moment, but she could only remember what she *thought* she'd felt. Could she trust that child's wide smile on her face? Was that a hint of anxiety darkening her eyes, or was it just the glare of the sun? Had she known then that her dad didn't love her, or had she been sweetly naïve, fooling herself before she even knew that was what she was doing?

"Fine," she told Rachel. "We'll take him."

It was a cold, clear evening, their breath coming out in puffs of frost as they carefully bundled their father into the car. He'd hemmed and hawed and resisted the whole endeavour, but Rachel had been that determined. Ben offered to drive, and their dad sat in the front, Rachel and Harriet in the back, like an odd, mismatched sort of family.

"Is *Quinn* coming to this thing?" Ben asked in the teasing voice of an older brother.

Harriet rolled her eyes. She didn't really mind Ben's joshing; he was clearly so pleased for her. "He said he'd meet us there."

"Quinn?" their father demanded. "Who is Quinn?"

Rachel and Harriet exchanged uncertain glances.

"He's Harriet's boyfriend, Dad," Rachel told him, and Harriet squirmed inwardly at the term because even though the last week with Quinn had been wonderful, she didn't entirely trust it. Trust him, or maybe herself. Hearing Rachel say it out loud—he was her *boyfriend*—made her feel exposed, vulnerable, like she'd claimed something she couldn't actually prove.

"Hmpph," their dad said, and turned to look out the window.

Well, that was entirely predictable, Harriet reflected on a silent sigh. Why would he care that she had a boyfriend?

Why would he care about any aspect of her life at all when he never had before?

It didn't hurt anymore, she reminded herself. At least, it didn't have to. Quinn had shown her that.

They drove in somewhat prickly silence into Mathering; Harriet was seriously wondering whether this evening was going to go well at all. What was Rachel hoping for? Some facsimile of happy families at the eleventh hour? Harriet already knew it wasn't going to happen.

And it didn't. They parked the car on a side street, and then walked, each of them holding one of their father's arms, into the town square, his gait unsteady and slow. It seemed like most of Mathering was out for the tree lighting, bundled up in hats and scarves. Agatha had set up a stall with mince pies and mulled wine, and one of the pubs had another, pulling pints. Harriet nodded friendly hellos to people she knew, and, for a few moments, as she stood there in the cold, she felt happy to be exactly where she was.

For so long, she'd resented being left in Mathering. She'd been the one who had chosen to stay, more or less, and yet she'd been willing to blame anyone and anything—her sister, her mother, her lack of A levels—for her sorry state. It had felt easier, or maybe stronger, but she'd never truly believed it inside.

Inside, she'd felt like a failure, for never daring to go anywhere or do anything. For being too afraid, too unsure, too insecure. She didn't feel that way anymore, she realised, and it wasn't just because she had a *boyfriend*. It was because Quinn had essentially held up a mirror up to herself, and shown her what *he'd* glimpsed there, not what she'd learned to see on her own. She wanted to trust that reflection in the same way she wanted to trust their relationship, but both were hard.

"Hey." A hand came down on her shoulder, squeezing lightly, and she turned to see Quinn stepping towards her before he dropped a light kiss on her mouth in a way that still felt entirely new and surprising—and wonderful. His arm came around her back as he smiled down at her, his eyes twinkling with warmth and good humour.

"Hey, yourself," she said back, conscious of Ben's and Rachel's unabashedly avid stares as they watched this little exchange. They had yet to see this New and Improved Harriet in action, the one with a Boyfriend, definitely with a capital B.

"I haven't met you, I don't think," Quinn said, holding out a hand for Ben to shake. "Quinn Taylor."

"Ben Mackey," Ben replied, and they shook hands, each man seeming to take the measure of the other. Harriet and Rachel exchanged amused glances. This was new.

"And this is my dad, Peter Mowbray," Harriet said, trying not to burden the words with too much import.

"Mr Mowbray, lovely to meet you," Quinn replied with his usual alacrity and enthusiasm, and no sense that he knew how fraught this relationship—or lack of it—was.

Peter grunted and gave a nod. He was looking tired and, Harriet thought, a bit confused, his shoulders slumped, gaze darting around uncertainly, and she wondered if coming into town was a bit too much for him. Rachel, she feared, couldn't see it; she seemed to think that a cup of mulled wine and a little enthusiasm would make their dad snap out of it somehow.

"Aren't the lights pretty, Dad?" Rachel remarked in an overly interested voice, like she was talking to a toddler. Their father ignored her. "Dad?" Rachel pressed, her tone turning just a little strident, and Harriet wanted to tell her to stop, that she couldn't make him into something he'd never been, never mind something he would have stopped being, even if he had, once upon a time. "Don't you think?" Still no response. "Isn't this nice? I could get you a cup of mulled wine—"

"Rachel," Ben said quietly, his face filled with compassion. Quinn glanced at Harriet, a question in his eyes, and she shrugged her answer. Everyone had their own brand of quirky, she realised, including her sister. Clearly, she wanted to make this a moment to remember, and it wasn't going to be one, at least not in the way she hoped.

"Dad—" Rachel put a hand on her father's arm, and he shook it off, so hard and so suddenly that Rachel went stumbling back, and almost fell down, until Ben caught her, pulled her upright, while Rachel stared at him in shock.

"Get off me!" he screeched, and raised his arm as if he was intending to hit her. Rachel gasped and stumbled back against Ben, who put his arms around her protectively. Slowly their dad lowered his arm, his whole body trembling, while Harriet and Quinn looked on, stricken.

Her father started to speak again, but what came out this time was a string of gibberish, impossible to understand. He looked around wildly, his face full of fear as well as anger. Rachel, Harriet saw, was crying quietly, Ben's arms still around her.

"Dad," Harriet said gently, stepping forward. "Dad, it's okay." She didn't dare touch him, but she tried to keep her voice and gaze steady, before something really unfortunate happened. He swung around to stare at her, his eyes wild, before something calm and cold came over his face, like a curtain dropping down. Instinctively Harriet took a step back; she'd never seen him look at her like that, not with indifference, but with something almost like hatred.

"Don't call me that," he said, and this time the words were completely clear.

Harriet froze, even as her heart started to thud in hard, heavy beats. "Dad," she said again, and he shook his head violently.

"Don't call me that."

The whole world felt suspended, like a held breath, no one moving or speaking, as she stared at him. "Why not?" she whispered, and when the answer came, it was as if she'd known it all along. Maybe she had.

"Because you're not my daughter."

Harriet could only gape silently as Quinn sprang into action. "Mr Mowbray?" His voice was amazingly genial. "I think maybe it's time to go home?"

"Who are you?" Her dad—except not her dad, not anymore—asked irritably. He had dismissed Harriet entirely.

"Nobody important," Quinn replied easily. "But would you like to go home?"

Her father stared at him for a moment, and Harriet watched as his face collapsed into lines of weariness and sorrow. "Yes," he said, and his voice sounded slurred and so very tired. "Yes, I want to go home."

THE NEXT HALF hour passed in a dazed blur, a haze of numb unreality. Somehow, they all made it back to the car—Quinn included. As they helped their father, Harriet turned to him.

"You should go." Her voice sounded wooden.

"Harriet…" Quinn's face was soft with compassion. "I want to help you."

"I know. I really do. But I need to…to talk to my…" She couldn't even frame the words. He wasn't her father. He never had been. "I'll see you soon," she promised, and Quinn enveloped her in a tight hug. She burrowed herself into him, feeling as if she wanted to disappear entirely, be *subsumed.* Quinn seemed to understand that sentiment, at least a little, because he held on to her as if he were fusing her to himself.

Eventually she forced herself to step away. She wondered if this would change anything between her and Quinn—how much of her dysfunction did he really want to deal with, especially so early in their relationship? She didn't have the head or heart space to think about that now. She had to focus on her family. Her father. Except, of course, that wasn't what he was.

They drove in grim silence back to Embthwaite Farm; her dad had fallen into a doze, snoring softly, and when they got to the farmhouse, Rachel helped him upstairs while Harriet walked straight to the dining room, took out the bottle of brandy that was in the dusty liquor cabinet, and had a slug straight from the bottle. She closed her eyes as it burned down her throat, all the way to her gut.

"I'm so sorry, Harriet." Ben's voice was quiet behind her. Harriet didn't reply, didn't even open her eyes. "I don't know that you can trust what a man in the advanced stages of a terminal brain tumour says," he offered hesitantly, and she let out a hard, cold laugh, a sound so unlike her usual self, except she didn't even know what that was anymore.

"Really, Ben? That old saw *again*?"

"I always thought you had his eyes," he said quietly, and tears stung those very eyes that she now knew *couldn't* be like her father's. She pressed her hand against them, willed the tears back. She was not going to cry. Not about this.

"Well, clearly you were wrong," she told him, her hand still covering her eyes. "It actually makes perfect sense, you know. I think some part of me knew all along. I'm not really that surprised." Even if she felt rocked to her very foundations. "It's a relief, really," she continued, her voice starting to sound strained. "At least there's a reason, a good one, why he never cared about me at all."

"Harriet—"

"You know it's true."

He let out a long, weary sigh. "I don't know anything, really," he said. "I know you've always felt your dad didn't love you, but I don't know that it was actually the case."

Harriet let out a ragged laugh, high and wild. "*Really*, Ben?" she demanded. "You're saying I'm wrong?"

"No. No, I'm not. I'm saying sometimes I saw him looking at you when you didn't see it. You weren't there when he told me that he knew you'd handle things after he'd gone, because you were the dependable one, the one he trusted."

She whirled around. "*What...*"

Ben gazed at her steadily. "It's true."

Harriet raised a warning finger. "Don't lie to me."

"I'm not."

"He didn't say that," she insisted and Ben kept her gaze.

"He did."

Harriet shook her head slowly. "I don't believe it. I can't." Her voice broke on the words. "After all this time...you're saying some part of him really cared? I never felt it. Not once."

"I'm not saying you did, or even that you should have," Ben replied. "Only what I knew and have observed. Maybe you aren't his biological daughter, Harriet, and for a man like him, that would be a hard truth to accept, but he did care about you in some way. It's not much, but maybe it's something."

All Harriet could do was keep shaking her head. Some part of her wanted to believe it...and yet she didn't know if she could. She'd never felt it...had she? She tried to think back over the years; thirteen years they'd lived together, just the two of them. Yes, there had been some gruff thank yous when she'd brought him a cuppa or put a plate of eggs in front of him. Occasionally, they'd shared a smile or even a laugh, usually about something inane in the paper or on the telly. It wasn't much, but like Ben said, she supposed it was something.

And yet she'd wanted so much more. She'd deserved so much more, or thought she had, but now that she knew the truth. She wasn't even his...

And her mother had left her with him, anyway. The

truth of it hit her like a sledgehammer, thudding through her, sending her reeling, a double betrayal. *How* could her mother have done such a thing? Knowing what she had, never telling Harriet? It was impossible, and yet it was.

The faint thawing of feeling towards her mother hardened once more, frozen into something solid and cold and immoveable. No explanation would ever be good enough for that.

"You should talk to him, at least," Ben said. "Maybe there is more for him to explain."

"Like what?" Harriet shook her head. Of course, there were questions she wanted answers to—like who her real father was. How long her father had known she wasn't his. Had her mother told him right from the beginning? But she didn't want those answers from her father. She wasn't sure she could bear to look him in the eye ever again.

"I can't answer that question," Ben told her. "Only you can."

"Well, I don't want to right now." She sounded childish and she didn't care.

"Understood," Ben said quietly, and then, after a few moments when neither of them spoke, he withdrew from the room. Harriet let out a gusty sigh and almost reached for the bottle of brandy again. She felt both empty and full; numb and overwhelmed. She didn't want to think and yet her thoughts churned relentlessly.

Then she heard a creak on the stair, footsteps to the door. A pause, a breath. She knew it was Rachel, and she tensed, because she really could not take any big-sister wisdom right now. The sense of healing and completeness she'd felt with Rachel earlier seemed as if it had shattered into a thousand pieces. They weren't even full-blooded sisters anymore; they were half-sisters, and Harriet felt as if they might as well be strangers. Melodramatic, perhaps, but it was how she felt in this moment, when the certainties she hadn't even known she'd depended on so much had been swept away.

She opened her mouth to warn Rachel off from saying something well meaning but unhelpful, but no words came. And no words came from Rachel, either, as she crossed the room and swiftly, before Harriet could protest or even make a sound, she wrapped her in her arms—tightly, without words.

Harriet found herself hugging her sister back, just as tightly. Neither of them spoke, and yet it was enough.

Chapter Fifteen

HARRIET STOOD IN the barn, breathing in the remnants of the scents of hay and animal. The stalls were empty, the last of the farm's dairy herd having been sold off that morning, the cows loaded into a trailer before they'd rumbled away with a farmer towards Kirkby Lonsdale. There was nothing left.

She stood there, blinking in the dim light, one hand wrapped around a post. It was strange to think she'd never again come into this barn to see her dad seated on a milking stool, crouched by a cow, the animals rustling and lowing, the swish and squeeze of the milking machine the only sounds in the quiet, dim space. It wasn't something she'd particularly thought she'd miss, and yet she found she did, simply because it was gone.

It was the day after her father's revelation, and she hadn't seen him yet. Hadn't had the strength to confront him, ask for answers, or even look him in the eye. She hadn't talked with Rachel, either; after they'd hugged, Rachel had started to speak, but Harriet had shaken her head.

"I can't," she'd said simply. "Right now, I just can't."

Quinn had sent her a text later in the evening, asking her how she was, and as much as she'd wanted to, she hadn't been able to respond to that, either, because the truth was, she didn't *know* how she felt, and she found she couldn't even think about it. She'd spent a long, restless night staring at the ceiling, sleep not even to be thought of, her mind a complete blank, which was comforting, at least. She knew she wouldn't be able to keep the thoughts, the realisations, at bay forever, but this brief respite felt essential.

When dawn had barely started to silver the sky, she'd got up, showered and dressed, gritty-eyed with fatigue, and headed down to the kitchen. Fred had been in his usual place in front of the Rayburn, his plumed tail thumping a staccato beat on the slate floor as he'd glanced up at her.

Impulsively, Harriet had dropped to her knees in front of the dog and put her arms around him, burying her face in his shaggy fur. His tail had beaten the floor harder. A sound had escaped her, something close to a sob, but then she'd sucked it back in.

"Hey, Fred," she'd said softly. After another few seconds, as she'd struggled to keep her composure, she'd risen and set about making a pot of tea. She'd had a feeling she was going to need several cups this morning.

Halfway into her second cup, Rachel had come down, belting her dressing gown, her expression cautious.

"How are you?" she'd asked as she reached for a cup.

"I don't know." Harriet had taken a sip of her tea. "I've just been sitting here, staring into space for the last half hour."

"They're coming over this morning for the rest of the herd as well as all the milking paraphernalia," Rachel had said. "I can sort it, if you want."

Harriet had known her sister was trying to be considerate, but it was hard not to feel a little stung. Not to second-guess everything. *Am I not part of the family anymore?* she'd wanted to ask. Cry. But she feared she knew the answer already; she wasn't.

In the end, they'd both helped with the transfer, and now the barn was empty, and Harriet still didn't know how to feel. She thought about heading over to the hotel, to help out with the preparations as well as to see Quinn, but even though she thought it would be good to keep busy, she found she still couldn't summon the energy.

Every so often a thought would flicker through her mind like a minnow, darting and swift, and then it would rise up to smack her right in the face. Her mother had had an affair. She was the daughter of a woman who had walked away thirteen years ago, and never come back. She had no blood ties to the Mowbrays, to Embthwaite Farm, to the rich history of this place that she'd once been proud to be part of. She'd have to change the name of her bakery business, she thought dully. *Embthwaite Treats.* No longer. And what about her biological father? Who was he? Did he even know she existed? Would he care?

Eventually she turned and walked out of the barn, outside. The sky was leached of colour, the air wintry. She breathed it in, let its sharpness into her chest, to wake her up. This didn't change who she was, she told herself. Who she'd become. It didn't have to. It would take time and effort to get past this, she knew. Not to sink back into her old habits of letting herself be defined by other people's choices, but she'd learned a lot, in large part thanks to Quinn, to his zest for life and his ability to have moved past his own hardships. She could move on from this. She could choose to. She glanced at the house, saw that Rachel was hovering by the kitchen window, her face pale and anxious. They would need to talk sometime, Harriet knew, but not yet.

She walked around to the front, tiptoed into the front hall, and scooped up her keys; she was in the car, driving down the lane before Rachel had twigged that she'd gone.

As she pulled up to the hotel, she felt something in her settle. She was glad to have left the farm, to be in this place, a hive of activity, with workmen coming and going, as well as employees. In some ways, Harriet knew, she wasn't really needed anymore, now that Quinn had an army of staff at his disposal, but she was still glad she'd come. She wanted to see him.

Downstairs, various people were bustling to and fro—everything was, amazingly, coming together just as Quinn had wanted. Dodging workmen and staff, Harriet wandered through the downstairs rooms—the sitting room with its squashy sofas, the puzzle already in its box on the table, waiting to be opened and put together by guests, just as Quinn had wanted. There was a magnificent Christmas tree in the corner, ten feet high, bushy and green, ready to be decorated. The dining room, with its family-style table that seated twenty-four, so all the guests could eat together, was swathed in white linen and red velvet ribbon. The games room, its glass cabinets well stocked with a variety of board and card games, the felt-covered tables ready for use, a bowl of walnuts with an old-fashioned nutcracker next to a snifter of brandy. He'd done it, she thought, smiling and shaking her head in wonder. He'd really done it.

"Harriet."

She turned to see Perry standing in the doorway of the games room, arms folded and unsmiling. Instinctively, Harriet straightened.

"Hi, Perry," she said, trying to sound friendlier than she felt. The other woman was practically glaring at her, and she thought she really could have used a respite from such naked animosity right about now.

"What are you doing here?" Perry asked, and Harriet recoiled, just a little. She'd been coming here several times a week for the better part of month, so why was Perry acting like she wasn't welcome?

"I thought I'd see how everything was going," she said, determined not to let Perry's unfriendliness get to her. "And to see Quinn."

"He's busy."

Harriet blinked. "I'll just say hi, then. Do you know where he is?"

Perry refolded her arms, like she was settling in. "Busy," she said again, and Harriet shook her head slowly.

"What is it that you have against me, Perry?" she asked, and saying it felt like a liberation. Why not be confrontational? Could things get any worse than they already were? Her new mottoes rang through her mind—*so what?* and *why not?*

She'd live them out right here, right now.

Perry pressed her lips together. "I don't have anything against you, per se," she allowed grudgingly.

"*Per se?*" Talk about the faintest of praise.

She sighed. "Look, Harriet, it's just... I know what Quinn's like more than you do. He's funny, he's charming, he bowls women over without even meaning to. But this..." She gestured to the space between them. "Is a blip."

"What," Harriet asked slowly when it seemed she wasn't going to say anything more, "do you mean by 'this'?"

"Mathering. The hotel. You, frankly." Harriet kept her expression neutral with a lot of effort. Part of her was incredulous; another part of her actually wanted to laugh. *Really, Perry, on today of all today, you need to tell me I'm a blip?* "Quinn's working through some stuff," Perry continued, "getting it out of his system. He's had some...bumps, and he's figuring his way through them. But he's going to go back to his old life soon." She paused. "Where he belongs."

This type of confrontation, Harriet thought, was something she really didn't need right now, on the heels of last night. She took a deep breath, let it out slowly. "Has he said that," she asked, "or is that just you?"

Perry took a step towards her, her eyebrows drawing together in something close to a scowl. "I know Quinn better than anyone. We met when we were eighteen—just kids. We've been through a lot together. This isn't who he really is." She nodded towards the games room, but Harriet knew she meant the whole inn, all of Mathering, everything he'd built here...including a relationship with her. "Or what he really wants."

"When I hear that from him, I'll believe it." Her voice shook only a little. She was too tired, too raw, for this.

"He won't tell you," Perry replied, "because right now he believes it is. That's how Quinn is. He's obsessed with something until he isn't. He's like a little kid in a candy store, skipping from one thing to the next. It's not that he's shallow; it's just that he's searching."

"Maybe he's found something here," Harriet replied, trying to keep her voice steady. "And I don't even mean me, Perry, but the hotel. His vision. Look around you. It's amazing what he's done. And what you've done, too." She frowned as a sudden thought occurred to her. "Why did you come here and help him with it if you're just waiting for him to go back home?"

Perry glanced away. "I told you, we go back a long way. And…I was worried about him."

Harriet raised her eyebrows, surprised. "Worried?"

She was silent for a long moment. "What you need to know," she finally said carefully, "is that Quinn is fragile. He hides it with his enthusiasm and energy and all that, but inside he's…wounded."

Perry wasn't, Harriet realised, saying anything she hadn't thought, at least in part. She'd seen the way his ready smile would drop like a mask, the flashes of sorrow or darkness that passed over his face. And yet…he had got *past* all that, hadn't he? He seemed as if he had; she'd taken encouragement and hope from the fact that he had. But was Perry really saying he hadn't? Or was she trying to scare Harriet away? "Are you trying to warn me off?" she asked. "Because you know, so am I, frankly. Pretty fragile, that is." She kept Perry's gaze with a level stare of her own. And if Quinn really was so *wounded*, well then, he should be able to tell her so himself.

"I'm not warning you off," Perry said finally. "I'm just

telling you. I don't want him to get hurt, and…I don't want you to get hurt, either." At Harriet's surprised look, she shrugged. "It's not that I don't like you. It's just…this is temporary. I want you to realise that."

"So, what do you think Quinn will do?" Harriet asked after a moment. "Leave this place to a manager and head back to America, back into the gaming world?"

"Something like that, or maybe sell this place." Perry shrugged. "As for the gaming…" Her expression darkened. "I hope he goes back to it, but I don't know." Her expression firmed. "But if you think he's going to settle down to life as lord of the manor in this backwater… Sorry, but no. He had a wobble, back in San Francisco, it's true." She paused. "I don't suppose he told you about that?" By the way Perry asked the question, Harriet was pretty sure she already knew the answer. She didn't reply. "Well, it's not for me to say," Perry continued. "But for a little while, he felt like he had to get away from it all, and he did. But he's going to come back. He was in the middle of developing a game, his best ever, when he left. It's all there waiting for him, when he wants it, which he will."

Harriet opened her mouth to respond, then closed it again without saying anything. She realised she didn't have the energy to argue with Perry. Maybe she was right, and Quinn would leave Mathering—if not in a few weeks, then a few months. She wouldn't blame him if he got tired of this place, of *her*. Part of her was expecting it already. Nobody stuck around Mathering. Nobody stuck around for *her*.

But she wasn't about to have a pity party about it; she was *done* with that, Harriet realised with a flash of determination. Done with feeling sorry for herself, for playing the victim. And funnily enough, it was Quinn who had helped her to see that.

"Thanks for letting me know," she told Perry, and she saw surprise flicker across the other woman's face. "Now I think I'll go find Quinn," she added, and turned and walked out of the room.

Her energised determination left her before she'd walked ten feet down the hall. As soon as Harriet turned the corner, she stopped, her shoulders slumping, dropping her face into her hands. Right now, Quinn felt like the one good, true thing in her life. But what if he wasn't?

Of course he isn't, Harriet. Did you really think you could keep the interest of someone like him? A dynamic millionaire who has been all over the world?

She wanted that old, mocking voice to shut up…forever.

"Be quiet," she hissed out loud, only to hear a familiar voice ask, "Harriet?"

She looked up to see Quinn striding down the hall, his expression wreathed in concern.

"H…hi," she managed before he came forward and folded her up in his long arms.

"Are you okay?" he murmured against her hair, and she closed her eyes.

I am now. "I will be."

He released her, holding her by the shoulders, slightly away from him, as he peered down into her face. "Do you want to talk about it?" he asked seriously, and she shook her head.

"I just want to blank it right now." She tried to smile at

him. "What's the best way to blank something out?"

He grimaced. "Normally I would say play a video game."

"*Yes.*" Harriet realised that was exactly what she wanted to do. She wanted to immerse herself into Quinn's world, to understand him in a way Perry didn't seem to think she did. "Can we play *Wilderwood*?" she asked. "I've never even played video games, so I'll be rubbish at them, but can we?"

He looked surprised, and then a little torn, and Harriet realised that no matter what Perry had said, Quinn seemed to have turned his back on his old life completely.

"We don't have to," she said quickly. "It was just a random idea."

"No, let's do it," he replied with sudden, decisive conviction. "I haven't actually played in ages. You stop playing the games, you know, once you develop them. You get other people to beta test them. But let's do it. I'd like to show you that part of my life, anyway, even if it's over."

She laced her fingers through his, and he led her back to his office, which was its usual chaotic mess of papers, clothes, pictures stuck on the wall, incomprehensible notes scribbled in dark pen.

"Looking at this," Harriet teased him, "you wouldn't know that your hotel is actually coming together in the most amazing way."

He laughed. "A method to my madness." He let go of her hand to stoop in front of the desktop monitor, hitting a few keys before he rifled through one of the drawers for a couple of controllers, untangling their wires and hooking them up to the monitor. "Are you sure you're ready for this?" he asked, grey eyes glinting as he handed her a controller.

"I have no idea," Harriet admitted honestly. "But I'm going to try."

"All right, then, let me explain it to you." He angled the monitor towards her, and pulled two chairs up to it so they could sit together. "Okay, first the buttons," he instructed. "This one to move forward, this one to reverse, this one to jump—"

"Wait, wait." Harriet started laughing. "I'm already lost. You realise I've never even *touched* one of these controllers before? We did not do video games in my house."

"Probably wise," Quinn murmured. "They are pretty addictive. Okay, let's go through it again." Slowly he took her through the commands. "Now the game opens with an intro where you can practise all the commands, so don't worry that you'll get thrown right into it." He pressed a button on his own controller and the screen came to life—an artistic scrollwork of vines and flowers with *Wilderwood* written in flowing script.

"I like it already," Harriet said, and Quinn grinned.

The next hour seemed to fly past as Quinn took her through the intro, and then into the game. At first, Harriet felt completely disorientated, running into corners and getting completely mixed up as to where she was or what she was doing, but with Quinn's gentle instruction, she slowly started to get the hang of it.

The game was completely immersive, an entire world that was a cross between *Lord of the Rings* and the *Chronicles of Narnia*, with magical creatures, monsters to fight, towns and cities to explore, treasure to find. Harriet let out several screams as she was accosted by wyverns, fell into a swamp, and discovered a box of treasure.

"I thought there were other players, though?" Harriet said when she'd fought six orcs and won, gaining a ruby ring and a short sword. It had been very satisfying. "Who were out to get me?"

"We're on single-player mode," Quinn told her. "I thought you didn't need that added stress."

"You're right, I didn't," she replied with a laugh before putting down her controller. "It's amazing," she told him with quiet sincerity. "Really, truly amazing. And you designed it all yourself?"

"Not entirely by myself, but yeah, mostly." He glanced at the screen, which was frozen on her character stats. "But at the end of the day, it's just a game."

"Is that you or someone else speaking?" Harriet asked, feeling the words instinctively, and Quinn's eyes narrowed as he swung back to look at her.

"What do you mean?"

"I don't know," Harriet replied honestly. She thought of all that Perry had said, but didn't know how to mention it now, if she should or even if she wanted to. "Only that you're clearly very talented, Quinn," she said instead. "Why did you walk away from it all?"

"I told you why." He tossed the controller on the desk, and stood up, running his hands through his hair. He seemed restless, edgy in a way Harriet hadn't really seen before, and she had a feeling she had referenced that so-called wobble. Well, she would respect Quinn's privacy. If he didn't want to talk about it, that was okay. But she still wondered.

"Do you think you'll ever want to go back?" she asked.

"No." His answer was swift and firm. "I can't, anyway."

"What do you mean?"

"I burned my bridges." Perry hadn't seemed to think so, but Harriet wasn't about to mention that. Quinn turned to her with a smile that didn't reach his eyes. "Let's not talk about this anymore, okay? It's old news. I'm glad I showed you the game, but I want to look to the future."

Could she fault that? Harriet wanted to look towards the future, too. She'd been mired in the past long enough, dwelling on old hurts and grievances. Maybe Quinn felt the same.

And yet, as he helped up from her chair and drew her into a gentle kiss, Harriet couldn't help but wonder: how long would this last?

How long had *anything* lasted for her?

Chapter Sixteen

'IT'S BEGINNING TO Look a Lot like Christmas' blasted from the Bluetooth speaker as Harriet fairly flew around the kitchen, determined to be merry. It was just four days until the Christmas party, and she'd been flat out with preparations, which had been a very good thing, because when she was busy, she found she didn't have to think—about her father, her mother, the fact that things between her and Quinn felt good, very good, but also tenuous. Was that just her usual insecurity, or something deeper? They hadn't talked any further about Quinn's past, and yet Harriet still had the feeling he was holding on to some secret, some big thing he didn't want to tell her. What could it be? Did she even want to know? She'd kind of had enough of secrets lately.

Two weeks on from the revelation, she still hadn't spoken to her father. It was easy to avoid him, as he was sleeping a lot, and Rachel had, by silent, mutual agreement, taken over the small duties Harriet had been doing—bringing him breakfast or cups of tea, checking on him periodically throughout the day. Even though Harriet knew she was trying to be thoughtful, it felt a bit like she was being cut out. She wasn't his blood relation. She had no part of his life anymore.

"How are the cookies going?" Rachel asked as she came into the kitchen for a tea refill. Harriet was filling freezer bags with her latest batch of matcha balls. She'd decided to make as many cookies as she could ahead of time; the matcha balls and lemon slices froze well. The others she would make the day before, in what would be a baking frenzy.

"Good," she replied in the brisk and slightly repressive tone she'd started using with her sister without making a conscious decision or even meaning to. She whirled away from where Rachel was standing by the kettle to stick a bag of cookies in the freezer.

"Harriet..."

Uh-oh. Her sister's tone did not bode well. It was serious, slow, with intent. They hadn't had a proper talk since the Christmas tree lighting; Harriet still didn't think she could manage it, even as she'd sensed, time and time again, her sister gearing up for a heart-to-heart. She'd managed to avoid one so far, simply by the fact that she was so busy, spending as much time she could at the hotel or with Quinn, and otherwise giving off 'too busy to talk' vibes while baking in the kitchen.

But now, despite the fact that she was sliding cookies off baking racks like she was trying to beat the world record, Rachel seemed to have decided now was the time for a talk.

"We need to talk," she stated, confirming Harriet's suspicions. "You've more or less been avoiding me for the last two weeks, but...time is running out. Dad seems..."

"He's not my dad." The words came out of Harriet quickly, almost viciously. She hadn't realised just how much she meant them until they'd been said.

Rachel frowned, her forehead furrowing, her face crumpling a little. "Harriet, he is your dad. Regardless of…well, biology, he was your father for the last thirty-one years."

"Well, he certainly didn't act like it," Harriet fired back. "And now I know why. So what is there to talk about?"

Rachel shook her head slowly, looking hurt, although Harriet wasn't sure why that was. Shouldn't she be the one to feel wounded, excluded? Rachel had their father's love, the farmhouse, everything. Harriet was the one who had been left with nothing.

"I'm still your sister," Rachel stated quietly. "Aren't I?"

"Half-sister," Harriet replied before she could think through the wisdom or sensitivity of such a remark, and Rachel's face crumpled all the more.

"Really?" she said, her voice vibrating with hurt, and Harriet finally came to a stop, a bag of cookies in her hand, a sigh escaping her as she briefly closed her eyes.

"I'm sorry. You're right. Of course you're my sister." Guilt curdled her stomach as she realised how hurtful her snarky remark must have been. And yet…it was still the truth. "It's just…" Harriet tried to explain. "I'm processing this as best as I can, okay? But it's hard."

"I know," Rachel softly. "I can only imagine…but it doesn't have to change anything, Harriet. It doesn't for me, I promise."

"It obviously did for Dad," Harriet returned, unable to keep the bitterness from corroding her voice. "The fact that I'm not his biological daughter obviously made a *very* big difference to him."

"Well, it shouldn't have." The words burst out of Rachel with the same swift viciousness with which Harriet had spoken. "I mean, I know Dad's always been a bit...ornery, but I didn't actually think he was *cruel*. But this is cruel. To treat you differently all these years... It's not fair."

"I'm sure he thinks it's fair," Harriet replied. She appreciated her sister's strength of feeling, but it didn't change things—and not in the way Rachel was hoping for things not to be changed. Her father had treated her like a stranger for most of her life, or as good as. His will proved that all the more. That, Harriet knew, could not be changed.

"There's something I need to tell you," Rachel said, and Harriet tensed. What more could be revealed? "I got in touch with Mum."

"Oh." The breath left her in a rush. "What did she say?"

"She was shocked. She seemed a bit sad...I don't know. We only spoke briefly. I just said I thought she ought to know. She thanked me, and she asked me a couple of questions, and that was it."

"Okay." Why, Harriet wondered, did this information hurt her? "Did you tell her that I know...about my birth, I mean?"

"No." Rachel was quiet for a moment. "I figured that was something you should talk about with her yourself. It isn't my place to say."

"Thank you."

"I have her number if you want to call her."

Harriet started to shake her head, and then relented. She didn't want to be like her father—the man she'd called her father—digging into an opinion, a belief, and becoming so entrenched you couldn't change. You couldn't bend or accept. "All right," she said, and Rachel smiled.

"I'll text you her contact details."

Harriet managed a nod. "Thanks."

Rachel reached over and squeezed her arm. "We'll get through this, Hats. We will."

She nodded again, and even managed to pat Rachel's hand before she removed it. "I know," she replied, and she almost believed it. She thought she might, with time.

Their sweetly sentimental moment was broken by a knock on the front door, and Harriet slipped away from Rachel to answer it with a small, apologetic smile. She tucked her hair behind her ears as she opened the door, expecting an Amazon delivery man or maybe Ben, but it was Quinn.

"Oh!" Harriet stared at him in surprise. "I wasn't expecting you."

"Is that okay?" Quinn asked. He looked wonderful—rumpled shirt, well-worn jeans, the usual Doc Martens. His hair was still a little long and wavy, his face creased into a smile, his grey eyes alight.

"Yes, it's more than okay."

Quinn opened his arms, and as easily as breathing, and Harriet stepped into them. He enfolded her, drawing her close, and she breathed in the smell of him, so grateful to be there.

"Why did you stop by?" she asked as, after a long and wonderful moment, she stepped back. "I thought you were crazy busy with hotel stuff."

"I am, or was, but I think everything is mostly in hand

now, and I feel like I'm just getting in the way. So I decided I'd come and see you. I thought you might need a break from the cookies."

"Well..."

"There's still four days until the party," he reminded her. "You don't have to do all the work today."

"I know, but five hundred cookies, Quinn—"

"How many have you baked so far?"

She thought for a moment. "Two hundred?"

"Then you can definitely take a break." He reached for her hand, twining his fingers through hers. "Come with me."

"Where?"

"Surprise."

She let out a laugh, shaking her head even though she knew she was going to say yes. She felt like an adventure, an escape not just from baking cookies, but from dealing with reality. "All right," she told him. "Let me just get my coat."

"Where are you going?" Rachel asked as Harriet went back into the kitchen to get her coat and handbag.

"I don't know," she admitted. "Quinn's surprising me."

"He certainly seems one for surprises," Rachel remarked, not sounding entirely approving. Harriet had already told her about their useless day in York.

"Well, I could use a few surprises in my life," she replied. "Good ones, that is." She hurried out of the kitchen before Rachel could reply.

"So, when are you going to tell me where we're going?" she asked once they were in Quinn's car, pootling down the drive. It was a beautiful winter's day—the sky bright blue, the sun glinting off the frost-covered fields, the distant, rolling moors lightly dusted with snow.

"When we get there."

She laughed. "Really?"

"Really."

Harriet glanced out the window. "Everything's actually in hand at the hotel?"

"Seems to be."

"And you're not stressed?"

He glanced at her, amused, eyebrows raised. "Do I seem stressed?"

"No," Harriet admitted. She considered asking him about what Perry had said, and what he most definitely hadn't, and then she decided she did not want to spoil a perfectly beautiful day with all that stuff. "I wish I could be like you," she said instead.

Quinn was silent for a moment before he replied, "How so?"

"You seem so…unbothered. I feel like everything snags on me, as if I'm covered in thorns. I can't just let things roll off."

He was silent again, his face drawn into a thoughtful frown. "Well, I suppose it takes some practice," he said finally, although Harriet had the sense he'd been thinking about something else.

"Well, I'm going to practise today," she told him, determined to keep things light. "No thinking about my parents, my birth, all that. I'm just going to enjoy… What is it we're doing again?"

"Ah-hah." He laughed, wagging a finger in admonition. "Sneaky. But I'm not telling you."

Forty-five minutes later, Harriet found out anyway.

"Ice skating!" she exclaimed as Quinn pulled into Yorkshire's Winter Wonderland, just south of York, complete with an ice-skating rink, Santa's grotto, vintage fun fair, and chalet café. It was like the one in the city, only bigger and better.

"Do you like ice skating?" he asked seriously. "It was a bit of a gamble."

"I haven't done it enough to know."

"Me, neither. I figure we could clutch at each other to keep ourselves upright." The grin he gave her was deliberately Big Bad Wolf-ish. "Not a bad way to spend an afternoon."

"No," Harriet replied, blushing. In the last few weeks, they'd kissed quite a bit, and it had been absolutely lovely, but they'd never gone further than that, which was frankly fine by Harriet. She knew she needed to take things slow. Maybe Quinn did, as well. This relationship was new for both of them, after all.

He bought their tickets, and moments later they were lacing up their skates before clopping their way onto the ice. The second Harriet stepped onto the slick surface, she almost landed flat on her back, her feet shooting out from under her, before Quinn thankfully rescued her, drawing her against his chest until she had her feet, wobbly as they were in skates, under her again.

"Clearly you're better at this than me," she told him, and he laughed softly.

"Nope, I'm just holding on to the railing still."

Harriet eyed the expanse of ice with decided unease. "You know," she told Quinn, "you do not want to break your arm or leg just days before this big Christmas party."

"I won't," Quinn assured her with far more confidence than Harriet felt. "Because I'm going to hold on to the railing, and to you, the entire time." He grinned as she twisted up to look at him. "If I'm going down, we both are."

"How chivalrous of you," she teased.

"I'll fall first, cushion the blow."

"Wow, thanks." She reached out to hold on to the railing herself. A few smug show-offs were whizzing by, doing figure-eights with their hands behind their backs as if they'd been born with a pair of skates on.

"They're unbearable, aren't they," Quinn murmured, and Harriet laughed because she'd been thinking the same thing. "Let's take this slowly," he told her as he pushed off, very slightly, from the railing. "Hand in hand. Sort of walking at first."

"Okay."

They started, edging their way across the ice like baby giraffes. Once Harriet wobbled and threw her arms around Quinn, who held her easily while staying upright.

"Are you just pretending you don't know what you're doing?" she asked suspiciously. "To make me feel better?"

"Absolutely not. I would never be so patronising." He smiled at her as she righted herself. "I'm just trying to move as little as possible." His expression gentled. "We're in this together, Harriet."

Something in her eased, loosened. There was a metaphor here, for how life felt now—shaky, treacherous, uncertain, and yet…there was Quinn. Quinn standing next to her, as tall as an oak, as solid as a rock, holding her hand. Showing her the way.

"I don't know what I would do without you," she blurted, and then let out a little gasp, mortified. You definitely weren't supposed to say things like that three weeks into a relationship.

But Quinn just smiled, a slow, satisfied curving of his lips, before he lowered his head and brushed a kiss across her mouth. "Good," he said.

THEY SKATED FOR an hour, managing to mostly stay upright, before retiring to the chalet café for hot chocolate. Despite the inherent tension of being on skates for the last hour, Harriet felt wonderfully relaxed. She had a new security in her relationship with Quinn that she hadn't felt before, or at least she hadn't trusted it. Now she did, or at least she was starting to.

That warm, relaxed, almost sleepy feeling continued all the way home; Quinn drove most of the way with one hand on the wheel, the other loosely entwined with hers. Fields and moors blurred by under a darkening sky as Harriet leaned her head back against the car seat and fell into something close to a doze, only to blink the twilit world back into focus when Quinn squeezed her hand and said, "Looks like you have a visitor."

"What…?" Muzzily Harriet pushed her hair from her face and she peered out the window as Quinn drove up Embthwaite Farm's lane. A silver sedan was parked in the drive next to their beat-up Land Rover, and a woman was getting out as they came into the forecourt.

A gasp escaped Harriet as the woman straightened, pushing her silver hair away from her face as she closed the door of the car.

"Harriet?" Quinn asked in concern, and she could only shake her head, unable to frame sentences, form words.

The woman standing there was her mother.

Chapter Seventeen

QUINN STOOD IN the empty foyer of the Mathering Manor House Hotel, flipping through the gilt-edged pages of the guestbook he'd had placed on the console table. They were all blank now, but soon, he hoped, they would be filled with effusive comments of people who'd had a lovely time, promising to come back soon.

The opening party was tomorrow night. He hadn't seen Harriet since he'd left her on the doorstep of Embthwaite Farm, staring at her mother in complete shock. At least, that's who Quinn had assumed the woman was who had looked back at Harriet with a wary sort of hope. This had been confirmed later that evening when Harriet had texted him to explain. He'd messaged her asking if she wanted to talk, but she hadn't. Quinn already recognised the pattern; when something emotive and difficult happened, Harriet retreated. Heaven knew he understood the instinct. He shared it, although in a way his was even more damaging. He didn't just retreat; he blew things up. Left destruction in his wake.

He told himself he was happy to give her some space, even though he missed her. Even though he worried that the longer she stayed away from him—three days now and counting—the less solid and sure their relationship seemed.

He'd tried to distract himself from such worries with the busyness of the hotel, but he now had enough people in position that the place felt like it was running itself, or would be, once the guests started to arrive. His new housekeeper was extremely competent, as was the head of desk. Perry, too, although they hadn't had quite the ease of relationship they had before. Quinn missed that, too. But he was determined to focus on the future…a future with Harriet, when she got over this bump or blip or whatever it was, and they were back together.

The last few weeks with her had been manic, but wonderful. He'd been working pretty much all the time, and when he hadn't been, he'd been with Harriet, up until she'd seen her mother and decided she needed her space. They'd had snatched moments—taking a walk in the grounds, going for a drink in the pub—Toby at the Tickled Trout as silent as ever—and that afternoon ice skating, when she'd told him she didn't know what she would do without him, a confession that had made Quinn feel as if his heart were a balloon, filling up and floating in his chest. They'd even played *Wilderwood* again in his office, joshing good-naturedly as they'd raced around the made-up world. If Harriet wasn't careful, she'd soon be hooked on the game.

He'd been reluctant at first to share it with her, that whole sorry part of his life, and especially how it had ended. He'd walked away from it for good, had told himself he'd never go back. That he didn't want to, and he *didn't*, yet sometimes he felt as if the life he had left behind, a deliberate choice, hadn't been enough. He still hadn't left *himself* behind. The doubts. The fears. The sense that no matter what he did, or how successful he was, it wouldn't matter. All the same stuff Harriet seemed to have struggled with and was now getting over. The stuff she thought *he* was, because he'd learned how to put on a pretty good front. Harriet didn't realise it, but he was a fake. He always had been. But he was trying to be more honest now.

With a sigh, he turned away from the guestbook to wander through the empty rooms of the hotel, all of them ready and waiting for guests. He should feel triumphant now, he knew, certain of his success. The hotel was fully booked for Christmas, two hundred guests coming to the opening party, inquiries from two national newspapers about running pieces on the place. All Quinn had to do was bask in his success.

The trouble was, he acknowledged, he wasn't doing that at all. He wanted to focus on the future, but he still felt mired in the past. It had been like this countless times before, of course. At the pinnacle of achievement, he'd felt emptier than ever. It hadn't been enough. It never was.

Why would he think this would be any different, just because he'd changed careers, continents, even? *He* was still the same, and maybe he always would be.

His father's voice echoed in his ears, as if he were right there in the room. *Video games, Quinn? That's what you're going to spend your life doing? I despair of you. You're useless. You've always been useless.* And on and on and on, in a thousand different ways, a thousand different times.

Quinn had laughingly told Harriet he prided himself on being useless, but she'd seen right through him, cut to the heart of the matter. If he chose to be useless, then it didn't matter if his father claimed that he was. It was his choice…except it never really had been.

And even now, with all this laid out before him, he still felt the same sense of futility, of failure. He'd thought he wouldn't, had hoped and prayed and *willed* it…

And yet here he was. A sigh escaped him, long and lonely. He thought of calling Harriet, or even heading over to Embthwaite Farm to see her, but she hadn't wanted to see him, with her mother there, and in any case, he didn't want her to see him when he was like this—depressed, despairing, in many ways his true self. He'd just become very good at fooling people. Fooling *her.* What would she think, *feel,* when she discovered the truth? That he was a fraud? That he'd built this whole hotel in a desire to give people the opportunity to be real, when he wasn't being at all real himself?

Maybe she would walk away from him.

The self-pitying thought had him stopping in his tracks. Maybe, he told himself, she wouldn't.

He'd decided to be different this time, he reminded himself. He wasn't going to sabotage himself before someone else could. He wasn't going to pull the plug on his hopes and dreams before someone could dismiss them all as worthless.

He *wasn't.* And for the first time, he actually believed it. Harriet thought he'd helped her without realising how she'd helped *him.* He was not going to pull the self-sabotage ripcord this time, not with Harriet in the picture. Not with Harriet to believe in him, even if that belief was misplaced, because, well, maybe it wasn't. It didn't have to be.

"Quinn?"

He turned to see Perry standing in the doorway of the library, where he'd ended up, staring into space. She was wearing her pyjamas, her expression unhappy and worried.

"What is it?" he said automatically, because it was clearly *something.*

Wordlessly she handed him her phone. Quinn squinted down at it, everything in him stilling as he painstakingly read the headline. *Gaming Millionaire Washes Up in Yorkshire.* The words beneath danced before his eyes, but he could guess their gist without needing to laboriously read it. He'd been discovered. He'd known he would be eventually, had prepared for it mentally, or thought he had been, and now he didn't feel surprised or afraid as much as relieved. Well, fine. He could weather any smirks or speculation. He didn't think anyone was going to cancel their reservation over this.

He scrolled down the article and saw that they'd linked the video of him at that wretched party. He'd thought, or at least hoped, that it had been banished to the outer circles of YouTube, but some keen journalist had managed to unearth it. He clicked on it as Perry made some small sound of protest.

"It's fine," he told her, and dispassionately he watched the video—taken on someone's phone—of him smashing wine glasses. Shouting into the void. Generally making an absurd, humiliating, unbearable scene in front of a hundred avidly horrified partygoers.

"It looks worse on video than it really was," Perry said when all three minutes and forty-five seconds of it had played, the scene ending with him being escorted out by security.

"Does it?" he asked with a huff of hard laughter as he handed back her phone. "Well, I knew this was going to happen eventually. What news site was that on?"

"*Yorkshire Live.*"

Yorkshire Live? He'd assumed, or maybe just hoped, that it had been some American outlet, some gaming site, even. Contained, still separate. But *Yorkshire Live*...the local news website. Realisation trickled through him. He didn't care about faceless guests or the great, anonymous mob of online viewers commenting and speculating on Reddit or Twitter, but he did care about Harriet. About what she thought...about him. Had she seen that article, that video? Was she wondering what on earth had got into him, who he really was?

Was *that* why she hadn't been in touch? She'd last texted him two days ago, telling him she was busy, how she needed time. He'd thought it was because of her mother, but what if it was because of him?

"When did that article come out?" he asked Perry.

"Two days ago."

The words thudded through Quinn. Harriet had to know—he was sure of it now. And she hadn't been in touch; she'd done her utmost *not* to be. What was he supposed to think?

There seemed to only be one possibility.

"I don't think this will affect bookings," Perry offered, and Quinn shrugged as he turned away.

"I'm not worried," he said.

"You seem worried."

"Well, I'm not." The words came out quick, sharp.

Perry sighed, long and low. "Quinn, I care about you, you know?" she stated quietly. "And I've seen this pattern before. You get so close to success, to happiness, to finding whatever it is you're always looking for, and then you blow it up before you can try to take hold of it. Boarding school, college—"

He made a scoffing sound. "You didn't even know me in boarding school."

"I know enough about you," she returned levelly. "I was there when you decided to drop out of Stanford as soon as you learned you'd made Phi Beta Kappa. I mean, who *does* that? You get the highest academic honour possible, and then you just walk away?"

Quinn shrugged; what else could he do? What response made sense, one that didn't sound insanely absurd, because it was? He wrecked things, right at the point when they were finally being successful. When he was.

"I was also there," Perry continued steadily, "back in San Francisco, when you basically wrecked anything good in your life. Kasey—"

He shook his head. "Kasey was interested in my money, not me." The most serious of his relationships, yet nothing on what he felt for Harriet.

"Maybe," Perry allowed, "but you sabotaged the relationship before you could find out. Same with the others…and the same as the way you sabotaged the best thing in your life, Quinn…Q Games."

The words hung in the air before settling heavily around them, unable to be unsaid. Perry had never accused him outright of wrecking Q Games, even though it had been blindingly obvious at the time. She'd bailed him out of jail when he'd been arrested for causing a disturbance at that party; she'd been silently accepting and unquestioning when, the day after, he'd told her the sale price of Q Games had dropped by a third, and she'd even agreed to come with him to Yorkshire when he'd asked her, although there had been absolutely no good reason to…except for loyalty to him.

"I'm sorry," he said in a low voice, and Perry shook her head.

"I'm not asking for an apology."

"I owe you one anyway—" More than one, really.

"You owe yourself one, Quinn." Perry took a step towards him. "Don't mess this one up, okay? You've worked hard with this hotel. I wasn't convinced about this idea at all, as you're well aware, and the only reason I came along for the ride because I was so worried about you, and because I care about you, you know?" She sighed, raking her hand through her bright pink hair. "And you've convinced me. You're happy here." She paused before adding, "Harriet's made you happy, not just the hotel. I was sceptical at the start; I admit it. Mainly because I wanted to go back to San Francisco, to the way things were, and she felt like a threat to that—"

"I was basically blacklisted, Perry—"

"I know," she cut him off, "but those attitudes don't last forever. Time in tech is in warp speed, and you're too talented for that world to turn its back on you…but maybe you should turn your back on it. I wasn't convinced at first, but I see it now." She smiled faintly. "I even tried to scare Harriet off, and she wasn't having it. She's a good one, Quinn. A keeper."

Quinn frowned, his unease about Harriet deepening. "You tried to scare her off? How?"

Perry had the grace to look a little abashed. "I told her you were getting something out of your system, and that you'd be heading back to San Francisco soon." She grimaced. "I wanted it to be true."

Was that why Harriet was keeping her distance now, or part of the reason, at least? Quinn wanted to talk to her, but he was afraid to. What if this article had changed things between them?

"I don't think she believed me," Perry continued. "And it was a while ago now." She held up a warning finger. "Don't mess this up, Quinn. I mean it."

"I know you do." Unexpectedly, Quinn pulled his friend into a hug. Perry wasn't a touchy-feely kind of person, and she stiffened for a second before she hugged him back, quickly. "Thank you, Perry, for having my back for so long," he said. "You've been a good friend, and I, frankly, have been a crap one."

She shook her head. "That's just you beating yourself up again. You've been a great friend, Quinn. You have always cheered me on, picked me up when I was down. You brought me into Q Games at the ground level, and even gave me a percentage of ownership—"

"Before I devalued it by thirty per cent," he felt compelled to say.

"It was your right to do what you did," she replied quietly. "You know that, don't you? You're the one who designed that game in the first place—"

"It was a stupid thing to do," he said on a sigh. "Although I'm not sure I can even regret it now."

"You shouldn't," Perry told him firmly. "I don't."

"Really?" He couldn't help but sound surprised.

"Really," she told him.

A long, weary sigh escaped him as he shook his head. "I've made a mess of so many things."

"Not of this," she replied. "Not with Harriet."

He nodded towards the phone. "And if she's seen that?"

Perry shrugged. "Then she's seen it. So what?"

Yes, Quinn thought, fighting a fresh tidal wave of despair, but would Harriet feel that way?

HARRIET HAD DONE a very impressive job of avoiding everything—and everyone—for the last two days. She hadn't spoken to her mother, father, or Rachel since Quinn had dropped her off after ice skating, and her mother had looked at with a wary weariness and said, "Hello, Harriet."

Harriet, her body practically vibrating with tension, had walked by her without a word, into the house, away from everything.

She'd stayed closeted in her room while Rachel and her mother had conferred in hushed voices downstairs. When she had finally emerged, she'd given them both forbidding looks and shortly informed them that she did not want to talk about anything.

They'd eaten dinner in silence. Harriet had gone back up to her bedroom. There had been three texts from Quinn on her phone, all of them full of tender concern, and somehow even that felt like too much to take. She just couldn't process all these *relationships.* And so, she'd texted Quinn, telling him she needed time…even though she wasn't sure time would actually help all that much.

What had helped was baking cookies. Lots and lots of cookies. When she had her hands in a big batch of dough, her mind blissfully emptied out. It also helped that her mother skirted around her, silent, uncertain, and Rachel was trying to give them both space they were taking—to stay apart from each other.

Until now, the afternoon of the second day, with the party tomorrow, and her mother came quietly into the kitchen while Harriet was taking a break from baking and was drinking a much-needed cup of tea.

"Any left in the pot?" her mother asked, smiling uncertainly. It was the first time she'd spoken to Harriet since greeting her on the drive two days before. Harriet had made sure she couldn't; there had been no opportunity.

"Yes, help yourself." Her voice was flat, abrupt. Her fingers trembled as she put down her cup. She watched covertly as her mother poured a cup of tea, added a splash of milk, and then sat down opposite Harriet.

"I know you don't want to talk," she stated in a calm, quiet voice. It was not a voice Harriet recognised all that well, because the mother of her childhood had often been either withdrawn or emotional, on the verge of fury or despair. "And I want to respect that," she continued. "But I just wanted you to know that when you do want to talk, I will be willing. More than willing."

So many questions bubbled up in Harriet's throat, burning like acid. She stared down at her hands, clenched around her cup. "I don't really want to hear what you have to say," she managed to choke out. "But it would have been nice for you to have told me, at *some* point, that I wasn't Peter Mowbray's biological child." She risked a glance at her mother, surprised to see her face drained of colour, her blue eyes wide and shocked. "Instead, he told me himself," she finished, and then found her throat was too tight to manage anymore.

"Harriet…" her mother murmured. One hand fluttered towards her before falling to the table. "Oh, Harriet. I never thought he would actually…" She trailed off, shaking her head, as if she couldn't bear to finish that thought.

"Why shouldn't he have told me, since you wouldn't?" Harriet filled in. *How could you have left me with him, knowing that I wasn't even his?* No, she wouldn't ask that. She hadn't been a child, after all, even if she'd felt like one. She'd been seventeen, almost an adult. She'd *known* that, and yet, it had still hurt. More than she'd ever wanted it to.

"Oh, Harriet." Her mother's voice was full of sadness, redolent with it. "He shouldn't have told you, because it simply wasn't true."

"What?" Harriet stared at her blankly. It was just about the last thing, the very last thing, she expected her mother to say. "What do you mean?"

Briefly her mother closed her eyes, then opened them to stare at Harriet with a matter-of-fact directness. "You *are* Peter Mowbray's biological daughter," she stated. "Of that there is absolutely no doubt, I promise you."

What…? Harriet's mind reeled, rejected. *It couldn't be…*

"Why, then?" she rasped. "Why did he think I wasn't? Why did he act as if I wasn't, for all my life?"

"Oh, Harriet." Her mother shook her head, her silver bob swinging against her cheekbones. She was fifty-three years old, and age had not dimmed her beauty. Arctic blue eyes, high cheekbones, an elegance to her face and body that Harriet had always envied. Both she and Rachel had taken after their father in their colouring…except, of course, she couldn't have, because—

"I'm not." She leaned forward, one hand clenched into a fist on top of the table. "I can't be." It suddenly became important to insist on this, to prove it, because if it had all just been one big mistake…yet how could it have been? "Why would he think I wasn't?" Harriet demanded.

"Because…" A small, sad sigh escaped her mother. "Because I told him you weren't."

Once again Harriet was left reeling. "Why on earth would you do that?" she whispered, slumping back in her chair.

Her mother glanced down at the table, tracing the grain of the wood with her fingers. "It was a stupid and immature thing to do," she admitted in a low voice. "I know that full well, and I regretted it instantly."

Harriet just shook her head. She was not able to think of a single coherent response.

"We were arguing," her mother continued in the same low voice. "It was just after you'd been born. I was twenty-two years old, Harriet, and I'd had two babies in the space of fifteen months. I'm not sure I was entirely of right mind. In fact, I know I wasn't." Another small, sad sigh escaped her.

"And I'd found out something about your father that hurt me dreadfully. And so, in retaliation, I told him you weren't his." She looked up at her, her expression agonised now. "He was furious, in the cold, stony, silent way only your father could be. He walked out of the room before I could say another word. He refused to talk about it again, but I still tried. When he seemed as if he—he wasn't interested in you when you were still just a baby, I told him you were his. I promised, I wept, I swore. I'd never had an affair, or anything close to an affair. I told him we could have a paternity test done, whatever he wanted to prove it. He refused, refused even to speak of it." She shook her head. "Still, I'd hoped he believed me, I thought he would…"

"But you must have known how he always favoured Rachel," Harriet pointed out, striving to keep her voice level when part of her—a large part—felt like ranting, raving, falling to pieces.

"Yes, but I thought that was because *you* favoured *me*. Right from when you were tiny." Her mother smiled faintly. "You always wanted me rather than him. Do you remember? You were my little shadow."

"I don't want to talk about that." She knew she couldn't bear to remember, not now.

"All right," her mother replied quietly. "I understand. I…I didn't think he'd held on to that stupid notion all these years, Harriet. I really didn't. At least, I hoped he hadn't."

"Even though he clearly preferred Rachel?" Harriet demanded. "Even though he ignored me for much of my childhood—"

"He ignored all of us," her mother replied, her voice rising, breaking, like waves on a rocky shore. "I know he seemed a bit more interested in Rachel at times, but he hardly lavished her with attention. I don't think she ever felt he did. He wasn't that sort of man."

No, he hadn't been, but Harriet had still felt it. Hadn't she? Sometimes she felt as she thought her father probably did right now, as if all the pieces of reality had been scattered, the jigsaw of her life upended into unrecognisable parts. But there were still some hard facts, she reminded herself, like the will he'd made, cutting her out.

She shook her head, weary of the way her mind was racing. "I don't know what to think anymore," she said.

"Harriet—" Her mother leaned across the table, one hand outstretched as if she wanted to touch her. "I'm so sorry—"

"Harriet." Rachel came into the kitchen, her expression grim. Harriet had thought she must have overheard her conversation with her mother, except her sister looked startled to see the two of them sitting there together. Then she held out her phone. "There's something I think you need to see."

Chapter Eighteen

QUINN WASN'T ANSWERING her calls, or even her text messages. They hadn't even been *seen*, which alarmed Harriet, because no matter how screen-free the hotel was meant to be, Quinn had always been eminently, wonderfully reachable…until now.

When Rachel had come into the kitchen, holding her phone like it was a live grenade, Harriet hadn't wanted to know. She hadn't wanted to deal with her mother's apology, either, to accept or reject it. She hadn't been ready to make a choice, to set things in stone, because that's how it had always been before. A lifetime decided in a reckless moment—such as her father believing her mother's lie. If she was even meant to believe her mother was telling the truth now. Who could really say?

And so, because she hadn't wanted to deal with all that, she'd taken Rachel's phone, swiped and seen, or really squinted, because the video Rachel was showing her was dark and blurry, but clearly of Quinn. He was at some glitzy party in some neon-lit bar, the shadowy shapes of people around, gawking, filming on their phones, tittering quietly. While he was *ranting*. She hadn't been able to make out everything he'd said, only certain words—pointless, stupid, *useless*—and then he was hurling wine glasses from the bar onto the floor, while people gasped and stepped back to avoid the smashing glass.

She'd watched the whole thing, until it cut off after two burly security guards had hustled him out of the room. Rachel had watched, as well, hovering by her shoulder, her mother seated at the table, silent but apprehensive.

When it had finished, she'd handed the phone back to Rachel without a word.

"Well?" Rachel had demanded, and Harriet had stared at her levelly.

"Well, what?"

"Aren't you *concerned*?" Rachel's voice had risen into something of a squeak of outrage. "I mean, I'm not trying to put you off him, but—"

"Really?" Harriet had cut across her, her voice hardening. "Because it sounds as if that's exactly what you're doing."

"*Harriet.*" Rachel's face had creased with hurt. "I'm *not*. But, looking at this video, I mean, warning flags much? He's clearly unstable—"

"No, he's not." Harriet had been surprised at how calm she'd felt. The video, she'd realised, hadn't surprised or shaken her at all. She'd been expecting something like this—something to explain Perry's dark hints, Quinn's reluctance to talk about the past—and now that she'd known what it was, it had only felt like a relief. "I know he's not," she'd continued, "and I should know far better than you."

Rachel had let out a huff of something like exasperation, mingled with concern. Harriet had known her sister meant well—at least she'd hoped she did—but she'd had quite enough of being undermined, well intentioned as it might have been.

"This is my relationship, Rachel," she'd reminded her. "I didn't tell you how to feel about Ben—"

"Ben never—"

"I don't care." Her voice had risen sharply, and Rachel's eyes had widened. "I appreciate your concern," Harriet had added in a more level tone. "Although I don't appreciate you searching up some video from the depths of the internet—"

"I hardly did that!" Rachel had protested. "It was the headline story on the *Yorkshire Live* website."

Harriet had briefly closed her eyes as she'd stifled a groan, imagining how Quinn would react to having his humiliation splashed around so publicly, in a place as small as Mathering. Really, there hadn't been more exciting news in Yorkshire than a hotelier having a strop online, and that months ago? Apparently not.

"Who," their mother had asked mildly, "are we talking about?"

"My boyfriend, Quinn," Harriet had told her flatly. "*My* boyfriend. So, thank you kindly, Rachel, but you can now Butt. Out." Capital B, capital O, as Quinn would have said.

Harriet had started out of the kitchen, only to have Rachel catch her arm. "I'm just trying to look out for you—" she persisted pleadingly, her voice caught between apology and defensiveness.

"I appreciate that," Harriet had replied, "but let me assure you, you don't need to make up for any more lost time. I'm an adult and I can manage my own relationships, thank you." She'd shaken off her sister's arm, tempering it with a small but somewhat cool smile, and then had walked out of the kitchen.

That had been yesterday afternoon; now it was the day of the party—seven hours and counting—and Quinn seemed to have gone AWOL. Harriet was desperate to head over to the hotel and look for him, but she had about a million cookies to bake—well, two hundred. She'd been in the kitchen since six o'clock that morning, checking her phone every few minutes, the low hum of anxiety she'd felt earlier now a loud, shrieking whine of genuine fear. Why hadn't he been in touch? What was going on?

She was, unfortunately but predictably, remembering every unhelpful—or not—thing Perry had ever said, about how Quinn was interested in things—or people—until he wasn't. How he'd had a wobble, been fragile, moved on like a kid in a candy store. Had the article on *Yorkshire Live* made him decide to move on from this? From *her*, like she'd been half expecting him to all along, even as she'd tried her best to believe in him, in *them*?

She remembered how Quinn had warned her, right at the beginning. He wasn't good with people. He disappointed them. He'd basically told her what he was like, so why was she even surprised that he seemed to be ghosting her now? That she hadn't been enough to hold him?

"Let me help."

Harriet straightened from in front of the Rayburn, blowing a strand of hair from her eyes. Rachel stood in the doorway, looking entirely penitent.

"I just need to get this done," she said as she turned away from the oven. She had six more batches of cookies to bake, the gingerbread to ice, the matcha balls to dust in glitter sugar, the Linzer stars to fill with jam... Plus she had to arrange all the cookies on festive trays and transport them to the hotel.

"I know you do, and that's why I'm asking if I can help." Rachel took a step into the kitchen. "I'm sorry about earlier. I was completely out of line, saying all that about Quinn."

"Well, maybe you were right," Harriet replied wearily. "Not about the warning flags or anything, but...he hasn't been in touch with me for days now. Maybe he's decided, what with all this palaver, it's not worth the bother."

"It's...?" Rachel queried with a frown.

"*I'm* not," Harriet clarified flatly. "He's been keeping a low profile since he arrived in Mathering, and I understand why now, but it might be that now the lid's blown off the whole thing, he doesn't want to bother with all the fuss and speculation." *With me.* She couldn't say it, but she certainly felt it.

Slowly, her face creased with concern, Rachel shook her head. "Harriet, I don't think that's what's going on here," she said. "If anything, Quinn is avoiding you—and I'm not saying he actually is—because he's embarrassed, and he thinks you won't want to bother with him."

"You can't know that."

"It seems like a pretty good guess. He didn't tell you about the video, did he? The party?"

"No, but he...hinted at it, I suppose. Anyway, it doesn't matter to me!" The words burst out of her. "I have a meltdown once a day, practically. He was under stress, he was questioning the whole world he'd become immersed in... I don't blame him, Rachel."

"Then maybe you need to tell him that," her sister replied gently.

Harriet shook her head. "He won't even reply to my texts."

"Then go over to the hotel!" Rachel exclaimed. "Beard the lion in his den. Be honest with him, and let him be honest, too. Harriet, this is too important not to try."

Not to try. Wasn't that what she'd been doing for most of her life? *Better not to try than to try and fail.* That wasn't a motto for a meme or a mug, but it was one she'd chosen, if only be default, to live by, and it wasn't inspiring at all.

In fact, it was plain *stupid.*

Harriet blew out a breath. "I've got all these cookies…"

"Then let me help," Rachel insisted. "I'm not completely useless in the kitchen. If you give me instructions—detailed instructions—I can manage. You've done most of the work already."

Harriet managed a small, wry smile as she glanced at her sister. "You've certainly changed your tune," she remarked. "Yesterday you would have had me running a mile from Quinn—"

"I've had a change of heart," Rachel admitted. "And something of an epiphany, thanks in part to Ben, who gave me a good talking-to."

"And what was this epiphany?" Harriet asked, curious.

"That I'm trying to rescue you from something, because I feel guilty for not being there when you were younger. So, part of me wanted Quinn to be the bad guy so I could be the good big sister." She grimaced. "That was Ben's armchair psychology, anyway, and it does have an unfortunate ring of truth about it. I really am sorry."

"That's okay," Harriet replied, realising she meant it. Rachel had been well intentioned, if misguided. She didn't want to blame her sister now. She didn't want to blame anyone for anything, maybe not even her mother. She wanted, Harriet realised, to try.

She glanced around the kitchen, which looked like a bomb site—a mess of mixing bowls, open sacks of flour and sugar, cookies in various stages of baking, cooling, or being decorated on every available surface.

"Are you sure…"

"Yes," Rachel said firmly. "But give me detailed instructions, please. Very detailed. I don't want to mess this up."

"I can help, too." The voice coming from the doorway was soft, hesitant. Harriet glanced over to see her mother looking almost shy. "I'd like to," she said quietly.

Could she really afford to entrust all her cookies—the biggest order of her business so far—to her sister and her mother? Could she really afford *not* to?

Maybe it was paranoia, or maybe it was instinct, but Harriet couldn't shake the feeling that it might be make-or-break with Quinn. That he needed her, or maybe she needed him, but it was really, really important to find him.

"All right," she said with a nod. "I'll go. I'll leave instructions. It should be straightforward, but…"

"We'll be fine," Rachel assured her.

"We'll try," her mother added with a faint smile.

Try. Wasn't that all anyone could ever do? Wouldn't that always be enough? *Just try.* That, Harriet realised, was a far better motto to live by than *so what?* or *why not?* Just try. Try with everything.

"Okay," she said, and she reached for a pen and a pad of paper and began to write.

Chapter Nineteen

QUINN HAD NOT come out of his office for nearly thirteen hours. It was, he acknowledged, not a good sign—or a good look. He feared he might be starting to stink, at least a little. After he'd seen that video on *Yorkshire Live*, after he realised that Harriet had probably been blanking him, he'd retreated. Retreat, he told himself, was better than sabotage, which had been his usual and unfortunate MO in the past. Wreck something before anyone else could. Wreck it because you weren't worthy of it in the first place.

Hadn't he always known he wasn't worthy of Harriet? He'd just put a good face on it, and she'd almost, *almost* been convinced. It was a thought, a fear, he was trying to suppress, but it kept barging into his head, just as Perry kept trying to barge into his office.

She had knocked—thundered, really—on the door several times since he'd closeted himself in there last night.

"Unlock this door, *please*, Quinn. Your guests are arriving today. The party is tonight." She'd sounded both exasperated and pleading. "Everything is working out, you know. No one cares about that stupid video—"

"I know they don't," he'd called back wearily. "Just…give me a minute, Perry, okay?"

She'd thankfully left him alone, but the minute had stretched to an hour, which had stretched to several, and here he still was. He wanted to leave his office. Heaven knew he needed a shower. He wanted to attend his own party, celebrate his own success. He wanted to be *normal*, but he didn't trust himself because he knew it wasn't how he'd acted in the past. And he really, really didn't want to wreck another good thing—the best thing—in his life. Again.

And so, he stayed.

He'd toyed with the idea of calling his father, just to get it out of the way. Rip off the plaster, lance the old wound. His father would tell him he was stupid and useless yet *again*, but then at least he wouldn't have to wonder, or worse, hope that *this* time, his father would have said something different. That this time what he'd done, what he'd achieved, would have somehow been enough to satisfy not just his father, but also himself.

He was thirty-four years old, he reminded himself. He should not have to keep trying to win his parents' approval. It was ridiculous; it was pathetic. And, in many ways, he honestly felt he'd moved past it. Most of the time, he knew, he lived a successful, interesting, enthusiastic sort of life. He *enjoyed* things. He genuinely felt the world held both promise and magic. It was only when he was on the cusp of his own success, when things were really going his way, that he exasperatingly tipped over into a futile sort of sabotage. He'd identified the tendency years ago, after some much-needed therapy, and it had helped, although maybe not enough, because here he was.

Except, this time he really did want to be different…because there was Harriet. And yet…*Harriet.* He'd switched off his phone several hours ago, after days of nothing from her, figuring it was better to absent himself completely than to keep checking and fearing, or worse, *knowing.* But maybe he should just face the worst, turn his phone on, and see the lack of messages from her for himself, and then somehow find a way to move on…

A knock had him stilling. It wasn't Perry's determined rat-a-tat-tatting, but a soft rap, a gentle one. And then a voice he knew so well—

"Quinn? Will you let me in?"

Harriet. She sounded kind, and worried, and not like she wished she'd never met him, which had to be a good thing. Quinn's heart turned over, swelled with hope, even as, for a few seconds, he simply sat where he was, paralysed by the circling of his own thoughts. Why had she come? Dare he hope?

"Quinn," she said again, a statement this time, a certainty.

"All right," he told her, a smile in his voice, "but I'm warning you, I'm in need of a shower."

"I don't care." She sounded fierce.

He went over to unlock the door and was nearly knocked off his feet as Harriet rushed at him, wrapping her arms around his waist, pressing her cheek against his chest. She really didn't care about the lack of a shower, Quinn thought as his arms closed around her. Holding her felt like a relief.

"Why have you been hiding in here?" she demanded, her voice muffled against his chest. "Is it because of that stupid video?"

So, she had seen it…*and yet she was here.* "I don't actually care all that much about the video," Quinn confessed on a sigh. "I mean, yes, it's more than a tad embarrassing, and I'd rather someone hadn't filmed me on their phone."

She peered up at him, the ghost of a smile on her face. "I'm starting to understand why you want this place screen-free."

"Well, there is that." He glanced down at her, taking in her golden-brown eyes, the freckles across her nose, those lush lips he was aching to kiss. "Why did you come here?" he asked quietly.

"Because I was worried about you," she replied simply. "You weren't answering my messages—"

"I turned off my phone." He paused and then admitted, "When you hadn't been in touch in two days, I thought it was because of the video. That you were…reconsidering."

"I didn't see it until yesterday afternoon." Her arms tightened around him. "I wasn't in touch because I felt like my head was going to explode, with my mother coming back, and then some things she said…"

"What did she say?"

"I'll tell you later, but you really wouldn't believe it. The drama." Harriet shook her head slowly before pressing her cheek against his chest once more, which was, Quinn realised, exactly where he wanted her right now. "But I think we both went into some kind of retreat mode, for different reasons, maybe, but essentially the same instinctive and self-protective response." She glanced up at him, her eyes, her whole face, soft with compassion and love. "I don't want to be like that anymore. That's why I'm here, Quinn."

"I went into retreat mode because it seemed better than the alternative," Quinn told her. He knew he needed to be honest now—about everything. "I admit, it's still not a great choice, but the truth is I have an unfortunate tendency to…wreck things. Self-sabotage, according to certain self-help books. Just when everything is going well, I wreck it on purpose. Which sounds crazy and stupid, I know, but…" He shrugged and spread his hands.

Harriet stepped away from him, closed the door, and leaned against it, her expression thoughtful, alert, waiting. "Is that what happened with Q Games?" she asked gently.

He nodded. "And before that, as well. Getting kicked out of school—it wasn't actually because I was doing badly academically, although I wasn't doing all that great. But then I got the help I needed, and I started doing well—I joined the computer club, I got straight Bs, and that was when I acted out. Enough to get expelled. At eleven, I couldn't explain my behaviour. I knew my dad wasn't satisfied with what I'd achieved, but I don't think I could completely connect the dots. I'm not sure I could explain it at sixteen, either, when it happened again." A sigh escaped him, low and heavy, before he continued.

"The headmaster brought me into his study to ask me why I'd been such an idiot—I'd cheated on a test I didn't need to. Very stupid. He seemed so sorrowful." Quinn could still remember the look of confusion in the older man's eyes. "'You had so much going for you, Quinn,'" he quoted. "'Your grades have improved, you're doing amazingly well in computer science… Why cheat for no reason?'" He sighed. "I couldn't give him an answer. I just felt…angry. But also strangely satisfied, while at the same totally not. I was my own worst enemy. I knew it, and I didn't care."

"I know how that feels," Harriet said quietly, and he was so very grateful for her understanding and compassion.

"I started to identify the trend when I dropped out of college," he continued, "right after I was awarded Phi Beta Kappa—an academic honour, one of the highest there is. Something my dad would have actually been proud of, I think, but maybe that's why I wrecked it. Because I was angry with him, or wanted to show him that I didn't care? I'm not even sure. A few years later, I started sabotaging relationships—I had a girlfriend, Kasey. We weren't very serious, because I didn't let us get serious. I think I probably could have, though, if I'd let myself. I started ignoring her, getting absorbed in work, until she broke up with me. She told me I'd acted as if I was pushing her to do it, and that's when I decided I needed some therapy to figure out why I was intent on wrecking every good thing in my life. The therapist helped me to understand the why—a lack of self-worth, the impulse to wreck something before someone else does it for you, et cetera—but knowing something and changing it are two separate things."

"They certainly are," Harriet agreed, her tone heartfelt.

"Q Games was the pinnacle of self-destruction," he stated flatly. "And I'm not even talking about the party. That party was to celebrate its sale—for fifty million dollars—to one of the bigger gaming companies. Everyone was thrilled, of course. I was going to be onto bigger and better things. We all were. The company was especially excited about a game idea I was selling to them—an amped-up version of

Wilderwood. I'd almost finished it, but during the sale they'd asked for some changes. They wanted to make it more…well, explicit, I suppose. More gore, more violence, more sex, that kind of thing."

"Sex?" Harriet repeated, sounding bemused. "In a video game?"

"Trust me, it can happen. Sexy elves are definitely a thing."

"I had no idea."

He let out a soft laugh. "Anyway, it felt like they were taking my idea and trashing it. It wasn't what I wanted, and I hated that I felt like a sell-out. But the sale was about to go through, and I figured it wasn't really my idea anymore." He let out a slow breath and then took another. "But at that party I just finally…snapped. I'd been struggling against the whole tech world for a while, I think. In college, I was with a bunch of geeky guys who loved gaming, but money and a certain sort of fame turned everyone into people like my parents—shallow, obsessed with status, with money, with *things.*" His voice throbbed with the memory of how trapped he'd felt, how disappointed that he was part of the kind of world he'd tried to escape.

"I hated it, and I hated that I might become like everyone else and start obsessing in the same way. That was the last thing I wanted. So, I had a bit of a tantrum at the party, which was *not* cool, and then I did something even worse." He paused, Harriet's compassionate gaze steady on him. "I went to the office and deleted the code of the new game. All of it, every backup, everything. I had reason, I suppose, in that I didn't like the way the game was going, but it was a stupid, irresponsible thing to do. The company that was buying Q Games knocked fifteen million off the price when they found out. Perry and a few other employees had stock options. They were not happy, although Perry said she understood. She's always understood."

He scratched his cheek. "I don't know if I was doing it to wreck things or to save myself. Maybe both. Over the years, they've sometimes felt like the same thing. But after the sale went through, I left to go backpacking. I just needed to completely unplug from the whole world, from everyone. No phone, no internet, for three months. I was completely off the grid…and it gave me time to think." It had been a painful time in many ways, but a good one, as he'd started to accept the part of himself that was so self-destructive. Started…and yet he was still a very flawed work in progress. Yet Harriet was still here, listening. Caring.

"Then I saw the ad for this place," he finished, "and the idea of the hotel was born, a place where I could be myself, where others could be themselves. Perry has said she hopes I'll find what I'm searching for here, and…" He kept his gaze on her as he finished with quiet certainty, "I think I have. But maybe now that you know I'm such a basket case—"

"Oh, Quinn," Harriet replied on a trembling laugh, "I'm just as much of one. All of humanity is, really. Show me a person who's got it all together and I'll say they're just a good actor."

"I was a good actor," he admitted quietly. "At least, I thought I was, but maybe I didn't fool you."

"You showed me something incredibly valuable," Harriet corrected him. "That you can move on from the hard things in life. That you can change. Yes, you've had your moments, but we all have, and you're still moving forward. You're still enjoying life and finding the good things in it, and you've shown me how to do that, too. How to have fun. How to enjoy. And," she continued, her tone turning almost fierce, "you're *making* good things…like this hotel. I needed to learn those lessons, and you taught them to me, Quinn."

"And you taught me that you can endure all the crap that's thrown at you in life and still keep soldiering on. You've *never* walked away the way I have, Harriet." He admired her deeply for it.

"I don't know if that was endurance or just a sense of powerlessness," she replied honestly. "I've stayed in Mathering for as long as I have because I've been so afraid of trying and failing. Of venturing out and then having to scuttle back, a failure. It felt safer simply to stay."

He took a step towards her, drew her back into his arms. "Stay *and* take care of your father," he reminded her gently. "You may see it as a coward's choice, but I see it as a noble one, far braver than going away."

A shudder escaped her. "I have a lot to tell you about all that," she said. "But it can wait. We have a party to get ready for." She peered up at him. "If you feel up for it? I want to celebrate with you, Quinn."

He quirked an eyebrow. "And do you trust me not to sweep all the champagne flutes to the floor?"

"As long as it's not my cookies…" she replied, her eyes glinting with her smile.

He let out a shout of laughter and hugged her tightly to him before he pulled away to brush her lips with a kiss. "It wouldn't be," he promised. "Even I have my limits."

HARRIET STOOD ON the edge of the hotel's library, a glass of mulled wine in her hand, her heart swelling with pride and affection as she glanced around the crowded room. Outside snow had started to fall softly, the big, downy flakes wonderfully festive, and perfectly fitting. A small five-piece orchestra had been set up in the entrance hall, and was playing Christmas carols as guests circulated, exclaiming over all the wonderful little touches around the hotel. Creamy candles glowed in their sconces, and the lights on the five different Christmas trees stationed throughout the downstairs twinkled merrily. A champagne fountain was set up in the dining room, along with a buffet including, of course, her Christmas cookies.

Her mother and sister had done an amazing job finishing them all off, although admittedly the icing was *slightly* sloppy. That was okay, Harriet had realised with a smile. It didn't need to be perfect. Nothing did…including people. They were all works in progress, fumbling and stumbling their way forward, helping each other up when they needed to. Today she'd helped Quinn…and he'd already helped her in so many ways. Love, she was realising, wasn't about presenting your best self to someone to be burnished and admired, but rather revealing your true self, even your worst self, and having them accept you. Love you…just as you were.

Because she did love Quinn, even if she hadn't said the

words yet, and she thought he loved her. It was a wonderful feeling—not that heady, fizzy one of before, but of something solid and true settling deep inside her, *righting* her.

It also gave her the courage to think about talking to her mother—and her father. Forgiving them and finding a way to move forward. Maybe, after all these years, relationships could be salvaged, saved. It didn't have to be too late.

"Well." The harrumphing sound next to her had Harriet turning to see Agatha hovering by her elbow, and barely reaching her shoulder. "I think I managed this all right."

"*You* managed it?" Harriet repeated in smiling surprise, and Agatha nodded smugly.

"How do you suppose all these guests got here?"

Harriet laughed softly. "I'm sure you had something to do with it."

"You bet I did." She nodded towards Quinn, who was on the other side of the room, chatting with some guests. He wore a plum-coloured waistcoat and a velvet smoking jacket and as he threw his head back and laughed, Harriet thought he looked like a character out of *Cluedo*. Her heart swelled with love for him.

"You didn't do too badly there," Agatha remarked shrewdly. "Your Mr Millionaire."

"I don't know that he's a millionaire anymore," Harriet replied. Quinn had sunk every last penny into this place. "But I'll take him."

"You deserve some happiness, lass," Agatha said quietly. "I always thought it a shame, how your parents pulled you between them."

How on earth had Agatha twigged that? Harriet wondered. The woman clearly had secret superpowers.

"Well, everyone makes mistakes," she replied, "especially when they're in love."

Agatha gave her an appraising look. "That's very forgiving of you."

"Yes," Harriet agreed, smiling. "It is."

There would be time later to talk to her parents, and to figure out if this warm, fuzzy feeling was real and would last. They still had conversations to have, painful ones, but not at Christmas.

"Excuse me, Agatha," she murmured and, placing her glass of mulled wine on a waiter's tray, she headed over to Quinn.

He caught sight of her when she was halfway across the room, his whole face lighting up, the people he'd been chatting to completely forgotten. The grin that stretched across his face was so wide and genuine it made Harriet feel like laughing aloud.

"You are looking very dapper, Mr Mystery Millionaire," she teased as his arms came around her, and it felt as if the whole world had blurred to the twinkle of Christmas lights, the softly falling snow…and the two of them.

"And you are looking equally dapper, if women can be called dapper," he replied. "Or maybe I should say beautiful. Heart-stoppingly gorgeous, in fact."

She'd splurged on her dress on a shopping trip to York, a deep ruby-red velvet with a faintly daring neckline that nipped in at her waist and swirled about her calves. She felt beautiful in it, especially with Quinn looking at her the way he was, his face aglow with appreciation.

"Shall we dance?" she asked impulsively, and he quirked an eyebrow.

"Nobody else is dancing."

"I know." She gave him a mischievous smile, feeling reckless and happy in a way she so rarely had before—like she could do anything, be anything, she wanted to. And she *could*, with Quinn by her side.

His answering grin was one of pure delight. From the hall, they could hear the strains of the orchestra playing 'Hark the Herald Angels Sing'. It wasn't exactly something you'd hear at a disco, but so what? Why not?

Just try.

"All right, then, my lady," Quinn pronounced, and as one they began to move about the room. At first, people looked at them slightly askance—a combination of amusement and uncertainty at this couple suddenly gallivanting about the library—but Harriet found she didn't care, and she didn't think Quinn did, either. They were celebrating, after all.

"Now *this* is how to act at a party," he told her as he whirled her around, and Harriet laughed, a sound of joy, of hope.

There were still things to figure out, she knew, and things to be decided. And there was a future to find—with Embthwaite Treats, with Quinn, within herself. It was all possible. It was all there, waiting.

As Quinn continued to whirl her around the room, Harriet gave in to the spinning sensation, the sheer, wonderful magic of it. Out of the corner of her eye, she saw a few other couples gamely start to dance, as well, and she reached up to twine her arms around Quinn's neck as she kissed him.

"I think we've started something," she murmured against his lips, and he tightened his arms around her waist as he kissed her back.

"I know we have," he murmured back, and it sounded like a promise…one Harriet knew they both would keep.

Discover Harriet and Rachel's mother Anna's story in the third book in the Mowbray Sisters series, Sunset over Embthwaite Farm*!*

If you enjoyed *Christmas at Embthwaite Farm,*
you'll love the other books in the…

The Mowbray Sisters series

Book 1: *Return to Embthwaite Farm*

Book 2: *Christmas at Embthwaite Farm*

Book 3: *Coming soon!*

Available now at your favorite online retailer!

More books by Kate Hewitt

Keeping Up with the Penryns series

Book 1: *A Casterglass Christmas*

Book 2: *A Casterglass Garden*

Book 3: *The Casterglass Heir*

Book 4: *The Last Casterglass*

The Return to Willoughby Close series

Book 1: *Cupcakes for Christmas*

Book 2: *Welcome Me to Willoughby Close*

Book 3: *Christmas at Willoughby Close*

Book 4: *Remember Me at Willoughby Close*

Christmas at the Edge of the World

The Willoughby Close series

Book 1: *A Cotswold Christmas*

Book 2: *Meet Me at Willoughby Close*

Book 3: *Find Me at Willoughby Close*

Book 4: *Kiss Me at Willoughby Close*

Book 5: *Marry Me at Willoughby Close*

The Holley Sisters of Thornthwaite series

Book 1: *A Vicarage Christmas*

Book 2: *A Vicarage Reunion*

Book 3: *A Vicarage Wedding*

Book 4: *A Vicarage Homecoming*

Falling for the Freemans series

Book 1: *Falling for Christmas*

Book 2: *Falling Hard*

Christmas Around the World series

Book 2: *A Yorkshire Christmas*

Available now at your favorite online retailer!

About the Author

After spending three years as a diehard New Yorker, **Kate Hewitt** now lives in the Lake District in England with her husband, their five children, and a Golden Retriever. She enjoys such novel things as long country walks and chatting with people in the street, and her children love the freedom of village life—although she often has to ring four or five people to figure out where they've gone off to.

She writes women's fiction as well as contemporary romance under the name Kate Hewitt, and whatever the genre she enjoys delivering a compelling and intensely emotional story.

Thank you for reading

Christmas at Embthwaite Farm

If you enjoyed this book, you can find more from all our great authors at TulePublishing.com, or from your favorite online retailer.

TULE
PUBLISHING

Made in United States
North Haven, CT
08 November 2023

43783334R00161